Double Figures

ALLAN McCREEDY

SAPHRIM

SAPHRIM

ISBN: 978-1982096748

For Colm and Ben.

CHAPTER 1

Clark Radcliffe didn't really know what a London city analyst did. He had an idea it was something to do with money and predictions, something that revolved around the financial district in the heart of the City of London. In truth he had very little interest. But that was all about to change.

"How are you today Dad?" said Clark after letting himself into his parent's rustic country house on a bright autumnal Sunday morning, his arms filled with the day's newspapers.

"Your sister called again last night," said his father.

Clark nodded and dropped into the high backed rigid Parker Knoll chair, his father having commandeered the generously cushioned leather recliner. Not that Clark minded given his father was the one convalescing from a heart attack. "And where's Mum?" he asked.

His father laughed. "Don't worry Son. Your mother's taken with going back to church these Sunday mornings, what with me feeling a bit stronger. She seems happy enough to leave me alone for a couple of hours. Thank goodness, that's what I say." He laughed again, a deep hearty laugh. Clark laughed too. He knew his mother meant well, and indeed she did well caring for her husband, but he knew too that she could be overpowering, domineering and in his case cold and unforgiving.

It was the first time Clark had visited the shores of County Down in nearly four weeks. He had a difficult relationship with his family, one grounded on a divergence of opinion on his journey to adulthood. He was trying to make things different.

Clark folded his arms and stretched his long legs out as far as they would reach, curious why his father had mentioned speaking with his sister the moment he arrived. "And how is Amy?" he said with little enthusiasm, having had little meaningful conversation with her in years other than the infrequent terse phone call across the Irish Sea to report on their father's condition.

His father looked at him. "Not good," he said, quickly looking away through the large landscape window at the back of the room over the fields and drumlins towards Strangford Lough. "It looks like this thing with Spencer is worse than I thought."

Clark nodded. He didn't know Spencer Livingstone even though his sister had been living with him in London Greenwich for many years. He had never met him. Indeed he wondered if his father ever had.

It seemed his father wanted to tell him Spencer's story regardless. "He invested some of the firm's money in a bad deal, even though it was his role to analyse and advise others, not to invest himself, or least not invest the firm's money."

Clark wondered if he could be any more disinterested, but his father continued. "To try and make amends," he said, "Spencer thought he would pour his own money back into the firm. But he decided to invest it first. And he lost again."

Clark sighed. "Why should you be concerned about this, Dad?" he said, "Why should I be concerned about this?"

His father dropped his eyes to the floor and said slowly, "Spencer has asked your sister to remortgage her property portfolio to help him."

Clark sat forward in his chair, suddenly interested. He ran his long fingers through dark thinning hair as he stared at his father. Amy was a successful Accountant in London. She had worked hard and earned well. Making money on the sale of her first home she had invested in a small letting property that had ridden the market and too returned a good profit. And so she had continued. Property development had started as a pastime, and eventually became a passion. She devoted all her free time to it, time when she was not working with her financial profiles in the City. According to their father she owned three properties outright and mortgages on a further three. All the properties had long term reliable tenants and the rental income together with her not insignificant salary allowed her to comfortably service the portfolio. Despite their differences Clark was proud of her.

"Do you know this guy Spencer, Dad?" he said.

"No Son, I've never met him."

"Have you spoken with him even, on the phone?"

His father shook his head. "No, I know nothing of him, other than what your sister has told me." He looked away again towards the window. He rubbed his nose on the back of his hand. "My only daughter has lived with this man for years and yet he is stranger to me," he said slowly.

Clark forced a smile. "I'm sure it will be okay. Amy is a sensible woman," he said in an attempt to provide some comfort although he was sure he was in no position to offer any. He lifted himself from the chair and rested his hand on his father's shoulder before slipping into the kitchen and returning with two mugs of instant coffee. His father nodded his thanks.

A shrilling ring startled Clark as he sat back in the rigid chair, a loud and deliberate ring from the landline phone that sat on the sideboard against the wall opposite the large landscape window. His father started to rise.

"Stay there," said Clark quickly. He lifted the wireless handset from its charger and handed it to his father.

"Hello?" said his father. A long pause and then, "Amy, calm down. What's wrong?"

Clark sat on the edge of his chair, elbows on knees. He stared at his father.

"Amy, Amy, The line is breaking up. I'm not hearing you," his father was saying. And then the handset dropped to his lap. His father stared ashen faced to a spot on the wall.

"What is it Dad?" said Clark.

His father turned his head towards Clark, his breathing deep and uneven. "I don't know Son," he said slowly, "It's your sister. She sounds distraught. I couldn't make out what she was saying." After a moment's silence, "The line went dead." And then his eyes closed. He slumped in his chair, his head falling onto his chest. Clark jumped from his seat and lunged forward lifting his father's head back against the headrest, his own heart pounding. His father's lips drained of colour.

"Dad," he shouted and dropped his ear to his father's open mouth. He heard a shallow breathing, a breathing that began to increase slowly in intensity and volume.

His father opened his eyes.

Clark blew out a long breath. "Are you all right Dad?" he asked quietly.

"I'm fine. This sort of thing happens all the time," he said curtly, "The doctors have told me to expect it. Your mother normally just gives me a glass of water and makes sure I have taken my medication."

Clark nodded. He did not think a doctor would tell a patient to expect to pass out. Nor did he expect his mother's routine response to be to offer a glass of water and to check on medication. But he didn't want to create a fuss. He would check with his mother. "A glass of water then?" he said as he walked towards the kitchen.

He was heartened when he returned. His father's face was back to colour and he was merrily flicking at a magazine, smiling at some article about a former sports star who fancied his chances on a televised dancing competition.

"Tell me again about Amy's call," said Clark as he handed over the water.

His father shrugged, "We lost the connection. I suppose she will ring back."

"Maybe you could call her?" asked Clark.

His father shook his head.

"Maybe I could call her?" he then said.

His father shook his head again, more vigorously. "No, probably best not to," he said.

Clark sighed and returned to the kitchen to freshen up the coffee. He contemplated leaving for Belfast, heading back to his own home. But he couldn't leave his father alone, not after the scare. He would wait for his mother to come home. Perhaps she would show some forgiving given she was coming home from church. Somehow he doubted it. But he hoped.

He stared out into the distance losing himself in thoughts of the life he'd had many years before, a happy life exploring the very fields before him, running home to the warm embraces of his family. He sighed and managed a smile. Good times indeed, different times.

Clark jumped as he heard a car door slam and turned brusquely towards heavy footsteps crunching on the loose driveway stones. He drew a deep breath and leaned against the worktop. He put on his best welcoming smile, ready for his mother. But the front door did not open, instead a loud rap against frosted glass. "I'll get it," he shouted and marched down the hall.

His mouth dropped as he opened the door. There stood his sister Amy, shaking with tears streaming down her face. She stared. Clark tried to say something, but couldn't. He stepped back and nodded.

Amy dropped her head and brushed past him into the lounge. Clark closed the door gently and leaned back against the wall, dropping his own head to the floor before pushing himself away and beginning a walk down the long hallway towards the bathroom, stopping to glance through the door to the lounge. His father had risen from his chair and was holding his daughter tightly. She in turn was holding her father, her head buried in his shoulder. Clark could hear her sobs, and could hear his father's soothing words. He wished he could be part of it.

"Come in Son," his father called sensing him in the doorway.

Clark stepped slowly into the room. Amy lifted her head and glared at him. Clark managed a tight smile. He opened his mouth to speak, to say something, anything, but again nothing came out. He nodded.

Amy held her stare.

"It's all right Amy, Clark knows," their father said to break the silence. And then he winced.

Amy broke away. "What do you mean, Clark knows?" she said turning her stare to her father. "Clark knows what? You mean you have told him?"

Her father looked away. "I'm sorry Amy. I thought he might be able to help."

She began to shout. "Dad, how could you." She pointed at Clark. "How on earth could he help?"

"Amy, please," her father said.

Clark needed to say something. "Amy," he said, "Dad meant only good by telling me." He stepped forward and took his father by the shoulder and guided him to his chair. "You need to sit Dad, to rest," he said, more for the benefit of his sister.

He turned to face her and held up both palms. She took a step back, her hands on hips. The tears had run dry. Her eyes were tight, her lips pursed, and her small nose twitching.

He shook his head. "I'm sorry Amy," he said. Nodding to his

father he hurriedly left the room, pulling the front door tightly closed behind him deciding he would call his mother later to talk about his father's turn, something to look forward to.

Clark passed a shiny black BMW as he reversed his morose Toyota out the driveway, surmising it most likely be the sort of car Amy would hire at the airport. He noticed too another car parked on the other side of the road across the gateway to the field opposite, a car with two men inside who appeared to be plotting their whereabouts on a map. They glanced at Clark and then quickly looked away. Clark paid little attention, well accustomed to Sunday day-trippers exploring the narrow roads around the Lough.

He drove towards Belfast unable to shake his sister from his mind. He knew she was suffering, knew she was distressed. She had come home to her father in search of solace, clearly needing her family. He was family. And yet she had dismissed him. He thought back to the many years before, playing together in the garden, chasing through the fields, exploring the rock pools at the Lough shore. Even though she was four years younger they had been inseparable.

He felt a tear run down his cheek.

On Belfast's Ethel Street he fortuitously managed to find a space to park immediately outside his mid-terraced house. The street was forever congested, residents and commercial vehicles from businesses on the adjacent cosmopolitan Lisburn Road continually competing for what little space was available.

As he climbed from the car he nodded at Vince, his next door neighbour recalling he should invite Vince and his housemate Ryan in for a drink, to be neighbourly. He would get round to it eventually.

Clark hung his overcoat in the small hall, leaving the car keys in the coat pocket and threw himself on the sofa in the only downstairs room, a functional open plan space that was an all-in-one sitting room, dining room and kitchen. It was a compact home but he liked it. It suited his needs. And it was all his. No mortgage.

Thoughts of his sister came back to him. He sighed while shaking his head and reached across the room for his Gibson J200, a present to himself way back when he had come into some money. He let his fingers walk across the fret board while he picked the strings, bluesy seventh chords producing a sorrowful melody that seemed appropriate.

A glance at the clock on the fireplace and he thought about meeting Siobhan later, about taking another step in their fledgling relationship. Siobhan was, like him, a computer consultant although she was an employee of a multi-national firm whereas he was freelance, albeit with the majority of his work coming through the one firm. They had much in common, their paths having first crossed recently when Clark was investigating embezzlement accusations in a government department, an investigation that taught him a lot about himself and those with whom he shared his life. He only hoped his feelings for Siobhan were more than the feelings of someone on the rebound.

He had been looking forward to his night with Siobhan, to their meal in the city centre, but now he wasn't so sure. He didn't think he would be much company. He decided to call her.

Siobhan answered almost immediately.

"I'm sorry," he said and went on to explain what had happened at his parents' house and that he had much to think through.

"Don't worry," she said, knowing Clark and his sister had their difficulties even if unsure what they were. All she knew was that they hadn't really spoken for years. She knew they had exchanged a couple of phone calls when their father was taken ill and she knew they had met fleetingly over the same period. If she was honest she found it hard to understand how siblings could not be the best of friends, the best of confidences, like it was with her and her sister. Siobhan had a twin sister, not quite identical and certainly not alike in personality. They lived together in the same rented house in Kerrsland Drive in the East of Belfast, although their careers and working patterns meant there were often long periods when each was in the house alone.

"Thanks Siobhan, for understanding," said Clark softly and hung up quickly before dropping his head in his hands. He would make it up to her.

He lifted his head at the sound of a car reversing outside and rose towards the window, in time to see a gleaming black coupe squeeze into an impossible space behind his own saloon. He sighed as a tall figure wrapped in a dark olive woollen coat and matching beanie hat climbed out and met his eye through the glass.

"Clark, we need to talk," said his sister Amy as he opened the door.

CHAPTER 2

Clark led Amy into his house taking her coat and hanging it on the hook beside his. She folded the hat into her oversize Burberry bag as she sat on the sofa and began fidgeting with her watch strap, eyes on the floor. Clark sat on the club chair opposite.

"Nice house," she said, "small, but nice."

"Thanks," said Clark realising it was the first time she had been in his house, a house that he had owned for more than a decade. "I'll show you round upstairs if you have ten seconds to spare," he added managing an awkward smile.

Amy returned the smile. "I'm sorry," she said quietly.

"It's all right," said Clark although not sure what she was apologising for.

"No, it's not all right," she said, "I spoke with Dad. He told me all about you, about how successful you have been now that you are freelancing. I am sorry I didn't know, or perhaps I refused to listen to Mum and Dad in the past if they tried to tell me. I am sorry that I doubted Dad's reason for telling you."

She looked at Clark and held his eyes. "I think you might be able to help." And then her floodgates opened. Tears flowed. Clark rose quickly and stepped towards her. She too rose and fell into his outstretched arms, her head nestling against his broad shoulders, her arms encircling him. Clark allowed his arms to embrace her, to pull her close. He gently rubbed her back. He didn't know what else to do. He closed his eyes tight, choking back his own tears.

"I'm sorry," Amy said again through her tears.

"I'm sorry too," said Clark softly, maybe too softly for her to hear. He knew he was apologising for the years that had passed, for the years that he had allowed the gulf to develop. He had missed her, and he would do whatever it took to make amends.

"Tell me," he said gently.

She lifted her head and smiled before stepping back and sitting on the edge of the sofa. Clark dropped onto the club chair and nodded. She took a deep breath and proceeded to tell the story pretty much how their father had relayed it. She told how Spencer had invested a sum of the firm's fee income in a venture he was sure carried low risk and high return. He knew he shouldn't be doing it, that it was against the ethics of his organisation, but he was so convinced by its opportunity and also naively thought it could help him swing a partnership with Rubenstein Roberts. But the investment failed. He then invested his own money in another ill-judged investment. It too failed and word began to get out that the respected firm of Rubenstein Roberts had a rogue in its midst. The Partners had given Spencer one chance at redemption. They offered that he should restore the firm's financial status, but with legitimate means and that he should rebuild his reputation as a sound and reliable investment adviser. And that meant no personal investing on markets. So he had asked Amy to bail him out, and as all Amy's capital was tied up in property he had asked her to sell or remortgage. Amy didn't know what to do. She wanted to help but she didn't want to compromise her own business interests.

"But that's not all," she said to Clark, "there's more that I have not told Dad." Clark raised his eyebrows.

She looked to the floor, the first time she had been unable to look at him since she had begun her story. "It's not that I don't trust him," she said, "but throughout the whole thing Spencer has shut me out. He would work away in his study for hours at a time. He would disappear to meetings and then close up when I asked him about them. And this was so unlike him. We have much in common, Clark, we share many interests. We both work in finance and discuss regularly what's going on at work. In many ways we are each other's professional conscience.

"We enjoy sharing a bottle of wine of a night and helping solve each other's work problems. But with this it has been different." She broke again into tears, heavy tears.

"Amy, it's okay," said Clark.

She shook her head. "I think I want to help him," she said, "but I need to be sure I am doing the right thing."

Clark nodded slowly. "You said he would disappear into his study for hours at a time?"

Amy nodded. "And when I called in to check on him, to leave a coffee or a glass of wine he would get flustered. He seemed to be studying spreadsheets on his laptop every time I went in. That in itself was unlike him. He usually printed documents and worked off hard copies, taking notes in the margins, penning some thoughts, that sort of thing. When I asked if I could help he ignored me. When I asked what he was looking at he said they were just company forecasts.

"One time I asked him if I could find the forecasts online and take a look at them independently and we could talk about them. He said they weren't available online, that he only had them on his laptop. I found that odd.

"Why did he do what he did Clark? And why did he not involve me? For goodness sake I know my way around spreadsheets and company accounts. I could have helped him." Her voice trailed off; no doubt reliving the many conversations she had with Spencer over the matter. And Clark understood the concern. If Spencer was so unwilling to share with her then why should she rescue him?

"So how can I help, Amy?" he asked.

She looked at him again, with sad yet hopeful eyes. "I think if someone examined the information he based his decisions on I might take some comfort. I have no idea what I suspect but there is certainly something suspicious about making financial decisions on documents that are not publically available, and indeed documents whose source is indeterminable."

"So you would like me to examine the computer documents?" said Clark.

Amy nodded.

Clark was indeed intrigued. He just wasn't prepared for what his sister asked next.

"Could you go and meet with Spencer, in London?"

Clark hesitated. "Sure," he said slowly, "whatever it takes."

"Tomorrow?" she said.

Clark looked at the clock on the fireplace.

"Tomorrow?" he said.

"Look, I know it's a lot to ask, short notice and all. It's just Spencer is in the City tomorrow, and he said he would be willing to…you know."

"Wait a minute," said Clark, "you have already spoken with him about me, about meeting me?"

Amy shuddered. "Yes," she said, "He called me earlier. I had hoped to speak with you first. I'm sorry. It just sort of came up in the course of the conversation. I told him you were a specialist in computer audits and you might be able to find something in the electronic documents that coerced him into investing as he did."

"And he said he would meet with me?"

"Yes, he seemed grateful. I don't know, but I get the sense he might agree that I should be certain before helping him."

Clark was troubled by being landed with this at the eleventh hour. But he couldn't let his sister see this annoyance. He wanted to do what he could to help her.

"Amy, I've got work tomorrow."

"I know, sorry." She shrugged her shoulders and looked to the floor.

Clark managed a smile. "Not a problem," he said, "I can drop an email to Fabian, one of the perks of freelancing. More importantly though, how am I getting to London tomorrow, aka, in a few hours time?"

"I'm sorry again, but I took the liberty of checking online earlier. There were still seats available to Gatwick at ten fifteen in the morning, and coming back on the last flight at seven forty."

"I better boot up my laptop and check they are still available then," said Clark with a smirk.

"And I'll arrange with Spencer to meet you somewhere convenient in the afternoon. And don't worry, I'm paying."

Not that paying was of any concern to Clark. He was just glad to be helping Amy. The flights were still available, although premium price was charged due to the lateness of the booking. Clark always thought this strange, thinking the airline should be grateful for selling remaining seats hours before departure and should not charge such a rate. The joys of modern day flying he thought.

He checked in online and printed off his boarding pass. He would have no need to check baggage. He remarked how he had just acted as his own travel agent and airline customer service agent. He wondered how long it would be until he could board himself onto the plane. Or fly it. He sent an email to Fabian Townsend, the Managing Partner at Chesterton and Williamson, the firm through which he secured most of his freelance work. He considered calling Siobhan but decided he would leave it until morning. He wanted an early night. He wanted to be fresh for his trip to London. He reminded himself he needed to talk to his mum about his dad's turn earlier that day. He decided though that too could wait until the next day, although Amy said she would let their mother know given she would be staying there for a few days.

Amy called Spencer and arranged for him to meet Clark at the Lamb and Flag in Covent Garden. It was a bar Clark knew, although it had been many years since he had been. He could find his way there from Victoria Station, a bit of a walk he knew but it would be a pleasant one nonetheless.

"Tell me more about Spencer?" Clark said, "What's he like? I've never met him."

Amy's face darkened to a deep shade of crimson. She looked away and began to bite on a finger nail. "I know," she said eventually. "You'll meet him tomorrow."

"How will I know him?" said Clark.

"Don't worry," she said, "He will know you."

Clark looked at her.

Amy stood and Clark followed. They held each other tight, Clark placing a soft kiss on her cheek. She smiled and he sensed her eyes beginning to fill again.

"Thank you," she said and turned to leave.

He waved her off and watched as she turned the black BMW into Northbrook Street and melted into the dusk.

Another car pulled out from across the road and sped towards Northbrook Street.

CHAPTER 3

Clark was up early, as always. He showered and dressed in chinos and sports coat, what he regarded his best smart casual ensemble. After a quick instant coffee and stale brioche he waited anxiously for the taxi to Belfast's City Airport.

Eight thirty Monday morning and the taxi began its fight into Belfast's rush hour, Clark silently cursing himself for not arranging to leave earlier and for not insisting on a mute driver. Mundane questions and anecdotes ensued despite Clark's failure to acknowledge or engage in conversation.

Inching its way along the Lisburn Road and through the city centre the taxi eventually picked up speed on the Westlink carriageway that connected the two main motorways. A few minutes after passing Harland and Wolff shipyard the taxi pulled into the City Airport, a comparatively small regional airport that delivered little in the way in international connections. Belfast's International Airport some ten miles to the north offered slightly more to the discerning globetrotting public. Belfast's choice of direct international destinations was however somewhat limited, a victim of demographics and commerce despite the best interests of local lobbyists. There was always Dublin.

Clark checked the meter and handed over the exact fare, nodding his thanks to the driver and making his way to the terminal building. He had no bags. He hadn't even worn his overcoat although he did sport a college scarf to assist his jacket in protecting him from the crisp morning air. He was hoping it would be a few degrees warmer in London.

His flight was called a few minutes after he had endured the security channel, a process he detested but tolerated. A nod to the inanely smiling and heavily made up woman inside the cabin and he made his way to his allocated window seat. He would have preferred an aisle given his long legs but it was a short flight. He would manage. A couple of suits squeezed beside him talking incessantly about helicopter views and strategic realignment pathways. Clark smiled to himself thankful he was not part of the conversation, and feeling sorry for whoever it was they were going to meet.

The flight was uneventful and swift, arriving at London's Gatwick Airport slightly ahead of schedule. He moved quickly through the arrivals gate, pausing briefly for some photograph to be taken and presented to him in a bizarre barcode format, a photograph he then had to hand over to gain access to the baggage reclaim hall. With no bags to collect he moved on, up steep walkways, round corners, across check in lobbies and down steps, eventually arriving at the train platform. The Gatwick Express was waiting, not that he expected anything different knowing the trains were scheduled to run every fifteen minutes.

He enjoyed travelling by train. He enjoyed the hypnotic hum as the wheels hurtled along the track. He enjoyed the ever changing scenery whizzing past the panoramic windows. On this occasion he enjoyed watching the London skyline as it raced towards him, the Gherkin Building, the dome of Saint Paul's, and the iconic power station at Battersea. His only distraction on the journey was the conductor who needed to validate his ticket, his online ticket that he had printed off the previous night along with his airline boarding pass.

After thirty minutes he was at Victoria Station, its vast concourse choked with hoards of travellers swarming to and from the numerous platforms. He checked the huge commuter clocks. Twelve thirty, plenty of time for the walk. Towards the pedestrian exit at Buckingham Palace Road he passed the concourse entrance to the Grosvenor Hotel, a hotel he had once stayed in on a business trip. He recalled checking into his room and then realising he had travelled from the aircraft at Belfast City Airport to the hotel room without ever setting foot outside. He smiled at the memory.

He continued towards the ornate Rubens Hotel, glancing across the road at the Bag 'O Nails bar again recalling a night spent on a stool chewing the fat with a client. He kept going, past The Royal Mews and eventually arriving at Buckingham Palace. He paused briefly. He noticed the Royal standard flying but couldn't remember if it meant the Queen was in residence or not. He imagined the former. He took a small digital camera from his jacket pocket and took a couple of snaps, something to show Siobhan, maybe. He knew he should invest at some point in a modern mobile phone that would double up as a camera, and save him carrying two devices. But his basic mobile phone had been good to him. It did what it was required to do, allowing him to talk to people and, if necessary, send a text.

He moved on through Green Park towards Piccadilly, a walk he'd taken many times and never once failed to be amazed at the array of people sitting on the grass, chatting, flirting, eating and impervious to the weather. He passed the Ritz Hotel and Fortnum and Mason. At Piccadilly Circus, by the statue of Eros, he pulled his A to Z London Visitor's Guide from his inside pocket, a small book that had been a companion for many years, dog-eared and out-dated but the main streets hadn't changed. He checked for Rose Street and confirmed all he had to do was cross Leicester Square.

He arrived at the Lamb and Flag forty five minutes before his scheduled meeting. He didn't' mind, he liked being early. He had been looking forward to seeing the Lamb and Flag again, not expecting it to look any different given that it had stood since 1772 and had strived to retain its authenticity. He recalled having spent a night there during his student days, a weekend in London on a budget. He recollected the turbulent ferry crossing and the arduous eleven hour coach journey, flying not an option back then. He remembered the youth hostel in Kensington and the dorm of many metal framed bunks. He smiled as the escapades came back to him. Jackson had been with him on that trip, as had a number of others, but he had no idea what became of them. Maybe someday he would look them up. He would though call Jackson when he got home. It had been a while since they had been out for a beer. Jackson Morrow was his oldest friend.

There weren't many in the bar despite it being lunchtime. A barmaid, small and round with dark hair pulled back in a tight ponytail greeted him with a welcoming smile. He nodded and headed towards a stool at the bar's corner, somewhere he could watch the door.

"Hi, what can I get you?" said the barmaid in an accent Clark found impossible to place.

He looked at the beer pumps. He thought he might give one of the ales a try. No point in sitting in a bar once frequented by Charles Dickens and drinking imported bottled beer that could be procured anywhere he thought to himself. "I'll try a pint of Seafarers," he said pulling the money wallet from his trouser pocket.

"Good call," she said and began to work the pump. "Do you come here often?" she asked.

Clark smiled at the line, a line he was sure had no connotation. Just idle bar chat. "No, not often," he said and looked away, not wanting to engage in futile yak with a barmaid. He hoped she would take the hint. He paid for the beer and folded his hands around the glass. It looked good, its amber hue appearing smooth yet mystifying. He took a drink, a long drink, more than half the glass disappearing. He nodded to himself. It was indeed good. He spun in his stool towards the wall fascinating at the array of framed pictures and plaques. He read each in turn. He spun further round and took in the cast iron fireplace, the copper coal shuttle and the booths beyond with their wooden pews distressed over many years of use, many years of providing rest for a myriad of patrons. He thought of the literary conversations and poetic recitals that might have taken place on those very pews.

He finished the beer and ordered another, the barmaid thankfully having given up her attempt to engage him. He checked his watch. He kept a watchful eye on the door.

He didn't have long to wait.

The door opened brashly and in came two men, both suited in navy, one sporting a bright rouge tie, the other orange. Both wore white shirts with cufflinks protruding below their jackets. Both carried similar black leather briefcases, two men very similar, but for one difference.

One was tall, with wide shoulders held back, a full head of hair, a presence emanating authority, control, and assertion. The other looked less confident. He was smaller, considerably smaller, round, bald, rosy cheeked and perspiring. They headed towards Clark.

It was the smaller rounder man who spoke first. "Radcliffe?" he said in a deep voice that seemed strangely out of place.

Clark nodded and held out his hand.

The man looked at Clark's hand and ignored it. "Thought it might be you," he said.

Clark looked down to his jacket and chinos thinking perhaps his dress had given him away. He looked at the near empty second beer glass on the counter and wondered what his sister had said about him.

"I'm Spencer. Spencer Livingstone," the man said but offered no hand. Clark looked briefly at the other man and then back to the man talking. He suppressed a smile as he thought of his presumption that it was the other man his sister was with, his tall, attractive, self-assured sister.

"Don't know why I'm here," said the man. "It was your sister's idea. Said you could help. Frankly it's none of your business. I don't know what she has told you but forget it. Tell her to get home." With that he turned and left. The taller man glared at Clark before turning and following Spencer.

Clark hadn't spoken. He sat dumbfounded. What was that? Was that really the man my sister has been living with all these years? The anger welled in him. He nodded a request to the barmaid for another beer and grabbed the mobile phone from his jacket pocket. He called his sister.

"Amy, what's going on?" he said as she answered the phone.

"What do you mean?" she said.

"Spencer came in here, was downright rude to me and left more of less telling me to butt out."

"What? Didn't you tell him how you might be able to help him?"

"No Amy, I did not. I did not even get the chance to speak with him. He said it was none of my business and to forget whatever you had told me. Then he just turned and left me standing like a lemon, him and some big guy with him."

"Probably Lance," she said, "Lance Oldfield. He follows Spencer everywhere, some sort of protégé. But Clark, I'm sorry. I know Spencer can be… difficult… but he said he would meet with you."

"And he did Amy. He met with me. He met with me to tell me to clear off. A waste of time this has been. I'll head back to the airport in a while. I'll see you later."

"No, wait Clark," said Amy, "I'll try to reach him. You wait there. He needs to apologise to you at least."

She hung up leaving Clark holding the phone to his ear. The barmaid brought the pint of Seafarers. He had a few hours before he had to make his way back to Victoria Station. He was enjoying the beer. He would at least make the most of that.

The bar was still quiet, unusually quiet he thought although he was comparing with the busy city centre bars at home. He was sure however the Lamb and Flag would get progressively busy throughout the rest of the day and into the evening. In the downstairs main bar there was just himself, the barmaid and a couple of tourists, or what he took to be tourists judging by the oversized Nikons and bags of souvenirs. The barmaid was having more luck extracting conversation from them.

After ten minutes the door opened and Spencer stomped in and marched towards Clark. The other man, who Clark then took to be Lance Oldfield, stayed at the door watching.

"I'm only here because of your sister," said Spencer.

Clark said nothing. He remained in his bar stool.

Spencer looked towards Lance, and then to the barmaid. He looked around the empty booths behind Clark. He blew a deep, heavy loud sigh and held out his hand, a move radiating much reluctance and distain.

"I suppose I owe you an audience," he said, "given you have come all the way here."

An audience, thought Clark. He nodded but remained silent.

"Spencer Livingstone, good to meet you at last, I suppose," the man said, introducing himself for a second time.

Clark accepted his hand, "Clark, Clark Radcliffe."

Spencer drew a long breath and again exhaled loudly before placing his briefcase on the floor. He fed a forefinger into the collar of his shirt, fidgeting.

"A beer," he shouted towards the barmaid, pointing towards the Seafarer's pump. An audible tut came from the other side of the bar.

"Your sister seems to think you can add something to our situation," he said, "but frankly I don't see how. I'm in perfect control of it, which is what I was trying to say earlier, but perhaps it came out wrong. For that I apologise."

So there we are, thought Clark, an apology, as insincere as it was. Spencer threw a note on the bar and reached for the beer. He took a long drink, paused, and then took another. The pint glass was as good as drained.

"We're done," he said, "it would have been better if your sister had not wasted your time. Or mine, for that matter."

He stooped to pick up his briefcase, glancing at Lance as he done so.

"Hold on a minute," said Clark, finally finding the opportunity and desire to speak, "You don't know me, and I certainly don't know you. I am here because for some reason my sister cares about you, and I care about her. She has told me you have asked her to help you. And God knows why, but she is willing to do it. She needs to be sure however that there is no alternative, that she is doing the right thing. She asked if I might be able to help."

Spencer's jaw fixed tight, heavy air pumping from his nostrils, his face reddening, "I'm sorry lad," he said dropping his briefcase back on the floor, "but how can you help? How can you possibly help? This is big league stuff, lad. This is big city banking. Your sister seems to be missing the plot, maybe something has got lost in translation?"

Clark could not help but notice that Spencer had yet to refer to his sister by name. "As I was saying Spencer, you don't know me. In fact do you know anything about me?"

Spencer looked at him, his face giving nothing away other than its crimson hue. Perspiration was running down his face, small droplets forming as the flow reached his chin. He continued to breathe heavily making no attempt to wipe his face. Clark wondered what might be happening under the arms of his shirt.

"I'm a computer analyst," said Clark, "and would be regarded pretty much as an expert in the field. I have consulted across the country including to Government Departments in Whitehall. And furthermore, I have a contract to provide expert analytical services to the police." He made sure his eyes stayed fixed firmly on Spencer. He continued, "My expertise lies in analysing hardware and software for flaws, anything untoward. So to answer your question, Spencer, I think I might be in a position to offer some help to you, on the assumption of course that whatever issue you might have has had some form of computer interface."

Spencer stared. He said nothing, but was clearly thinking. And then he nodded. A faint smile developed as he ran a hand over his face, finally removing the residue. He cocked his head towards the booth in the corner. "Let's sit," he said and waved two fingers to the barmaid and pointed at the booth. A classy request for two more beers thought Clark who was about at his limit for the afternoon.

Spencer waved the other man over. "This is Lance," he said when the man arrived at the side of the booth.

Clark nodded, waiting for a hand to be extended. None was offered. "Clark Radcliffe," he said keeping his own hands on the table.

Lance began to drop into the booth beside Spencer but he was met with a raised palm. "It's okay Lance. Leave us," Spencer said.

Lance stepped back. He looked at Clark and then back to Spencer. "Are you sure?" he said.

Spencer did not look at him. His eyes were on Clark. "Leave us," he repeated.

The tall broad shouldered man sulked out of the bar, the door slamming in his wake.

Spencer turned to Clark. "So you work at computers?" he said.

Clark nodded. He considered explaining that working at computers was probably an oversimplification, but decided against it.

"I'm sure your sister has told me about your chosen vocation before. I can't remember. She has said you could help, but as I have said I don't see how. But I'll give you a go."

Clark had heard enough. "Wait a minute Spencer," he said raising his voice, "This is not a job interview, or a trial. I am a busy man. I am here because Amy asked me to come. I am here for her, and quite frankly I am beginning to wonder why she would have anything to do with you. What is your problem Spencer?"

Spencer held both hands to his chin and stared at Clark. The barmaid left two beers on the table, smiling briefly at Clark but ignoring Spencer. Clark did detect a slight roll of her eyes as she looked at him, a sign of contempt for Spencer or a sign of pity for Clark having to endure him. It was probably both. The interruption calmed the tension.

"Yes Clark, of course," said Spencer, "point taken." He again ran his forefinger round the inside of his shirt collar. He looked over his shoulder as if to check for eavesdroppers, but there was no one in earshot. A few other customers had taken up residence on bar stools but they were well out of the way. He leaned forward. "It was a sure thing," he said, "shouldn't have failed. My source was impeccable. I don't know what happened, but it did."

Clark nodded.

"And then it happened again. Same source and it failed again. I am now where I am and have one chance of putting it right, of putting this behind me and moving on," said Spencer. "And I understand your sister's concern. I will do what I can to help you in allaying that concern." He sat back and looked at Clark.

Clark nodded again. He had just received Spencer's tacit agreement to his help. "You followed the same source twice?" he said.

Spencer nodded slowly.

Clark shook his head. "And you trusted this source, twice?"

Spencer looked away. He bent down to his briefcase and opened it, pulling out a CD ROM in its case. He handed it to Clark and lifted the beer to his lips, gulping its contents before setting the empty glass back on the table. He didn't say another word.

Spencer slid out of the booth and disappeared out the door into Rose Street.

Clark watched him leave before looking down at the CD case. He turned it over in his hands and slipped it into his jacket pocket, leisurely finishing his beer, thinking through what he knew. He needed to speak to Amy to tell her that Spencer had returned to the Lamb and Flag and they'd had a conversation, albeit brief. He needed to tell her Spencer had given him a disk. And he had to tell her exactly what he thought of Spencer. But that was something he would have to tread carefully with, given he and his sister were reconciling after many years estranged. Amy had been with Spencer for most of those years. She clearly felt something for him and for Clark to question her choice in partner would no doubt come across sanctimonious and spiteful. He decided he would wait. He would talk with his sister face to face. He sent Amy a text, brief and to the point, saying he had met with Spencer and had made some progress. He suggested they meet the next day for lunch.

The walk back to Victoria followed the same route as before, only in reverse. No stops this time for photos. The train was waiting when he arrived at the platform and he climbed into the second carriage, for no reason other than he always boarded the second carriage. It was probably something to do with assuming the first carriage would be for first class passengers. He didn't have a first class ticket.

He found an empty table with four seats and sat at the window facing the direction of travel as he was inclined to do. Aimlessly watching other trains and passengers he sensed someone sit beside him, and two others sit opposite. He turned and gave his fellow travellers a quick glance the way passengers tend to do noting they were well dressed in extravagant business suits, groomed and dapper. He then returned to his aimless study through the window. He felt a nudge on his elbow and turned.

"Hi," the man beside him said.

Clark stared. Strangers don't normally talk on trains. He looked across at the two men opposite. They both smiled and nodded. The man beside him pulled a sheet of note paper from his pocket and handed it to Clark. Clark looked again at the three men. They were all smiling warmly. He looked at the note and then quickly looked back at the men who then stood and slipped out of their seats.

"Take heed," the man who sat beside him said as they moved down the carriage and stepped off the train.

Clark looked again at the note. There were three words on it.

Leave it alone.

CHAPTER 4

Leave what alone? Leave alone any thoughts of investigating? Leave Spencer alone? Leave the disk alone? But there was no explicit mention of the disk or attempt to take it from him. And who was it advising him to leave it alone? The questions turned over and over in Clark's head the entire journey home. He needed to get back to Ethel Street. He needed to check the disk. But there was one thing he wanted to do first.

He took a taxi from the City Airport to Siobhan's house on Kerrsland. He hoped she would be pleased to see him, his having cancelled their date the previous night. He needn't have worried as the front door opened and she met him with open arms, pulling him close and holding him tight. He stepped back and looked at her, at the stunning figure in a tight Abercrombie charcoal dress falling to just above her knees, and high heeled Geiger boots rising to just below them. A gentle breeze wafted her dark brown hair away from her sultry features.

"Clark, how are you? How are things with your sister?" she finally said.

He realised he hadn't told her he was going to London. He had meant to call earlier. He told her everything, about Amy arriving at his house after he had called off their date, what she had told him, how he had agreed to go to London to meet Spencer and what he had learned from the meeting. He didn't however mention the note.

"All that since we spoke yesterday?" said Siobhan smiling, "Whoa, that's unreal."

Clark smiled too. He was tired, the afternoon beers a contributing factor. "How was your day?" he asked remembering it was something he should ask.

"Not as exciting as yours by all accounts," she said, "a day at the office, meetings and emailing." That was all she offered and Clark did not probe. He yawned.

"Hungry?" she said, "I was going to order Chinese?"

Clark smiled again and nodded. That sounded good. He stretched out on the sofa and fell into a light slumber while Siobhan ordered the food and prepared the table at the back of the room. They ate in comparative silence, Clark inwardly running over his meeting with Spencer and the episode on the train while Siobhan seemed to be processing what Clark had told her. She had poured herself a glass of sauvignon to complement the Kung Pao chicken. Clark had opted for tap water, the beer grogginess having set in. After the meal Clark sat on the sofa as Siobhan tidied the table and lit a small lamp by the fireplace. She pressed a couple of buttons on the small speaker system beside the light and her IPod came to life. Soft music filled the air, music Clark did not really care for but it suited the moment.

Siobhan pulled off her boots and dropped into his lap, wrapping both arms around his shoulders. "I know you have a lot on your mind," she said softly, "I know whatever it is going on with Amy is upsetting you." She leaned forward and gently bit on his earlobe. "If there is anything I can do you only have to ask," she whispered.

He smiled and pulled her towards him, kissing her hard and allowing his hand to slip down her back. She pulled away slowly, looked at him and smiled before melting into his touch.

Clark was awakened by early morning sunlight streaming through a gap in the curtains. "Good morning stallion," he heard Siobhan say. He turned to see her lying beside him, on top of the bed sheets and naked to the waist. She was smiling broadly. He smiled in response. What time is it?" he said.

"Relax Clark," said Siobhan as she gently rubbed his arm, "it's still early."

The smile fell from Clark's face as he bolted from the bed pulling on his chinos and shirt before racing towards the door. He shot a glance at Siobhan. She too was no longer smiling. "Clark?" she said.

He did not answer as he left the bedroom pulling the mobile phone from his trouser pocket and bounding down the stairs. He called a taxi and waited at the kerbside.

Back in Ethel Street he sat on his own bed, his head in hands. He thought back to his four year relationship that had recently ended. He had never stayed over in her house, never in the four years. But she had stayed with him. And now he had just spent the night at Siobhan's house. He shot up from his own bed and marched to the bathroom, banging the door closed behind him. Throwing his clothes in the laundry basket he stood for an eternity under the shower head that hung over his bath. The water was scalding hot, his skin blotching as the powerful droplets bounced off him. He would have to call Siobhan. He would call later.

And he had the disk to explore. He had arranged to meet his sister for lunch and she would no doubt expect him to have at least some idea what was on the disk. He thought about skipping work, perhaps going in later. But he had already missed Monday. There were only so many liberties he would allow himself to take. He would check the disk later, after work.

The bus made its way along the Lisburn Road towards the commuter terminals at Belfast's City Hall. After a short walk towards Bedford Street he arrived at Windsor House and the offices of

Chesterton and Williamson, the city skyline domineered by the monstrous office building. As a freelance contractor Clark was not afforded many office luxuries, but he did have a desk and chair, if not much else. His desk sat at the end of a bank of three in a large open plan office on the sixteenth floor, windows all around offering impressive panoramic views of the city. The other two desks at his bank housed salaried employees, two employees who sat opposite each other and to all intense and purposes despised each other. Their desks were overflowing with the best and most modern of equipment, large widescreen computer screens, computer docking stations and internet phones. Locking filing cabinets sat beside each of their desks. Clark had the impression that they used his empty desk for overflow and storage when he wasn't there.

"Morning," said Clark to no-one in particular as he dropped into his chair and began fishing the Dell laptop from his shoulder bag. He looked at Jimmy Callaghan whose eyes were fixed on some seemingly fascinating document in front of him. Jimmy said nothing, not even a grunt. Clark didn't care, nor did he expect anything else. Clark knew Jimmy didn't like him. He knew Jimmy despised the flexibility afforded to Clark through his freelance contract. Jimmy was envious too of Clark's access to Fabian Townsend, the Managing Partner at Chesterton and Williamson. Jimmy reported to a Director in the firm and rarely, if ever, was called to meet Fabian without the Director present. Jimmy was ambitious, of that there could be no doubt, but what he had in ambition he lacked in chivalry. He was around the same age as Clark and was always meticulously turned out in sharp cut Gucci and Hugo Boss business suits. His shoes were never anything but shining and his ties were forever loud and bold, yet appealing. Clark too liked to dress well. He appreciated good clothes and was quick to recognise what everyone wore, both men and women. His wardrobe almost exclusively housed Ralph Lauren, Armani and Hilfiger but his preference was for smart casual rather than formal business. He would of course sport a jacket and tie if he had to, more often than not along with a pair of chinos, giving him that American College look.

Clark turned and nodded at Deanna who did smile in return. "Good morning Clark," she said and turned back towards her computer screen. Clark stole a quick look at the smart black dress she wore. Ted Baker he thought. While small in stature and carrying a few too many pounds Deanna had all the right curves in all the right places. She was a few years younger than Clark and, just like Jimmy, was always well presented. She had mastered the art of gliding gracefully and effortlessly across the floor despite very high heels she invariably wore to compensate for lack of height. Clark liked Deanna, and she seemed to like him too. Although they were invariably genial towards each other they were in reality social strangers. Clark knew nothing about her. He didn't know where she lived or who she lived with, if indeed anybody. And she knew nothing of him. Yes, they did share conversations from time to time, usually over a coffee, but they tended to be work related, about what Clark was doing, who he was working for, what issues he was having with clients. Clark would seldom instigate conversation with her however, and when he did it was usually to ask for her advice or help on issues of company protocol, things that to him as a freelancer were alien, things like how to claim for expenses, how to manage the filing system and who might be available to help him with some photocopying.

Deanna, like Jimmy, was ambitious but was warm and hospitable with it. In Clark's opinion, for what it was worth, she was more capable, more analytical, and more productive. She too reported to the Director of Consultancy Services and not directly to Fabian Townsend, but she didn't seem to have an issue.

Clark sensed Jimmy looking his way. He lifted his head and quickly realised it was in fact his shoulder he was looking over. He noticed too that Jimmy was smiling. Clark turned instinctively and saw Annabel approaching, looking like a model straight off the pages of a Pirelli calendar. Only with slightly more clothes on, even if short and tight. Versace undoubtedly thought Clark in recognition and appreciation. Annabel's hair was long and blonde falling well below her shoulders. A subtle centre parting created an immaculate frame for her fine featured face, with its small pert nose, slender lips and mysterious brown eyes.

Annabel was a trainee with the firm, a recent Economics graduate who was starting on her professional accountancy training. She was enthusiastic, keen to make an impression. Jimmy seemed to have taken a shine to her, although Clark could not help but recall that Jimmy seemed to think his shine was a magnet to all and any female.

Clark had never spoken with Annabel.

"Hi Clark," she said as she sat on the edge of his desk, her back to Jimmy, the short black dress creeping further up her thighs to reveal yet more shimmering black nylon. She hooked one of her pointed high heeled shoes behind the other and leaned towards Clark. He glanced quickly at Jimmy whose wide smile had morphed into an open mouthed gape.

Clark nodded at Annabel and formed a tight smile, hoping his embarrassment was not obvious.

"We've never formally met. I'm Annabel," she said and held out her hand. Clark took it and shook limply, not sure if it was as a result of his unease or if he surreptitiously valued the delicacy of her hand, manicured and soft as it was. For some reason too he impulsively glanced at her other hand, her left hand. No rings.

"I'm Clark," he said, "but of course you know that seeing as you have just said 'Hi Clark.'"

She threw her head back and laughed. "Yes, of course," she said and leaned forward again, prodding Clark on the shoulder with her forefinger. "I believe you and I will be spending some time together. I believe you have some things to show me?" With that she pushed herself off his desk and melted into the distance.

Clark shrugged at Jimmy and went back to work.

A door behind him opened quickly followed by the thick booming voice of Fabian Townsend, "Clark, a minute please." Clark glanced at Jimmy and Deanna hoping for some sort of sign that they might have a heads up but both were meticulously beavering away with their paperwork.

He headed towards the door of Fabian's office, giving a polite nod to Charlotte his dictatorial secretary as he passed. Most of the Chesterton and Williamson workforce were pushed together in the large open plan space, the only exception being the Partners and Directors who each had their own offices, not particularly large or salubrious, but their own individual space nonetheless. The offices were in a uniform line behind where Clark sat. Charlotte also sat in the open plan but outside the door to Fabian's office. The other Partners and Directors too had secretaries sitting outside their offices, like officious gatekeepers and at the beck and call of their charges.

"You're late. No alarm clock in your house? And you didn't even turn up yesterday? Never mind, close the door and sit," barked Fabian when Clark had stepped into the office. Penny Critchlow was already sitting at the small conference table. She smiled and rolled her eyes. Clark nodded choosing to ignore the quips about his tardiness and his absence. He sat beside Penny. Fabian slid his rotund and dishevelled frame into a chair next to Penny.

Penny was the Director of Consultancy Services, an Accountant by profession, as were the majority of consultancy staff within the firm. Penny was in her early fifties and looked it, having long since given up trying to fight the onslaught of wrinkles, deep set crow's feet crawling from her eyes with no attempt to conceal behind makeup. She favoured loose fitting trouser suits over dresses, perhaps not a bad choice Clark had often thought. She had a no nonsense approach, firm but fair and always approachable. For this Clark held her in high regard, even though in practice their paths rarely crossed.

That was all about to change.

"A proposition," said Fabian to Clark as he looked at Penny.

"Detective Inspector McArdle has requested your services again to provide some data mining for an investigation. I am of course delighted at this request and the repeat business you are generating. I am however concerned about our ability as a firm to meet these requests. Now, I know you are the expert and will always be so but I think we need some contingency, some structure if this service is to prosper. I am therefore proposing that you now work through Penny in a more formal way than you are used to. That will mean work planning, fee scheduling, progress reporting, that sort of thing. You know how it is Clark. I have my fellow partners to satisfy."

Clark said nothing. He couldn't think of anything to say. This was not what he was expecting, or wanted. He had served his time in the public service, planning, reporting, and covering backs. He had left to freelance, to give himself independence, freedom.

"And you will need support. The firm will need you to have support. I want you to mentor Jimmy and Annabel in your line of business. As I said you are the expert but share with them what you do, take them to meetings, and let them do some initial analysis. And don't worry I have already arranged the necessary security clearance. That will be all for now. Penny and you can arrange the details."

Clark looked and Fabian and at Penny. He nodded. He looked over his shoulder to where Jimmy would be sitting on the other side of the door. He grimaced and then stood, leaving the office without saying a word.

He sat back at his desk and stared at his computer screen. He wasn't sure if Jimmy knew yet about shadowing him although Annabel clearly did, Clark now knowing what she had meant when she said they would be spending some time together. He looked up at the sound of high heeled shoes clicking across the linoleum floor at the far side of the open plan office. Annabel waved at him.

He checked his watch and pushed himself away from his desk. It was time to forget about Chesterton and Williamson.

It was time to meet his sister.

CHAPTER 5

They had arranged to meet in Ten Square, a popular modern bar and restaurant that was also a small boutique hotel. It was directly behind the city hall, and not far from Windsor House.

He sat at a table set for four with his back to the window and waited for Amy, mindlessly perusing the menu. He put the Fabian meeting out of his head and refocused on the one he'd had the previous day in London, purposefully slipping his hand into his coat pocket and removing the folded sheet of paper. He looked furtively at it again and frowned, just managing to hide it away before Amy arrived.

She looked good he thought, dressed in finery with minimal yet effective make up. Her long fair hair shone and flowed freely. She looked confident, and in control. Clark stood and they embraced, kissing each other's cheek lightly.

"Well, how did it go?" she asked when she had settled into the seat facing him.

"Let's order first," said Clark.

Amy had a quick look at the menu and made her choice of

Mexican chicken salad. Clark had already decided on a club sandwich. He called over the waitress, a pleasant woman who was undoubtedly well experienced in serving her customers, her wide smile never leaving her. Clark ordered for them both.

"And what can I get you to get drink?" she asked as she gathered the menus.

"Sparkling water please," said Clark smiling at her, her manner infectious.

"And I'll go for a glass of Pinot Gris," said Amy again with a smile.

"Nice lady," she said when the waitress had left.

Clark nodded. He looked at Amy as he gathered his thoughts, deciding there was no other way other than direct. "Amy," he said, "what redeeming features attracted you to Spencer?"

She smiled and leaned towards him. "So you two boys hit it off then?"

Clark managed a chortle but more out of relief at having got away with his opening gambit than an acknowledgement of humour. "Not really," he said.

"Listen, I know Spencer can be difficult, that he has let us say, personality traits that can be objectionable, unpleasant. But I love him, I really do. We have been together a long time. We knew each other a long time before we got together as a couple. We had a lot in common and were spending a lot of time together. It just developed naturally into the relationship it became."

She looked away for a moment. "To be honest it was never a physical attraction. He was always generous and supportive and for that I was really appreciative. I suppose I grew to love him."

"So you weren't attracted to his manly charm and good looks?" said Clark.

She laughed, and Clark was again relieved she did not take offence. "No," she said, "you know what they say, love is blind."

The waitress brought their drinks and set them carefully on small paper coasters depicting the logo of the Hotel. "Your meal will be along shortly," she said and left still smiling.

"So why have we never met him?" said Clark and then realised he shouldn't have expected to meet Spencer given he had not spoken with his sister in years. He knew though that their parents had never met him either.

Amy shrugged. "No premeditation," she said, "it just never happened. Spencer was always too busy when I was coming across. You know how it is."

Clark nodded but thought there had been nothing to stop Amy inviting their parents over to say with her and Spencer in Greenwich. He said nothing however.

The waitress was discreet in placing their lunch plates. They both nodded their thanks.

"Anyway," said Amy, "What did you learn from Spencer?"

Clark took a bite of his club sandwich and a long drink from his glass. He leaned forward. "Not much," he said. Amy looked at him. She opened her mouth to speak but Clark continued. "It was brief, and to the point. He showed me little or no courtesy and made a couple of statements that did little more than confirm what you had already told me."

Amy looked over Clark's shoulder to the window and the city hall beyond. She lost herself in thoughts for a moment and then looked at Clark once more. "I'm sorry," she said quietly, "for wasting your time, and for Spencer." She reached to her handbag for a handkerchief.

Clark then produced the CD case from his pocket. "He did give me this however," he said with a mischievous smirk as he placed it on the table.

Amy looked at the CD case and then back to Clark. "What?" she said.

Clark shrugged. "He gave me this CD. But as to what is on it I have no idea. He just handed it to me and disappeared without saying another word."

"And you haven't looked at it?"

"No Amy. Not yet," he said feeling decidedly guilty for his calling on Siobhan. Amy frowned, and with good cause thought Clark. She would have expected him to have at least looked at the CD by the middle of the next day.

"I'm sorry Amy. He did tell me one thing though that was interesting," he then said in hope it would make amends. "He told me the two investments that he made were on the advice of the same source."

Amy didn't say anything for a moment. "So someone advised he invest and he did?" she said eventually. "And the investment turned out to be unsuccessful so the same source advised him of another investment and he followed that too? And that was also unsuccessful"

"Yes," said Clark.

"Who was it?"

Clark shrugged.

She looked again out the window. And then froze.

"Clark," she said loudly, her voice shaking as she pointed over his shoulder.

He turned quickly and rose in his seat to look at whatever she was pointing at. He saw nothing untoward. He looked from left to right seeing only groups of office workers and shoppers carefully navigating their way along the busy footpath. He sat down again.

"What was it Amy?"

She pointed again towards the window, her face white and drawn. "There were two men watching me, two men just standing and watching."

"Clark looked again over his shoulder and then back to his sister. "Are you sure they weren't just looking for somewhere to eat?"

"Yes Clark, I am sure. They both nodded at me when I saw them. And then one of them mouthed something."

Clark leaned forward. "Mouthed what?" he said.

She was shaking her head. "I don't know. It looked like, '*Leave it alone.*'"

It was Clark's turn to freeze. He looked yet again over his shoulder before putting his hand into his pocket and pulling out the folded piece of note paper. He placed it in front of Amy. She looked and gasped, both hands jumping to cover her mouth.

Leave it alone.

"Amy, what is going on," he said.

She stared at him. "I might ask you the same thing Clark. What is that?" she said pointing at the note. "Where did you get it?"

He told her about the three men on the train. He described them as best as he could remember, not that he could remember much other than they looked smart in tailored suits and were well groomed. He could not picture their hair colour, or whether they were or were not of normal height. He didn't think any of them wore glasses, but he couldn't be sure. It had all happened so quickly, and unexpectedly.

"And when were you going to tell me this?" said Amy.

Clark shrugged again. "I was getting round to it, I suppose," he said although could not look directly at her. In truth he did not know if he was going to tell her at all. He thought, perhaps naively, that by not telling he was protecting her. But protecting her from what? She had come to him for help. She had a right to know.

"This is just typical Clark," she said holding both palms up to him, lips pursed.

"I'm sorry. I don't know what I was thinking. I should have told you," he said quietly, hoping he had not compromised the progress he had made with his sister over the last couple of days.

"Okay," she said nodding slowly, "but from now on, please tell me everything."

He nodded. "And you too?"

She nodded. "What do you want to know?"

"Like why there are men following ..." He suddenly stopped.

"What is it Clark?"

"Sunday, when I came away from Mum and Dad's," he said, "there was a car parked by the field."

She sat forward. "What are you saying?"

"There were two men inside, I'm certain." He thought for a moment. "And after you left my house on Sunday night a car pulled away from across the street." He didn't say any more. He thought through what he had just said. Amy was silent too.

"Do you think Mum and Dad are safe?" she said eventually.

Clark nodded. He had no reason to think otherwise. He and Amy had received what he was interpreting as warnings, but no explicit threat. "Just be careful," he said. "Keep your eyes open for anything suspicious. And don't tell Dad. Or Mum."

She nodded her agreement.

"Let's try and make some sense of this," Clark said and began to recap. "You came to Mum and Dad's on Sunday morning and, potentially, someone followed you. If so someone knew you were coming. Or someone followed you from London and came on the same flight. Someone then followed you to my house. I went to see Spencer in London and may or may not have been followed there, but I doubt it for no other reason than I did not book the flight until late. Of course there could have been a standby at the airport.

"Let's go with I wasn't followed. Were you then followed the rest of the day yesterday?"

Amy shook her head. She couldn't be sure.

"And in London Spencer arrives with another man, Lance. Now there's a curious one." Clark raised his eyebrows to Amy. She nodded.

"They go out of the bar," said Clark, "and then come back after a while. Spencer dismisses Lance, who didn't look too happy. Spencer gives me the disk."

Clark then picked up the disk and put it in his pocket. He continued, "Spencer leaves and then I head towards Victoria. And on the train three guys dressed to impress sit beside me and nonchalantly hand me this note." He paused. "But they did not mention the disk." He nodded slowly and looked at Amy. "I don't think they know I have the disk. No one saw Spencer give it to me. And just now two guys give you the same message I was given yesterday. Leave it alone. Leave what alone? If they don't know I have the disk then what is it?"

Amy too was nodding.

"We need to see what's on the disk," said Clark quickly and stood up. He waved the waitress over and asked for the bill which he paid from his fold of notes, leaving a generous tip. Unusual for him he knew but he was impressed with her service, her attention and her infectious smile.

Deciding to leave Amy's car in the public car park they ran across the road towards the bus stop for the 9c service to the Lisburn Road. They took seats at the rear of the bus and kept a watch on other passengers boarding. Reaching the gate to his small front yard Clark stopped and looked over each shoulder before opening the front door and letting Amy in ahead of him, checking over each shoulder again before himself going inside. He made sure the door was closed tight.

"Coffee?" he said after they had hung their jackets over two of the dining chairs. Amy nodded and Clark began to organise a cafetiere. He liked his coffee, and he liked it strong. He hoped Amy like it that way too.

"Are you not supposed to be at work?" she said.

"Don't worry," he said, "I can drop in later and close up the computer." He had other things on his mind. Finishing a report could wait, as could any notion of entertaining Jimmy and Annabel.

He set the coffee to brew and went up the stairs to his study, effectively the small second bedroom, to retrieve his back-up Dell laptop. He always kept two laptops, one he transported to and from work or to clients, and one he kept at home. The one at home was a recent replacement following a theft. He always preferred Dell models, finding them responsive, intuitive and practical. Downstairs he checked the window again, left and right. He set the Dell on the dining table and booted it hoping there would be enough juice in the battery. He lifted the CD case from his jacket pocket and sat slowly behind the computer, inviting Amy to move another chair around and sit with him. Neither spoke.

Clark inserted the disk and then held his breath as its contents came to life.

Amy sat forward.

CHAPTER 6

Four documents appeared as large icons, two word processed documents and two spreadsheets. Clark turned to Amy and she shrugged. They looked together at the icons, the word processed documents titled *TB1* and *WG1*, and the spreadsheets titled *TB2* and *WG2*. Clark clicked on the first, *TB1*. A page opened; a page with no heading or prose. Clark let out a sigh. The document held nothing other than a scanned copy of another document, blurred and difficult to read. It was a table, a table that looked to be taken from a brochure of some sort, a table titled *Thompson Braithwaite Potential Mergers and Acquisitions*. Thompson Braithwaite. TB. There were columns of names and columns of numbers, many numbers.

Clark looked at Amy. She was staring at the screen, stony-faced. He clicked on the second word processed document, another scanned table, *Wilson Group Sales*. The table showed only dates and numbers, very large numbers with zeros aplenty. Clark sucked in a long breath and pointed. Amy nodded silently.

Clark then moved the on-screen cursor and opened *TB2*, revealing a spreadsheet titled *Thompson Braithwaite Forecast*. *WS2* was, unsurprisingly, *Wilson Group Forecast*. The spreadsheets, like the other documents, were filled with large numbers, zero after zero.

"Well, what do you think?" said Clark to draw some verbal reaction from his sister.

"Thompson Braithwaite and Wilson Group," she said shaking her head. "No, not ringing any bells."

"What do you think we are looking at?" said Clark.

"Two different companies," she said slowly. "Spencer invested twice. These could be the companies he invested in." She paused for a moment. "But he invested at different times. Why would he have the information on the same disk?"

Clark nodded. "Don't worry about that Amy. I can check the dates the documents were saved."

She too nodded. "So he could have invested in one, and then received the information on the other afterwards?"

Clark nodded again.

"And where did he get this information?" Amy said.

"There's a lot we need to consider," Clark replied, "We need to find out more about these companies. You are the accountant. I imagine you will make more sense of the numbers than me. What I can do is try to mine into the documents' properties, try and find some clue as to who might have been involved."

Amy looked at Clark. "I noticed you said 'We'?"

He nodded.

"Thank you," she said softly.

Clark smiled. "I'll run you off copies," he said lifting the laptop and taking it upstairs to his study. He preferred hardwiring his computer to the printer rather than using the Wi-Fi option. No reason particularly, he just did.

Back down the stairs he gave Amy the document copies, having made a copy for himself as backup. The spreadsheets each ran for a number of pages. The scanned documents were single pages. She left them on the table and they moved to the sitting area with the coffee they had forgotten about, Amy to the sofa and Clark to the club chair.

"Have you any more thoughts about the guys following us?" Clark said.

Amy shook her head. "I just don't know. But one thing's fairly certain; it's something to do with Spencer and whatever it is he was involved in."

Clark nodded. "Did you notice anything unusual when you were home in Greenwich?"

She shook her head again. "No. No cars in gateways, no men staring through windows, and certainly no bizarre notes passed on trains." She paused and looked away, dropping her head into her hands. "In fact," she said slowly, "There hasn't been anything unusual until I came over here."

Clark thought for a moment and nodded again. He watched as she fought back tears and then said quietly, "Tell me more about Spencer."

She sat up and gently rubbed her face, letting out a long exhale. "I don't know what to say really. He's a workaholic, away early in the morning, home late at night mostly." She paused. "Of course I work long hours too but I do try and get home around seven, to cook a meal, relax, and do a bit of catching up on the property stuff. But more often than not I'm home alone. Spencer will arrive home from late nights at the office, dinner meetings, or just drinks after work and we might then have a light supper and talk about our day."

She looked away again for a moment. Clark did not interrupt.

"We do try to have at least one night in the week when we are both home early enough to enjoy a meal together, and we do aim to spend our Sundays together. But even then he disappears into his study. I suppose however it is something I have grown to accept. It is who he is. As I said he is a workaholic."

Clark looked at her and asked slowly, "Can you trust him Amy, I mean with his being away so much?"

She glared at him and he regretted asking. After a long moment she shook her head, "To be honest, sometimes I wonder," she said, "sometimes he is deliberately evasive… but… yes. I don't think I have any issues with trust. I accept and respect him for who he is, a workaholic who even when he is at home sometimes prefers to lock himself in his study." She shook her head again and choked back a sob, "Hiding away researching failed investments."

"I'm sure he didn't think they were going to be failed investments at the time," said Clark trying to sound as reassuring as he could.

Amy nodded. "That's the point," she said, "Why did such an experienced and renowned investment adviser invest personally in two failed investments? And did he advise any of his clients to invest in the same companies?"

It was Clark's turn to nod. "Yes indeed, many questions." He looked at Amy. "Does Spencer have many friends?"

She shook her head. "Not really."

"And you don't socialise with other couples?" said Clark.

She shook her head again. Clark said nothing as he reflected on the hollow life his sister seemed to have created for herself.

"He of course would have talked a lot about colleagues at work. But there was never any talk about anyone you could describe as a friend. Other than Lance Oldfield, that is. There was another guy he used to meet from time to time for a drink, a guy called Ronald Hawk. He works in another firm in the city so I suppose that would be the closest thing to a friend he would have if you disregard those he actually worked with."

"And what is Ronald Hawk like?" said Clark.

The makings of a smile formed on her face. "You know, I have no idea. I met him once, a couple of years ago, when Spencer and I had arranged a drink after work. He was with Spencer when I arrived at the bar and we were introduced. Then he left. I have never seen him since."

"And does Spencer see him much?"

She nodded. "He would mention him every week or so. I assume they meet up for lunch or maybe go for a drink before Spencer comes home. But I know nothing about him. Spencer will say he met Ronald for a chat but never elaborates, even if I ask."

"And Lance?" said Clark.

"Lance has been working with Spencer for a couple of years. When he joined the firm Spencer was appointed as his mentor."

Clark smiled on hearing the mentor reference. He thought of his imminent role in mentoring Jimmy and Annabel.

"Are you okay?" said Amy.

Clark nodded. "Sorry," he said, "It's just mentoring is something I have to look forward to."

She smiled. "Anyway, Spencer will take Lance to all his meetings. He talks a lot about Lance, about how diligent and meticulous he is, about the promise he shows as an analyst. I've met him a few times with Spencer, again when we were out for a drink after work. Seems nice enough although I have to admit I know nothing about him, if he's married, where he lives, what his interests are."

Clark thought that after two years someone should be beyond showing promise and should be demonstrating their potential. But he said nothing. "What about you Amy," he said, "have you any good friends you can spend time with?"

She laughed. It was hearty and genuine and warmed Clark. "And how do you think I survive? Of course I do. There's a group of girls from work and we meet up regularly for meals, catch a movie, and sometimes go to the theatre. And Natasha next door has become a good friend. Her husband works away a lot and we would drop into each other's houses for a coffee, or a glass of wine. Sometimes we'll head into the city together for a spot of shopping. I'm still friendly too with Kristen from university. We've kept in touch although we don't see each much these days. She's working in a small accountancy practice in Manchester, married now with two girls. We speak on the phone pretty often."

Clark nodded. He was reminded that he needed to call Jackson; a friend who just like Kristen was to Amy was a friend of his since university.

Amy sighed and stood, carrying the empty coffee cups to the kitchen. "I think I'll go back to Ballydorn and see how Mum and Dad are doing," she said over her shoulder before folding the document copies and slipping them into her handbag.

Clark nodded slowly, rationalising that Amy would be safe with their parents, and thought too their company would keep her mind occupied. In any case he wanted to start mining the documents on the disk, something he preferred to do when alone.

He stood and dropped the disk into his jacket pocket before calling a taxi to take them back to the city centre to collect Amy's car and to close out at Chesterton and Williamson's. They didn't have to wait long, late afternoon not renowned for peak taxi cab demand. Clark sat beside the driver who he was glad was more interested in the local radio news than attempting irrelevant and instantly forgettable conversation. Amy sat in the back of the taxi in silence staring at the traffic moving slowly through the city centre.

Clark left Amy on a soft seat on the ground floor reception and rode the lift to the sixteenth floor of Windsor House. He hoped there would be no one there, and was in luck; no Jimmy or Deanna. Charlotte however was still working away head down in front of Fabian's office, a signal that he was still inside strategising his next manoeuvre. Clark kept his head down too and was as silent as possible in shutting down and packing away his computer. As he reached the door to the foyer he looked back over his shoulder, and instantly regretted it. There was Annabel at the far end of the office waving, one hand on hip and a smile as wide as a face could endure. He pushed hastily through the door and prayed there would be a lift waiting.

Amy left Clark home in the BMW, Clark looking left and right and over his shoulder the whole journey. At Ethel Street he made sure

Amy was content to travel on to their parents alone before waving her off. He watched as she rounded the corner at the bottom of the road. He waited for any other car, but none came.

Bruce Springsteen's Lucky Town filled the silence in his living room. He liked low background music when he was analysing documents. It helped him focus, favouring the soft rock style of Springsteen and Adams, and the moody folk rock of Morrison and Dylan. He was not adverse either to the modern country offerings, as long as it leaned towards crossover rock rather than the traditional dead dog self pity style. Sat at his dining table he lifted the disk from his jacket and turned it over in his hands as he thought again of the note he had been handed the train, and the mouthed message Amy had received. *Leave it alone.* What did it mean? He knew he would get to the bottom of it.

He loaded the disk and stared at the four documents on the screen. He could feel adrenalin building as he started with the spreadsheets, deciding that *TB2* would be first for no reason other than alphabetical. He clicked on the icon and *Thompson Braithwaite Forecast* came alive.

The columns of names, dates and numbers filled the screen, names he assumed to be companies supplied by Thompson Braithwaite, although at that point he had no idea what Thompson Braithwaite supplied. Nor did any of the companies supplied mean anything to him. He would check online later. The dates and numbers he assumed related to sales to the other companies, but he didn't know if they were anticipated or agreed sales. There were however peculiarities that jumped out at him. Two companies showed large peaks against them in the third quarter of the year, seasonality peaks that Clark imagined should be expected in any business, but they appeared to be excessive. He reached into his work satchel and pulled out a reporter's notebook, an unused notebook and one he then designated as belonging to the investigation. He wrote the names of the two companies with sales peaks in the notebook together with the dates of the actual spikes; *Santexon* and *Rancode Holdings*.

He began to explore the tabs along the header of the spreadsheet but found nothing else to pique his curiosity. He clicked to explore the properties of the document, a function that would let him see when the document was created, when it was last saved and last printed. He took a note of each of these dates in his notebook. He explored further and found that the document author was a *J Wooten*, a name that he also recorded. He realised that the name would be the computer username, a name that could mean anything depending on the system on which the document was created, a pseudonym for example. It was nonetheless something worth noting. He found also that the spreadsheet had gone through a number of revisions, effectively changes made or information added. He noted this in his notebook along with the date of the last revision.

He opened *WG2*, *Wilson Group* Forecast, and after a quick scan noted a similar pattern, a number of company names with figures attributed. One company however showed figures far in excess of the others, a company called *Green Crab Commodities*. Clark made a note of this company. He noted also, as before, the date created, nodding to himself as he recognised the date to be some months after the creation of the *TB2* spreadsheet. He noted too the number of revisions and the date of the last revision. And he noted the name of the author, *C Hayward*.

Clark stared at his notebook, head in hands. He needed more on these companies, the companies that the spreadsheets belonged to and the companies mentioned within them. He needed to learn something about the dates the documents were created and to test for any significance. And he needed to learn something about the authors of the documents.

Clark was preparing to move away from the spreadsheets to the *TB1* and *WG1* scanned word processed documents when his Nokia buzzed. Reaching for the phone, and grimacing at being interrupted, he looked at the screen. It was Jackson, his oldest friend.

He had been meaning to call Jackson for some time but had been putting it off. They had been through a lot together, both good and bad. Jackson was one of the good guys, always going out of his way to help. But it had been a while since Clark had seen him. And it was all because of Tracey.

Tracey Fox and Jackson Morrow lived together and had recently become engaged, Clark agreeing to be Best Man. But he had not been able to make the engagement party. Or he had chosen not to go. And he had not seen them since. Unknown to Jackson Tracey had made a pass at Clark and Clark had responded. He had however stopped the situation developing too far. He had since chosen to bury his head and stay away. And now Jackson was calling him.

"Hi Jackson," he said, eyes closed tight.

"Hi," said Jackson. And then silence.

"I've been meaning to call you," said Clark.

"Yeah, me too," came the reply.

"Listen..., sorry about the engagement thing."

"Yeah, I know you can be busy."

Clark sighed.

"What about getting together?" Jackson said.

"Yeah."

"Tracey has been asking a lot about you."

Clark closed his eyes again and rubbed his temples, but said nothing. An image of Tracey flashed into his head, the slim frame, the short cropped hair coloured bright red, the comely demeanour; and the incessant talking, a trait Clark found both frustrating and appealing in equal measure.

"What about all of us heading out for a drink?" said Jackson breaking the silence, "You still with Siobhan?"

Clark grimaced again. He hadn't spoken with Siobhan since he had left her that morning, left her confused and upset, and no doubt angry. "Yeah, we're still together," he said hoping it was indeed true.

He would have to speak to her.

"I haven't seen her in a while either," said Jackson, "Still as stunning as ever?"

Clark managed a laugh. "Yeah," he said.

"Tracey is looking forward to meeting her."

Clark nodded as he realised Siobhan had never met Tracey. Siobhan had met Jackson in the early days at Clark's house, in the bar after work, and even on occasion she'd had lunch in the city centre with Clark and Jackson. But she had never met Tracey. "Yeah," he said.

"What about Friday night," said Jackson, "The Cloth Ear, seven thirty?"

"Sure."

"See you then," said Jackson and hung up.

Clark wasn't sure what he had agreed to. Burying the hatchet with Jackson? Facing Tracey? Facilitating Siobhan and Tracey's first meeting? Maybe all three. He would have to clear the air with Siobhan first, or there may not be a night out.

As he turned back to his computer and clicked on the first of the scanned word processed documents, the phone buzzed again. He sighed and pushed the answer button.

"Clark," said Amy quickly, "there are two men in Mum and Dad's house."

CHAPTER 7

Clark logged out of his computer anxiously waiting for the end of the shut down process. Clicking a start button to finish something was one of many strange computer phenomena he, like everyone else no doubt, accepted without question. And why did the shutdown process, like a boiling kettle, always seem to take longer when in a hurry? He pushed back his chair and lifted the disk, running to the door with heart pounding. He grabbed his overcoat from the hall and pulled it on, dropping the disk into one of its deep pockets and slamming the door behind him while he groped for his car keys. He then did something he had never done before. He leaped the low wall separating his house from next door and banged on the window.

Vince sat beside him in the front of the Toyota, Ryan squashed into the rear seat, his knees pressed tight into Vince's back. Both men were dressed as they always seemed to be dressed, tee shirts and jeans with light brown boots. No matter what the weather Clark had not seen them venture outside in anything other than tee shirts, broad heavily inked arms on display, with squat shaven heads resting on thick necks. Yes, they appeared frightening, threatening even, but

Clark had no reason to regard them as such. He had lived next door for many years and regarded them as good neighbours, quiet and unobtrusive. Not unlike himself. Vince and Ryan were friends who shared the rent and seemed to live simple lives that revolved around little more than going to work and frequenting their social club where no doubt beer, darts and snooker featured heavily. Vince drove a lorry making deliveries for a local garden supply centre, the lorry on occasion making an appearance on Ethel Street. Ryan's work seemed to be less obvious with Clark seeing him being picked up in a number of different vans at different times of the day, and sometimes leaving with Vince. Clark surmised he was taking whatever casual labour was available, helping out Vince when required or perhaps if he had no other work. They were two men who worked hard and bothered nobody.

"Appreciate it," said Clark as he drove along the Lisburn Road as fast as he could in the early evening traffic, the chaotic Belfast rush hour having just passed.

"No problem," said Vince, his eyes fixed firmly on the road in front. Ryan said nothing.

Clark tried to stay calm. The last thing he would need would be to run into the back of another car, or to be pulled over by traffic police. Of course, the police, he thought wondering if he should contact them. And tell them what? No, he quickly decided. He would wait, at least for now. He would speak with Detective Inspector McArdle when he had more of a handle on what was going on.

Clark had told Vince and Ryan there might be intruders in his parents' home and as they lived rurally he would appreciate some back up to check on them. They had followed him immediately; no questions asked and glad to be of assistance. They were certainly an enigma, and one for which Clark was grateful.

"Not keeping you guys from anything?" said Clark as he reached the clearer rural roads and the speed picked up.

Vince shook his head, "No, just going to the club."

Clark nodded. "I'll drop you there on the way back."

Vince nodded.

There were no other words spoken the rest of journey. Vince and Ryan had not asked where they were going. They did not know where Clark's parents lived, and Clark had not told them. They were seemingly content to sit and wait until they arrived at where they had to be.

Clark arrived in the car park at Whiterock, a picturesque beauty spot that overlooked the Lough with its sailboats and cruisers moored offshore for the sea hardy to enjoy. Dusk was beginning to fall, the view soon to be cloaked in darkness. He saw Amy's black BMW in the far corner of the car park and pulled up beside it. Climbing out of his Toyota he dropped into Amy's passenger seat. Vince and Ryan did not move.

Amy was pale, her eyes moist. She was breathing heavy. Clark reached his hand across and let it fall gently on her knee. "Tell me again what you saw," he said calmly.

She looked at his hand. Clark quickly removed it. She turned to him and then looked oddly at the outline of the two bulky figures squashed into his car. Clark managed a smile and cocked a thumb over his shoulder. "Back up," he said.

She shook her head. "As I told you," she said, "I was coming down towards Mum and Dad's driveway and there was a car parked beside the gate posts. I thought it odd as a visitor would surely turn into the driveway and park. And then I remembered you saying about seeing a car parked across the field gate on Sunday morning so for some reason I slowed and drove past the driveway and glanced up towards the house."

She paused, reliving what she had seen. "Clark, there were two figures standing at the window. I could only see their backs... I can't be certain... but it must be them... the same two from earlier..." She broke into tears.

Clark returned his hand to her knee. "It's okay Amy," he said,

"Let's go and see."

They decided to go in one car, opting for Clark's as it would be easier for Amy to climb in and join the other inhabitants rather than moving them. It wasn't something she looked particularly happy about but into the back she climbed and sat as close to the door as she could to put as much space between her and the tree truck thighs on the other side of the seat. She smiled an awkward smile. Ryan nodded.

Clark pulled out of the car park, making quick introductions as he did so. Vince turned and smiled. It was a warm smile and Amy responded in kind. Clark developed a plan on route and the rest listened.

The car was still parked beside the gate; an unremarkable silver Ford saloon that Clark was sure was the same one that had been parked across the field gate two days before. He drove into the driveway with Amy in the passenger seat. He had let Vince and Ryan off at a narrow country lane some fifty yards shy of the house, a lane not much more than tractor ruts. He had pointed them in the direction of the house. The plan, such that it was, involved Vince and Ryan crossing the field and stepping over the sheep fence into the garden, Vince to cover the front door and Ryan the back. Clark and Amy would drive towards the house feigning ignorance that anything was untoward. Clark was assuming that if there were two men in suits in his parent's house they were there to deliver a message, just like on the train or in the city centre. He had brought Vince and Ryan just in case. He had told them that the front and back doors were normally kept unlocked and to wait outside unless they deemed it appropriate to intervene. He hoped they could determine themselves when, and if, was appropriate.

Clark and Amy walked towards the front door, turning as they heard a rustle in the hedgerow. Clark nodded as Vince took up position. He suspected Ryan was already at the back door.

The front door was unlocked as expected and Clark and Amy

walked slowly over the threshold, towards the voices in the lounge.

"Hi Clark, Hi Amy," said their father from his usual chair. Their mother was sitting on the Parker Knoll, a blank look on her face, a visage of confusion. Clark wasn't sure if it was because of the two sharp suited men standing facing them or because he and Amy had arrived together. His mother, he was sure, was still of the view Clark and his sister had a lot of reconciling to do. Just like he knew he and his mother had a lot of reconciling to do.

Clark nodded at his father and at his mother and then stared at the two men. Amy stayed behind him.

"Amy and Clark," said the taller and considerably slimmer of the two men, "Glad you are here. We were just having a chat with your parents. I'm Brent by the way and this is Wayne." Both men were dressed in similar but not identical navy suits. Tailored, well tailored, with a look of Savile Row about them Clark thought. Their shirts were Hawes and Curtis with matching floral silk ties and cufflinks. Hand stitched leather soled Grensons shone in the electric light that lit the room. "Sorry we didn't get a chance to talk to you earlier in the City," he said and glanced at Amy with a smile. Clark was enraged and rocked forward but Amy's hand rose quickly to his elbow.

"These are friends of Spencer," said their father, "Over here on business. First time here and Spencer said to look us up. Pretty decent of them don't you think?"

Clark and Amy both looked at him and sensed the twinkle in his eye, a twinkle that only they would have recognised, a twinkle that said he was playing along. Their mother said nothing.

"We were just saying to your parents," said Brent, "that we were having lunch in Belfast when you saw you. We wanted to talk but you were both gone by the time we went outside."

Clark felt his cheeks flush at this reverse of the truth. He turned towards Amy and she put her hand again on his arm. She was shaking her head, a sign that Clark interpreted to let them have their say.

"We've never met. We don't know you. Why would we want to talk to you?" said Clark.

"No, indeed we have not," said Brent, "but we feel like we know you. We have heard so much about you." He pulled a folded foolscap page from the front pocket of his jacket and opened it to show two printed photographs, one of Clark cropped from an online group picture at a conference somewhere and one of Amy that looked more professional, probably from her firm's website Clark guessed. "A very good likeness," the man said as he waved the page in front of them.

Clark led Amy further into the room and nodded again at his mother. Amy sat on the arm of her chair and reached to hold her hand. Clark moved to between his father and his mother and Amy. He remained standing. "What do you want?" he said.

"Just to say Hi," said Brent with a broad grin and held out his hands in some form of conciliatory gesture. Clark's chest heaved in unison with his pounding heartbeat. Blood rushed to his head. He clenched his fists and took a step forward. The other man, the round one called Wayne, was quick despite his shape. He stepped in front of Brent and held up his hand. It was a subtle yet effective move. Clark stopped and rocked back on his heels. He nodded and stepped back to stand again between his mum, dad and sister. He had however learned something.

Wayne deferred to Brent.

His father spoke to alleviate the tension. "Everything's fine," he said, "These men have just been telling us about Spencer and the great asset he is to his firm, how the firm has thrived due to his success." He paused for a moment and then said, "And how important it is that he continues with the firm."

Clark looked at his father.

His father shrugged. "It looks like your sister is the only hope. The firm needs Spencer but they need him to right his wrongs first."

Brent was smiling and nodded. Wayne stood silently with his gaze fixed on Clark.

"Wait a minute," said Amy as she lifted herself from the arm of her mother's chair and stood beside Clark to face the two men. "Who are you? And why is any of this your business?"

"Who are we?" said Brent, the smile still on his face. "As your father has just said, we are friends of Spencer. We were here on business and thought we would introduce ourselves to your family Amy. After all you and Spencer have been together for years. He talks a lot about you. We feel we know you already. So why not try and get to know you better?" The smile was wide, too wide, and the hair was too black, the eyes too blue. And there was something about the complexion, too shiny, too conditioned. In all, he was too slick, too confident.

"How come I don't know you? Brent and Wayne you say? How come I don't recall Spencer having mentioned you before?" said Amy.

Brent shrugged.

"Does Spencer know you're here?" she asked.

Brent nodded.

Clark turned towards Amy and pointed towards the door. "Go call him," he said.

Amy turned but Wayne was quick. He stepped towards the door and stood with his arms folded. No smile. His hair was thin on a small head, an unusually small head for a man so wide. His nose was wide with narrow deep set dark eyes. Yet despite it all he too was well groomed, clean shaven, with flawless complexion.

Amy glanced to the floor beside her mother's chair. Her Burberry bag was still there, the phone safely stored inside. She stared at Wayne and then back to Brent.

"Say your piece and leave," said Clark, shoulders back and standing tall.

Brent stepped back and again opened his arms. "It's simple," he said, "the firm needs Spencer. But they need him to clean his slate.

His own assets will not cover him. He can't borrow." He looked at Amy, "But you can help him. And he would appreciate it if you could do just that, as would we. We know you can. And we are asking that you do."

Clark stepped towards him and stopped when he sensed Wayne moving in his direction. Wayne kept coming, brushing provocatively past him before halting beside his comrade.

"Are you threatening Amy?" said Clark staring at Brent.

"Not at all, as I said, we are asking."

"Well I'm telling you," said Clark, his anger getting the better of him, "get out now." He bounded forward and grabbed the tall shiny man by his tailored collar and pulled him towards him. Brent fell forward off balance and Clark let him drop to the floor. It happened too quickly for Wayne, despite the dexterity and speed of action he had demonstrated earlier. He stepped forward but Clark had jumped back, away from Brent. Wayne had too much ground to cover. Clark was ready for him.

Amy screamed and the lounge door crashed open. Vince thundered into the room and pushed Clark out of the way. He stood firm and Wayne froze. Wayne looked from left to right. He turned to Brent who had lifted himself to his feet and was brushing himself down. Brent nodded and Wayne stepped back. Brent looked to Amy and to Vince. A smile broke across his face and he looked at Clark. He shook his head. "Clark," he said, "I have been friendly. I have asked. But I think you have underestimated the situation. You have no idea who you are dealing with, have you?"

And then Ryan stepped into the room. He stood to the other side of Clark, who was then bookended between the two chunky tattooed men. It was Clark's turn to smile. "No," he said, "I don't think you have any idea who you are dealing with."

Brent moved his hand towards the inside of his jacket. Clark drew a sharp breath. But Brent let his hand fall to his side. He looked at Wayne and nodded towards the door. Clark and his minders stepped aside and let Brent and Wayne leave. They did not speak another word, even though the tall man could not erase the smile from his face.

Clark moved to the window and watched as the two men turned the corner at the bottom of the drive. A car engine started and drove quickly away illuminating the road and surrounding fields with its bright halogen headlights.

"We'll wait outside," said Vince as he and Ryan turned and left as silently as they had arrived.

Clark continued to stare out the window, hands on hips. He let out a long sigh.

"For goodness sake Clark, what have you got us into now?" snapped his mother, the first time she had spoken. Clark looked at her and then to Amy and his father. He smiled and Amy laughed. His father laughed too, a deep loud laugh. Clark began to laugh.

"Doris," said Clark's father to his wife through his laughter, "Are you going to blame Clark for the melting polar caps, and for world poverty?"

She looked at him strangely, "What on earth are you talking about Malcolm?"

"Clark is helping Amy," he said, "You can't pin this one on him."

She folded her arms and sat back in the chair. "Right, I think someone had better explain."

And so Amy told her about Clark having gone to London the previous day to meet Spencer and about encountering a number of well dressed men on the train who had more or less told him not to get involved. She told her about the men in Belfast city centre staring at her through the window of the restaurant, the same two men who had just left their house. She told her about the message that was mouthed at her; a message that seemed consistent with the one Clark had received in London. Their mother shook her head. Amy looked at their father. He stared at her. "I didn't know Clark had gone to London," he said, "I didn't know Clark had met Spencer." He looked sharply at Clark in the chastening way he had done many times before.

Clark shrugged.

"Leave it alone?" said Amy, "Leave what alone? It doesn't make sense. On one hand they are telling me, telling us, to leave it alone and then they are encouraging me, if I can put it that way, to sell up and help Spencer."

"Maybe the message is to leave alone the questioning of Spencer's motives and just sell up, and pay up?" said their father.

Clark nodded. "That's my thinking," he said, "Stop questioning, and don't investigate."

"Investigate what?" said their father.

"Nothing," said Clark and looked to the floor.

"No Son, it is not nothing. We are now involved in case you haven't noticed. Investigate what?"

Clark looked at Amy and she nodded. Their father was right of course. Two men had come to their house unexpectedly. Clark and Amy had arrived with two burly acquaintances. Yes indeed, they deserved an explanation.

"Spencer gave me a computer disk," said Clark, "He didn't say much but I think he suspects something suspicious about what is on the disk."

"Go on Son," said his father, leaning forward in his chair, captivated.

"I don't know yet as I haven't had much of a chance to explore but the disk contains a few documents, documents that I think may relate to the companies that Spencer invested in. I think what is happening now is we are being encouraged, to use Amy's word, to leave alone any investigation into these companies."

"But why?" said their mother sharply shaking her head.

"I don't know," said Clark and he turned to look at Amy, "But I intend to find out."

Their mother stood and headed for the kitchen muttering

something about a cup of tea. Clark could do nothing but smile. Some things never change he thought as he remembered his mother's answer to all crises over the years. Let's have a cup of tea. Clark glanced at his father who glanced back and shrugged. They waited in silence. She returned with a tray holding four Royal Albert teacups on saucers and a matching teapot with stream billowing from its spout. She set it on the sideboard beside the phone and left again for the kitchen, returning with a second tray adorned with lemon slices and fingers of Battenberg cake. Clark had to smile again. "Who are those two animals outside?" she said looking coldly at Clark.

"My next door neighbours. Here to offer a helping hand."

"Humph. I don't care much for your choice in neighbours," she said as if Clark, or indeed anyone, could choose their neighbours.

Clark looked away. "I suppose I'd better get them home," he said. "I'll order them a taxi." He went outside but returned a few moments later. "They're fine," he said, "They'll wait for me." He looked at his mum but she turned away from him. He turned then to his dad. "Tell me this," he said, "How long were those guys here, Brent and Wayne? What did they say to you? Did they threaten you in any way?"

His father shook his head. "No. They just walked up the drive and your mother let them in, said they were friends of Spencer. They showed us a couple of photographs, some sort of workplace photographs, showing them and Spencer together. Not that we have ever met Spencer but the man they were with looked similar to the man we have seen in photographs Amy has let us see over the years." He stared at Amy and she dropped her head. "They were very civil. Stood for over an hour and talked all about Spencer and Amy, all about London. They asked plenty of questions about Belfast, about Strangford Lough saying it was the first time they had been here and how much they were enjoying it. There was really nothing to be concerned about. In truth I was actually enjoying the conversation. And then you two arrived."

Clark nodded. If they were there for over an hour they must have arrived not long before Amy had driven past and called him. It took him just over half an hour to drive from Ethel Street. He was relieved no harm had come to his parents. They did not seem to have been in any danger although he was curious what Brent and Wayne really wanted at his parents' house. Did his and Amy's arrival interrupt any plan they might have had?

"You had mentioned earlier Dad that they had said how much of an asset Spencer was to the firm. What exactly did they say?"

His father rolled his head back in the chair and closed his eyes, clasping his hands together in front of his chest as he tried to recall. "I'm paraphrasing Son," he eventually said, "Apparently Spencer is essential to the firm. I can only imagine that whatever he does he is good at and the firm doesn't want to lose him, or perhaps they rely and depend upon whatever kudos, fees, or whatever he brings."

"But if he is so good why did he do what he did? Why did he invest the firm's money, and in a failed venture? What confidence could anyone have in his credibility as an analyst and adviser? And then he invested again, albeit his own money, in another failure?" said Clark shaking his head, bewildered.

His father shrugged and they both looked at Amy. She shrugged too. Their mother spoke, "Do you need some money Amy?"

"Thanks Mum," said Amy resting her hand on her mother's knee, "but if you are offering money I hope you have plenty." She smiled. Their mother smiled. Clark too smiled at the other two smiling. And then their father broke again into laughter.

"How much money have you got Doris? I sure hope you haven't a stash hidden away from me?" he said.

She glared at him.

Amy shook her head. "We are not talking tens of thousands of pounds here, not even hundreds of thousands," she said. "Spencer has got himself in a serious mess… But I know if I do what he asks he will be okay."

"But can you trust him?" asked her father, a question Clark himself had asked. Amy's eyes began to well. Her mother lifted her arm and placed it around Amy's waist.

"Right," said Clark. "We don't know what we don't know, but we do know..."

"For goodness sake Clark," said his mother abruptly, "What on earth are you talking about?"

He looked at her, sighed and held up both hands. "Hear me out," he said, "Spencer has asked Amy for help. Amy wants to be sure she is doing the right thing before she offers that help. Spencer has given me a disk and at the same time a number of guys, all of whom are well dressed giving the impression they have some form of business affiliation, appear to be advising Amy and I not to question what Spencer has done but at the same time they are encouraging Amy to fund his survival. But no one has mentioned the disk."

He paused and looked at Amy and in turn at his father and his mother. He looked back to Amy. "They don't know I have the disk. There must be something on it or else why give it to me? I need to learn as much as I can about it and frankly from my initial scan there is a limited amount I can do. I'll go home soon and look again but I am thinking I will need to speak again with Spencer."

Amy nodded slowly. "I'll see if I can draw anything from the hard copies of the documents."

Clark nodded and turned to his mum and dad. "But there are still two men floating about who know where you live," he said, "And no doubt they know that Amy is staying here. As it stands they are unknowns. I think it might be better if you went somewhere for few days." He turned back to Amy.

She nodded. "Why don't I take Mum and Dad to the Slieve Donard?"

"Perfect," said Clark. The Slieve Donard was a luxury and highly desirable hotel at the foot of the Mountains of Mourne, and backing onto the Royal County Down golf course. It would be a safe environment until Clark could establish what was going on. There were public spaces aplenty, spaces where they could relax, and in the case of his father continue to recuperate. And it was only forty minutes away.

"Right, I'll organise it now," said Amy and strode across the room to collect her bag before lifting her parent's laptop computer from the sideboard. "And I need to call Spencer and organise for you to go and see him tomorrow. No point in talking in the phone. Go and face him, ask him what is going on, try and get some answers. But be careful," she said raising her eyebrows, a warning Clark had heard before. She left the room with her bag and the computer.

She had taken him off guard. But yes, speaking with Spencer face to face was probably best given his arrogant intolerance and likelihood to hang up on any phone call. Clark however had his own work to go to. He couldn't just drop everything. Fabian, Penny, Jimmy and Annabel would be expecting him. He had gone that afternoon for lunch and had not returned, other than to retrieve his computer. And Annabel had seen him, had waved at him. He dropped his head into his hands.

"This is all getting a bit serious now Son," said his father. "Don't you think we should contact the police, not least that we seem to be arranging to leave our house following some kind of threat or intimidation?"

Clark nodded. "I know Dad," he said, "But I just want to know more about what is going on first. As it stands what have we got to tell the police?"

His father nodded his agreement, "Don't you have a friend in the police though?"

Clark laughed. "An acquaintance is perhaps the word you are looking for? Yes Detective Inspector McArdle is someone I do a bit of freelance work for. And yes he works in Financial Crimes so at some point he may well be someone to speak to. But for now let me find out more."

His father nodded again. Clark however had already given some thought to contacting McArdle, at least for an off the record chat. He would call him later. His mother was quiet as she sat glaring at him. He hoped she would be content by the prospect of a few days in the Slieve Donard Hotel with its spa and a la carte dinners.

After a few moments Amy came back into the room. "Right, all sorted," she said, "Two rooms in the Slieve Donard are waiting." Their mother rose from her chair and scurried from the room, no doubt with her mind on locating and packing a suitcase. Their father sat in silence.

Amy then looked at Clark and shook her head slowly, a look of concern and apprehension on her face. She pointed discreetly over her shoulder and Clark followed her into the kitchen.

CHAPTER 8

"Spencer has no idea who Brent and Wayne are," said Amy when they were safely out of their parent's earshot. "When I described them he still maintained he had no idea."

"What about the photograph they showed Mum and Dad?" said Clark.

"He has no idea where it was taken" She looked away and added quietly, "He didn't seem concerned when I told him I was frightened." She looked out the window into the darkness. Clark caught her reflection, seeing pain in her face. He stepped towards her and wrapped his arms around her waist, eventually dropping his head onto her shoulder. "I didn't tell him I was taking our parents away for a few days," she said turning towards Clark, tears dripping on her cheeks. He stepped back and released her from his embrace. "Why is that Clark?" she said.

Clark could not answer. He didn't know what his sister was thinking, didn't know enough about her relationship with Spencer. Indeed he knew nothing of her relationship with Spencer. And he knew nothing about Spencer, other than he appeared obtuse and patronising. But he had given him a disk, and this Clark had taken as a gesture that he wanted help. Clark was willing to take it at face value. "What about my meeting him again?" he asked.

Amy waited a moment for her tears to subside. "He wasn't particularly enthusiastic," she said slowly and looked away.

Clark was surprised by his own disappointment. He had resigned himself to meeting Spencer and teasing more information out of him. He had thought too that Spencer would want to meet him, to learn what he had garnered from the disk.

"But I managed to persuade him," Amy continued, turning back to Clark. "Even if he does make it sound like an inconvenience. He said he is busy all day tomorrow, and is out in the West End tomorrow night. But he said he will meet you there in the West End before he goes out. You probably won't make the last flight home tomorrow. Would you be up to staying over?"

Clark blew out a long breath. He thought again of Chesterton and Williamson. He nodded.

"I was thinking maybe of the Strand Palace Hotel, opposite The Savoy? It's in a great location. Functional, but has a great bar. Are you familiar with it?"

Clark nodded again.

"Okay. I'll organise flights and the reservation and let you know." She paused and looked at him. "And Clark, be careful."

"You too," he said and turned towards the lounge. His mother was holding a shirt in each hand, seeking her husband's opinion on their suitability for packing. He looked like he couldn't care less. Clark said his goodbyes and asked his mother if she could drive Amy to collect her hire car from Whiterock. She just looked at him. He slipped out the front door to round up Vince and Ryan.

There was silence in the car as they made their way back towards Belfast, Clark running everything over in his head, Vince and Ryan as quiet as ever. Eventually a voice from the passenger seat said, "Everything okay?" It was Vince.

"Yeah," said Clark.

"You know those guys?"

"No. And by all accounts Amy's partner Spencer doesn't either, even though they produced a photograph of themselves with him. Amy described them to Spencer on the phone but he doesn't know them. Doesn't know where the photograph might have come from."

Vince didn't say anything for a long moment. Then he turned to Clark and said, "I have their picture."

"What?" said Clark turning his head abruptly, almost careering into the oncoming traffic. A horn blared and headlights flashed.

"On here," said Vince nonchalantly. He held up his phone, "Snapped a shot in the room."

Clark smiled and held out his hand for a high five. Vince looked at him and Clark coughed, dropping his hand quickly onto the gear stick. "Don't suppose you can send it to me?" he said and then realised the basic functions of his Nokia probably didn't permit data transfer. "Can you email it?"

Vince looked at him again. "Sure," he said slowly. Clark dictated his email address and made another mental note to update his phone.

Twenty minutes later and Clark pulled up on Belfast's Dublin Road, just short of Shaftesbury Square. He had no idea where the social club was, or even what it was, but this was where they had asked to be dropped off. He put his hand in his pocket and pulled a number of twenties from his fold. He handed them to Vince.

"Thanks guys," he said, "I really appreciate it. Have a few beers on me."

Vince looked fleetingly at his hand. "No, it's okay," he said and opened the car door.

Ryan reached across from the rear seat and placed his hand on Clark's shoulder. Clark turned, startled, "Anytime," said Ryan. He nodded at Clark and climbed out of the car. Clark smiled and shook his head. It had been a long time since he had heard Ryan say anything. He watched them disappear into the distance.

It was approaching nine o'clock on what had been a long day. But he still had more to do. Constantly checking his mirror he drove slowly home where he lifted the disk from his coat pocket as he hung it on its hook. After closing the curtains over the lounge window he sat at the dining table, waiting for the Dell to come alive.

The first word processed scanned document was the table titled *Thompson Braithwaite Potential Mergers and Acquisitions*. Clark looked carefully at the list of names, names he took to be companies that Thompson Braithwaite had targeted. None of the names meant anything to him. He looked again, pushing his head forward so his eyes were only centimetres from the screen. Something looked off. Was that a faint blurred smudge around one of the company names? He nodded as he concluded the original pre-scanned document had the company name highlighted with a coloured pen. He looked eagerly at the column of numbers, a column labelled 'Net Worth' noting again a blurring around the number aligned with the same company, a company he took a note of: *Yerco*.

He began to explore the properties of the document, noting the date created. He flicked back in his notes and nodded, the date matching the last Thompson Braithwaite spreadsheet revision. The document author was the same: J Wooten.

In the second scanned document, *Wilson Group Sales*, there didn't appear to be anything highlighted, just a list of numbers Clark assumed were confirmed sales. He checked the document properties and noted the date created, flicking back in his notes and confirming that it too was a date shared with the last Wilson Group spreadsheet revision. He made a note of the document author, again the same as before: C Hayward.

Clark chewed on his pencil as he flicked through his notes, reflecting on what he had garnered. He had two companies that he decided to call parent companies, Thompson Braithwaite and Wilson Group, and four other companies he decided to call subsidiaries, Santexon, Rancode Holdings, Green Crab Commodities and Yerco.

And he had the names of two document authors, J Wooten and C Hayward.

It was time for the internet search engine to work its magic. As his fingers began to dance across the keyboard his phone rang, his Nokia that he had placed on the side of the table. He picked it up without checking the caller ID.

"Hello?" he said, his mind elsewhere.

"Hello Clark."

It was Siobhan.

Clark closed his eyes recalling the events of that very morning, the running from her house. He didn't know what to say. Siobhan came to the rescue. "I'm sorry," she said, her voice crackling.

Clark tried to speak but could only manage a dry croak.

"I shouldn't have allowed that to happen," she said, "It was too soon."

The tears welled in Clark's eyes as he reminded himself yet again how lucky he was, how special Siobhan was. "Siobhan…I…"

"I know Clark. I just wanted to say… I love you." And then she hung up.

Clark dropped his phone. She had said the words, words he had never heard her use before, and words he had not heard in a long time, words he had thought he would never hear again. His shoulders shook as he fought to control himself. But it was a battle he lost. He gathered himself and lifted a bottle of Corona from the fridge, deciding he would call her back. He wanted to hear her voice again. He would talk to her about what had happened with Amy and about what he planned to do the following day. The personal stuff could go unspoken. And that was what he did. He told Siobhan he was going to London the next day and would be staying over in the Strand Palace. He told her he would be home on Thursday afternoon and that she should come to Ethel Street and he would cook dinner. He remembered also to tell her about Friday night, about meeting Jackson and Tracey for drinks. She appeared excited, remarking that she was looking forward to meeting Tracey at long last, and that it was about time now that she was Jackson's fiancée. Clark said nothing in reply. She told him to be careful and he wished her a good night before ringing off.

He felt better having smoothed things with Siobhan, but he had other things to do. He had just settled behind the laptop when his phone buzzed again, this time a text message, a message from Amy saying she and their parents had arrived at the Slieve Donard Hotel and confirming he was booked on the Wednesday 14.25 flight to London Gatwick and on the Thursday 16.20 flight back to Belfast City. She included the flight number so he could check in online. She confirmed also his reservation for the Strand Palace. He sent a short return message telling her to stay safe and that he would be in touch.

The flight schedule meant he could go to Chesterton and Williamson in the morning and maybe orchestrate the afternoon and next day away on some form of work related matter. He was used to having flexibility to do such things and remained unsure what might change now that Penny Critchlow was in the mix. He would find out tomorrow. He considered too the expectation that he induct Jimmy and Annabel into his police investigatory work. He frowned. It reminded him however that he had intended to call DI McArdle. He looked at his watch. It was late but he dialled, undeterred.

"Financial Crimes, McArdle," came a deep booming voice from the depths of a portly frame, evidently not checking his caller ID.

"Good evening McArdle," said Clark.

And then a roar of laughter, "It's Detective Inspector McArdle to you Radcliffe."

"And it's Clark Radcliffe to you," said Clark laughing in return.

"And what can I do for you this fine evening?" asked McArdle.

Clark didn't want to get into detail over the phone. He said he was doing a bit of investigation into his sister's partner's business affairs and would welcome a chat with the DI.

"Sure thing. Funny enough I'm just finishing up a shift at HQ. Be with you in fifteen minutes. I take it you are at home?" said McArdle with enthusiasm that Clark read as gratitude in having his advice sought.

"Great," said Clark, "and yes I'm at home."

Clark returned to his notes and then suddenly remembered something else. He logged hastily into his email and there it was. The photo that Vince had sent; a grainy picture with the faces of two men in conversation, two men with polished faces, one thin and dark haired, the other small, round and thinning. The tailored shirt collars and colourful ties were visible. The background was his parent's magnolia painted wall with a box canvas print of a sailboat and sunset creeping into the corner. Clark smiled and nodded as he carried the laptop to his study to print copies.

Back downstairs he slipped Bob Dylan's Freewheelin' into his CD player reminding himself to make the time to convert his collection to MP3 when he heard a rap on his door.

And in he came, as rotund and red faced as ever, thick black hair dishevelled, the navy chain store sports coat lying open exposing a faded yellow shirt and aqua blue spotty polyester tie, off the shelf grey trousers gravely creased and dark rubber soled shoes badly scuffed. Clark smiled and shook his head.

"Well Clark son, what's happening?" McArdle said after following Clark into the kitchen and leaning against the worktop, forcing Clark to work around him in organising a cafetiere of coffee.

Clark told McArdle everything, from Amy arriving on Sunday morning to the trip to London on Monday and the events at his parents' house that afternoon, Tuesday afternoon. He showed him the note he had been handed on the Gatwick Express, and he told him about the same message Amy had received in Belfast. He added he was going to London the next day. And finally he showed him his notebook with the list of companies.

McArdle listened intently, alternating periodic nods with sighs. When Clark had finished he looked at him. "There is some serious stuff going on here," he said, "and I'm not sure I am happy for you to be dabbling in it."

Clark poured the coffee and handed a mug to his visitor. He leaned back against one of the dining chairs, his own mug in hand. He lowered his head.

McArdle continued, "Threatening behaviour, intimidation, and folk leaving their home to a hotel?"

Clark nodded and reached behind for a copy of the photo Vince had emailed. He handed it to McArdle who stared, thin lips pulled tight.

"Slick," he said reiterating a descriptor Clark had considered. "Certainly sharp dressers. And the three guys who gave you the note on the train?"

"The same," said Clark.

"Right, give me a minute." McArdle set down his mug and walked to the front door. Clark moved to the window and opened the curtains a chink. McArdle was sitting in the passenger seat of a silver Vauxhall saloon parked directly behind the Toyota. Although difficult to see in the dimness Clark was certain there was another figure in the car. DC Campbell he realised. McArdle was rarely without DC Campbell by his side, a younger slimmer man, and a man who rarely spoke.

Ten minutes later and McArdle was back. Clark had fresh coffee brewing. McArdle stood in front of the fireplace, hands on hips. "Right," he said, "I have spoken with Edward James, a DI colleague in the London Metropolitan Police. He would be a counterpart of mine in Financial Crimes, what they call Specialist and Economic Crime Command. I know him pretty well. We would meet up at conferences, and have shared some info on cases in the past. Good guy. He works closely with the Economic Crime guys at the City of London Police. He knows his stuff."

McArdle ran a hand across his face. "Here's the thing; it's not uncommon for corporate ranks to organise themselves for what they might call mutual advantage." He stared at Clark and added slowly, "They establish a structure and follow a strict set of rules..."

"Wait a minute," said Clark cautiously, "Are you saying like an organised gang?"

"Hmm," said McArdle with a careful nod, "They would indeed be organised and disciplined but they are underground, very secretive."

Clark was shaking his head. "Why? What's their purpose?"

McArdle shrugged. "Apparently these guys are good with the markets, investments and stuff. They enjoy the good life. And once they have it they don't want to lose it. They will do what they can to sustain each other's financial success."

It was Clark's turn to stare at McArdle. "Do what they can? What does that mean? Some form of money rigging cartel who insert pressure and influence or is it something more sinister?" He remembered Brent asking him if he knew who he was dealing with.

McArdle didn't have answers to Clark's questions. But he offered something else. He handed Clark a business card, a London Metropolitan Police card with the name of Detective Inspector Edwards James embossed upon it along with a set of contact numbers and addresses. "Make time to see him when you are in London," he said, "He will be expecting you."

Clark fell into the club chair beside his Gibson. "Expecting me? Should this not be official police business?" he asked.

McArdle remained standing and nodded slowly. "DI James and I will confer after you and he have spoken. For now are you satisfied your sister and parents are safe?"

Clark nodded.

"And you? Do you want to stay somewhere else?"

Clark shook his head.

"Maybe I can arrange patrol to keep an eye on this place?"

Clark then nodded again.

McArdle stepped towards the door. "So how's things at Chesterton's?" he said.

Clark, taken aback at the sudden change of subject, remembered Fabian telling him McArdle had asked for him to carry out some data investigation. He also remembered the mentoring. He looked up and managed a smile. "All change," he said.

"Is that so?"

"Apparently I have to build a team, what with your demands upon my time."

"Well there you go, who'd have thought?"

Clark looked at him and McArdle laughed. A wide smile spread across Clark's face. "So you are behind this?"

McArdle raised both his palms. "I might have mentioned in passing a bit of contingency, that's all."

Clark told him briefly about his meeting that morning with Fabian and Penny and that he would be expected to report to her. He told him he had to mentor Jimmy and Annabel. He told him as much as he knew about them, Annabel's demeanour and Jimmy's arrogance.

"Maybe arrange for this Annabel to do a bit of shadowing with Campbell," McArdle said with a smile as he pointed towards his car.

Clark laughed. "Perfect," he said. Jimmy would be pleased.

McArdle took another step toward the door. He nodded at the Gibson. "You play that thing?"

Clark smiled.

"The Troggs, The Searchers, The Tremolos," McArdle said, "That was my era." He looked at Clark. "Be careful Radcliffe." And then he was gone.

Clark's head was buzzing with confused images of dapper street gangs. He quickly shook away the thoughts. He still had the list of companies to feed into the internet.

CHAPTER 9

Clark awoke early the next morning, refreshed having slept well. He supposed the police patrol had passed by as agreed. It had been the small hours when he had finally made it to bed after finding something about each the companies on his list, the parent companies and the subsidiary companies as he was calling them, more information on some than others. His plan over breakfast was to review what he had found.

And he had to pack an overnight bag for London.

He sat at his dining table with a mug of coffee and opened his notebook. Thompson Braithwaite and Wilson Group were both conglomerates, both multinational multi-industry companies with headquarters in London. Both were listed on the London Stock Exchange, or FTSE the Financial Times Stock Exchange, among the top one hundred companies. Thomson Braithwaite was indeed a parent company with a number of subsidiaries and focused on pharmaceuticals, chemicals, natural resources and munitions. Wilson Group's concentration was far reaching and included food processing, tobacco, retail and hotels. Clark had scribbled a rough table in his book, a table that listed the four subsidiaries he had noted from before and alongside a note of their products. Santexon was an oil exploration and production company based in London but with interests across the world. Rancode Holdings was a production company with plants across America specialising in naval and land forces ammunition. Its headquarters however were in London. Green Crab Commodities was a gold producer based in South Africa but registered as a UK company with an address in London. Yerco was a food technology and processing company specialising in meat and poultry products. Again, while it had a large production presence in South America, it was headquartered in London.

Clark checked again each of the London addresses, the parent and subsidiary companies. They were all in the EC2 and E14 postcodes. EC2 was the City of London, the Square Mile. E14 was Canary Wharf. Clark nodded, noting that despite the numerous postcodes across London all the companies were headquartered in only two.

It was time to pack. He remembered the airline rules on container sizes for liquid in carry-on bags. He didn't have any toiletries in small enough packs but he had no intention of checking a bag in the hold for a one night stay. He would pick up travel sizes at the small departure gate shopping mall. His packing therefore amounted to nothing more than a tooth brush and a change of clothes folded into a rucksack.

After showering Clark dressed in his preferred smart casual garb, opting for a light blue Ralph Lauren shirt and navy V neck sweater, light brown Gant chinos, dark brown moleskin blazer and a pair of Forzieri camel and blue Italian leather shoes. He wrapped his checked scarf of many blue and brown shades around his neck and headed to the bus for Chesterton and Williamson, his overnight bag over one shoulder, his work satchel with computer over the other. The notebook and the disk were safely tucked among his change of clothes, his pre-printed boarding pass folded inside his jacket pocket.

Clark slipped quietly into the seat behind his desk, Jimmy and

Deanna ignoring his arrival. Not that he expected anything else from Jimmy, but it was unusual for Deanna. He connected his laptop to the Chesterton and Williamson network and was waiting for the boot up when he heard a faint whisper. He looked over his shoulder, but no one was there. "Psst, Clark," he heard and turned back. It was Deanna, was leaning so low he wondered how she could breathe. "Fabian's on the warpath," she said softly Clark, "shouted out everyone this morning. Wanted to know where you were. He has Penny in with him now." And then she went back to her work. Jimmy ignored the exchange.

Clark shrugged and began to work up a report he had been procrastinating over. He cared little for Fabian's moods swings. He was however concerned about having to leave in the early afternoon and about being away the following day. He wasn't yet sure what the formal arrangements were with Penny. He decided until he heard otherwise he would inform Fabian directly. As he read over the draft report everything went onto darkness, a sweet floral scent arriving at his nostrils. "Guess who?" said a soft quiet voice. He turned to find Annabel's face inches away from his. She had crept up on him and covered his eyes with her hands. She was leaning into him, blouse gaping. Clark didn't know where to look, but he smiled. She leaned closer placing a hand on each of his thighs. Her fine golden hair brushed his cheek. "I'm looking forward to seeing what you have to show me," she said faintly and stepped back slowly allowing her hands to fall away. She smiled and walked away. Clark turned back to his workstation, catching Jimmy staring down the room after Annabel, and Deanna staring at his bright red face.

"Clark, my office now," boomed Fabian Townsend. Jimmy and Deanna's heads shot down as Clark stood. Charlotte's head shot down too as he passed her desk and entered the lion's den. "Sit," Fabian barked pointing at a chair around his small conference table. He took up position behind his own desk. "Have you spoken with Penny yet?"

Clark shook his head.

"Of course not, because you haven't been here. You disappeared yesterday and this is the first I have seen you since. Care to explain?"

Clark opened his mouth but nothing came out.

"Let me spell it out," Fabian bellowed, "You are good. You are good for the firm but you are a loose cannon. We have had our flexible arrangement in the past but now's the time to rein you in. I am quite prepared to keep you on a freelance arrangement but you need to integrate more, to contribute at a corporate level, or else I will have no choice but to review the situation again. Am I making myself clear?"

Clark nodded. It was a threat. He suspected however idleness in the threat given it was he and he alone who had enabled the firm to secure the contract with McArdle and the police. It was his reputation, his skills, his experience. He was sure the contract with Chesterton and Williamson would terminate if he was to leave. But he liked the work. As a freelancer he worked for other firms, but it was the work with the police that he relished the most. And that work was only available through Chesterton and Williamson. He would play along, or at least try. "Okay," he said, "I'll speak with Penny now."

"Good. She will I'm sure make time for you. She has another assignment from DI McArdle that will need started. That will be all."

Clark didn't move. He took a deep breath. "Are you sure Jimmy and Annabel are best placed to work with me?" he asked, in his mind thinking Deanna would be a better choice than Jimmy. And Annabel was an unknown and concerning quantity.

Fabian nodded, fixing his eyes firmly on Clark. He said nothing for a long moment. And then he said, "Jimmy is ambitious. He is capable and analytical. He is extremely competent with information technology. I have given this much thought and I, along with Penny, believe he has all he attributes to learn what needs to be learned and to eventually deliver what needs to be delivered."

Then he turned away and stared at the wall. "Annabel," he said slowly and then stopped. He turned to face Clark again. "Radcliffe," he said firmly, "I am going to trust you with this information. No one else in the firm knows this. And I mean no one. Consider this a measure of my faith in you. You have a mature head and a calm manner. You keep yourself to yourself. You are an outsider, despite what I said earlier about integrating." He raised his eyebrows. Clark nodded. He knew what Fabian was getting at. He had worked in large organisations before. He knew about gossip and rumours. He knew that corporate loyalty meant little among the rank and file.

"Annabel is my brother's girl," he said. "She will go places but she has…let us say, issues, personal issues, attention issues. I'm no expert but my take is she lacks confidence, always seeking reassurance. I brought her into the firm to help her build a career, to develop the confidence she needs to get on in life. She is smart, came out with a first class degree from City University. But she became very disillusioned back home in London after a few rejections from training firms. So over here she is, and is doing well with her audit training. I want her to continue to do well, and to give her some experience on the consultancy side." He looked at Clark and again raised his brows.

Clark nodded. He had never known Fabian to be so open. He took some satisfaction that Fabian had chosen to share what he had with him.

"And Clark…," he said, "She is vulnerable. I've seen the way Jimmy watches her... Keep an eye on him."

Clark nodded again. He now understood. Mentor Annabel and manage Jimmy's libido. That was why Fabian had paired them together.

Clark left Fabian's office and rapped gently on Penny Critchlow's door.

Penny smiled and sat alongside him at her small conference table. Her office was almost identical to Fabian's. Clark imagined all the cellular offices occupied by the Partners and the Directors, all in a line and all with panoramic views across the city, were the same, uniform and consistent.

"How was Fabian?" she asked.

"Affable," said Clark, his face stoic.

She laughed and placed her hand gently on his arm. "His bark is worse than his bite."

"Is it?" said Clark returning the smile.

She laughed again, "No, not really." She lifted her hand from his arm. "Right, so I have to bring you into my fold, apparently?"

Clark smiled.

"I must say I know very little about your work, what with you having reported directly to Fabian, but with this contract with the police we need some structure, some formality to how we deliver the contract, and of course how we report our performance against it."

Clark nodded.

"And of course we need contingency. It will always be your expertise, which was after all why the contract was awarded in the first place. But maybe this is a growth area for us? Maybe if we can skill up a couple of staff they can help you?"

Clark nodded. "If the firm thinks this is a growth area, why not bring in already trained staff, maybe on a call-off freelance basis?"

Penny smiled and placed her hand back in his arm. "I know Clark, that makes sense and who knows, maybe at some point in the future that will be what is required. But this is business. We need to develop our capability at a lower cost and penetrate the market place before we increase our costs."

Clark smirked at the jargon. He realised however this was the private sector and Penny had to ensure her business was profitable.

Penny then handed him a folder. Inside was a chart showing his name among a group of staff, including Jimmy and Deanna, with an arrow pointing upwards towards her, the Director of Consultancy Services. Penny's name then pointed towards Fabian. Clark grimaced as he noticed the title of Senior Consultant against his name. Below his name was that of Annabel Hopkins with a dotted line pointing to him. The title of Junior Consultant had been attributed to her. Clark assumed she was employed in the firm under a different surname to protect her anonymity. Townsend would be her surname. Maybe Hopkins was her mother's name. The folder also contained a printout from an electronic timesheet along with a set of instructions on how to access and operate the system. Clark had no intention of wasting time on such matters.

"You will still be on a freelance contract," said Penny, "different to everyone else, but don't broadcast it. We do however need more consistency in our operational processes."

Or more control, thought Clark. "Will I still have freelance latitude?" he asked.

She smiled and touched his arm again. "Of course, why would that have to change?" He liked her and if he was honest he didn't really have any problem with working with her. He only hoped that would be the way it would turn out, that he would be working with her, and not for her. He was freelance. He didn't want to work for anyone.

"It has been agreed that Jimmy will be your wingman," she said. Clark frowned. "And Annabel Hopkins will be a trainee assigned to learn the ropes. I feel Jimmy will take to this line of work quite quickly. I see this as an opportunity for him to develop new skills that he can employ alongside his day to day consultancy work." She paused for a moment. "Annabel however I know little about. I hear great reports on her from the audit teams and I have been told she has demonstrated potential as an analyst and has expressed an interest in working on the consultancy side."

Clark nodded. It was a slightly different story to the one he had heard but he said nothing.

"Annabel will continue to be formally managed in the audit teams. Your role will be to mentor her in your data analysis work when and as required. Karl Thomas is her Audit Manager and you should liaise with him."

Clark sighed. He didn't want to liaise with anyone. His independence, everything he relished about his job, was starting to erode. "I need to be somewhere this afternoon, and tomorrow," he said, "on another job."

She sat back, her turn to frown. Eventually she nodded and reached under the conference table and lifted a locked aluminium flight case. She set it in front of Clark and handed him a sealed envelope with his name on the front. He opened the envelope and found a letter from DI McArdle stating he had confiscated a laptop from a building firm suspected of making undeclared payments for labour and supplies. He asked Clark to examine the laptop. The letter also contained the combination number to the flight case and had copies of evidence transfer documents stapled to it that no doubt McArdle needed to keep himself right, both legally and within the terms of the contract with Chesterton and Williamson.

Clark opened the case and removed the laptop. He handed the letter to Penny and left her office with the laptop under his arm, the flight case still on her table. In the main office he nodded to Jimmy and pointed to the vacant meeting room beside the foyer door.

"What's going on?" said Jimmy as Clark closed the door and sat at the table.

"Take a seat," said Clark and waited as Jimmy fell into the chair opposite. Clark glared at him, at his salon styled hair, his groomed brows and moisturised skin. He looked at his tailored white shirt with monogrammed pocket initials, at the buffalo horn cufflinks and at the matching tie clip over a striped burgundy and navy silk tie. He glanced down at his own sweater and trousers. "I have to introduce you to my work, apparently," he said.

Jimmy looked at the laptop and smirked. "So, show me," he said.

It was all Clark could do not to throw himself across the table. "First things first, you will be learning from me. You will do what I tell you and when I tell you."

Jimmy nodded but didn't shift his smirk. "So what are we waiting for?"

Clark shook his head. "Not yet. We need someone else."

Jimmy sat forward, "What do you mean?"

"Not just you Jimmy. The firm needs a team, not an understudy."

He looked over Clark's shoulder and through the glass panelled wall of the meeting room towards Deanna.

Clark smiled and said, "A team of people all equally skilled and experienced to assist me in delivering the contract to the police, a team of people who can learn from and support each other."

"Who?" Jimmy said slowly as he scanned the open plan office behind Clark.

Clark let the question hang for a long moment. "Annabel," he said eventually.

Jimmy looked at him and then towards Deanna. He began to nod and a slight smile returned, the nodding becoming more pronounced and the smile wider as he processed the information.

"Go and get her," said Clark abruptly, snapping Jimmy from his trance.

"Excuse me?"

"I said go and get her." Clark pushed back his chair and stood, moving to the corner of the room and standing over Jimmy. Jimmy stared. Clark stared back, unflinching. Jimmy stomped from the room and disappeared among the cluster of desks. Clark stayed in the corner of the glass cubicle and waited. He knew McArdle had instigated the need for more support and he suspected Jimmy had talked himself into the role. He also suspected Jimmy had expected to be the only one, to give him a commercial advantage should the function expand. Increased fee income would lead to corporate advantage when it came to promotion. He wouldn't want to share that advantage with others. He was ambitious, ruthless, and selfish. And Clark despised that in anyone.

Jimmy opened the door and let Annabel in head of him. Annabel stepped towards Clark and with her back to Jimmy winked at him.

"Let's sit," said Clark and pointed at the chairs. Jimmy regained his seat from earlier and watched as Annabel sat on the seat beside Clark.

Clark placed his hands on the laptop. Annabel moved her seat closer and swung her knees so they touched his, the short pencil skirt riding high. She leaned into him, the blouse again gaping. Clark didn't look. Jimmy stared.

"I want you to examine this," said Clark to Jimmy. "I will be back on Friday morning and I will expect a report on your findings."

Jimmy then managed to look at him. "What do you mean? Examine? Write report? Where are you going? Should you not be showing me?"

Clark glared at him. "You want to work in data mining and analysis? Show me what you can do. Show me why I should invest my time in showing you anything. As to where I am going, it is none of your business." He pushed the laptop towards Jimmy and stood, "And make sure you keep Annabel appraised of what you are doing." That brought a smile to Jimmy's face.

Clark nodded Annabel towards the door and led her to the foyer. She stood close to him, her gaze fixed on him. He moved back a step. "I'll be back on Friday," he said and paused, "Until then... be careful." He nodded and brushed gently past her. Deanna watched him but didn't speak as he shut down his computer and collected his overnight bag. He glanced at the meeting room. Jimmy was inside staring at the laptop. Annabel stood by the door, waving. Clark left silently and hailed a taxi to the City Airport for his flight to London Gatwick.

CHAPTER 10

As he sat on the plane Clark concluded he should have handled the Annabel situation differently. Fabian has trusted him with private and personal information. He had confided in him and all he done was to ask her to be careful, effectively passing her to Jimmy, someone he been asked to protect her from. And he hadn't even spoken with Karl, her Audit Manager. No, he hadn't handled it well.

Clark hailed the flight steward, a pleasant young man with the name of Toby on his name badge, and bought a small bottle of red wine. Long gone were the days of complimentary in-flight drinks he lamented, never mind seats with reasonable and medically approved legroom. He rarely drank red wine. He just took a notion that it was red wine he wanted, if for no other reason than to shake Annabel, and the guilt, from his mind. It seemed to work. The wine was good, or as good as cheap wine served at the wrong temperature in a plastic cup could be. He relaxed, his mind focusing on Spencer and the conversation they needed to have.

Clark had called his sister Amy earlier from the airport departure lounge after picking up his travel size toiletries. Their parents seemed to have settled well into the Slieve Donard Hotel, their mother having spent the morning swimming and soaking in the Jacuzzi, their father reading papers and drinking coffee in the lounge. Amy had managed to clear some emails and make some calls on work matters, even though she was officially on holiday leave. Amy had told him she had spoken again with Spencer who had confirmed their meeting in the bar of the Strand Palace Hotel. Clark had received also a text message from Siobhan telling him she was looking forward to seeing him the following night. He was equally looking forward to it.

After progressing quickly through Gatwick's arrivals he made his way to the train platform for the Gatwick Express, no pre-booked ticket this time. After buying a return ticket he made his way to the train's second carriage where he sat and watched the travellers running towards the train even though it was going nowhere, and wouldn't be for some five minutes according the platform clock. He looked at his ticket and reflected on its price, reckoning that at the same rate per mile it would cost him a small fortune to take the train the short distance from Belfast to Bangor to see his friend Ed, his wife Caitlin and Conor and François, their two adorable children. Clark smiled at the memories of three year old Conor on his knee and seven year old François at his side as he read bedtime fables of mice and monsters. Ed was someone else he would have to catch up with, now that he had finally made plans with Jackson. Ed was an old work colleague from his days in public service, and someone who had recently come through for him in an hour of need.

Clark kept an eye on passengers boarding the train, mindful of his last journey on the line. He was relieved when a family sat with him, the father beside and the mother and son opposite. Polite smiles and nods were exchanged, but no conversation. Not on a train.

He watched as green fields and rural dwellings hurtled past. In no time the familiar London skyline was upon him.

The concourse at Victoria Station was as bustling as ever, harried commuters jostling for position with disorientated tourists. Clark made his way to the underground, having decided on this occasion against the walk. He wanted to check into the hotel and gather his thoughts before meeting Spencer. He had a choice of the District and Circle lines as both ran towards Embankment, not the nearest Underground Station for the Strand Palace Hotel but one that avoided changing trains. Opting for the Circle Line he bought a single journey ticket and descended into the depths of London, the fusty stench that met him reminding him of why he generally preferred to walk, the experience further exacerbated by the seemingly unrelenting mass of bobbing bodies trailing suitcases and travel weary children in their wake.

The train itself was no better. He managed to side shuffle though the open door towards the far wall, fellow passengers already boarded reluctant to give any space. And forget about a seat, he was fortunate to locate an overhead grab handle. The doors closed and the bodies pushed closer together, body odour and perfumed fragrance fighting for supremacy. Clark was glad of his height, able to hold his head over the horde and stare aimlessly at the tube map positioned high over the windows. It was only a couple of stops to Embankment. He would cope.

Welcome air hit him as he reached the station entrance to Villiers Street. He took a moment to fill his lungs resolving then that he would walk back to Victoria the following day. He took another deep breath. Fresher air, he decided, rather than fresh air. This was London, a long way from the bouquet sea breeze and clean aqua aroma of Strangford Lough. He checked the map in his trusty London pocket guide and made his way towards Strand. A right turn and five hundred yards later he was at the hotel.

The receptionist was under pressure to check in a large group Clark assumed to be a number of families travelling together, American families of excited fathers, demure and petite mothers and adolescent children, jock boys full of testosterone and prim girls with tramline teeth. Clark was patient and sympathised when it was his turn at the counter, a gesture that was appreciated by Isabella according to the lapel badge, a name that suited her rhythmic and melodic Italian accent. She smiled warmly as she handed him the key to his third floor Club Room and pointed towards the lift. He nodded and smiled in return.

The room was functional, as Amy had said it would be, but comfortable as was the bed on which he threw himself and began to read through his notebook. With heavy eyes he checked his watch. It was after five o'clock and Spencer was not due until seven. He allowed himself to drift into a light slumber.

By six thirty he was standing at the bar, waiting for Luke the Australian barman to serve him a bottle of beer. Luke was clearly pleased to have a customer. He told Clark about his gap year and his travelling and that it was nearing the time to go home. Clark nodded along but really didn't care. He took his bottle to a corner table after Luke asked him why he was in London.

Clark heard Spencer long before he seen him, the heavy steps and loud breaths giving him away. "So you're here," said Spencer dropping his briefcase on the floor in front of the table. Clark nodded. Spencer blew out a long wheeze and pulled a brown leather club chair towards him. He sat opposite Clark who had positioned himself on the striped leather sofa bench that ran the length of the wall, allowing him full view of the room. Lance Oldfield stood at the bar entrance alongside another man who Clark did not recognise, a tall man with a midriff, slightly unkempt but with a commanding grace nevertheless. He smiled broadly and waved when Clark looked his way.

Clark ignored him.

"What have you got for me," said Spencer.

Clark looked at him. Slowly he shook his head. "You really are something else. Amy and her parents, and my parents for that matter, are in a hotel because they are frightened, intimidated in their own home. And your opener is to ask what I have for you?"

Spencer looked away smiling and shook his own head. "I'm sure they are fine. Now, why am I here?"

Clark pulled his lips tight and counted to ten. "How about thanks Clark for coming all the way over?" he said.

"Look Clark son," said Spencer, "I'm a busy man. I've somewhere else to be. If you want gratitude you have come to wrong place. Now, what do you want?"

Clark lowered his voice, "Why did you give me the disk?"

Spencer glanced briefly over his shoulder towards his companions and then dropped his head. "Did you find anything?" he asked in a near whisper.

Clark nodded and reached into his satchel for his notebook. Spencer held up his hand and pushed back his chair, stomping his bulging frame towards Lance and the other man. A hushed conversation ensued and Lance disappeared into the foyer, the other man following but not until he had waved and smiled again at Clark.

Spencer returned and sat, droplets of perspiration bubbling and dripping from his forehead. "Show me," he said eventually mopping his brow with a handkerchief produced from his breast pocket.

Clark sensed Luke the barman heading in their direction with his pad and pencil in hand. He waved him away and then pulled out his notebook and the disk. "Why did you give me this disk?" he asked again.

Spencer thought for a long moment and said quietly, "I got information from a source, a good source and I acted on it." He nodded at the disk.

"So this is it," said Clark nodding at the disk that he had set on the table between them.

Spencer nodded.

"This is all the information you based your decisions on?"

Spencer nodded.

"I would have thought your profession would have involved more detailed investigation that that. There's not much there. I'm not sure

I would want someone advising me on what to do with my money based on this information?"

Spencer sighed and lifted the handkerchief back towards his forehead. "It's there if you know what to look for."

Clark sat back. He nodded and slowly reached for his notebook. "J Wooten and C Hayward?" he said. "Who are they, your sources? Although you did say you had one source?"

Spencer looked over each shoulder. "Yes," he said, his eyes narrowing, "One source. Who are these people you've mentioned?" He panted and once more dabbed his brow.

Clark watched him and said slowly, "They are the authors of the documents on the disk."

Spencer's eyes dropped. He ran his finger around the inside of his shirt collar, an action Clark had seen before. Clark called over to Luke to bring two bottles of beer.

"All I know," said Spencer turning back to Clark "is someone gave me the disk, someone reliable, someone who had proved to be reliable over many years. I accepted and acted on the information in good faith."

"Who was it?"

"That I would prefer not to say," he said sharply.

Clark sighed and said nothing as the bottles of beer arrived. He thanked Luke and glanced towards the hotel foyer. The other man had moved back into the bar entrance and was smiling at Clark again. He waved when Clark caught his eye. Lance came around the corner and called him away. Clark asked Luke to take two bottles of beer out to the men in the foyer.

"Who's he?" said Clark to Spencer as he nodded towards the foyer.

"That doesn't matter. Now what else do you have?"

Clark shook his head and proceeded to read the two parent company names from his notebook, Thompson Braithwaite and Wilson Group. He glanced towards Spencer and detected a wince.

He moved on to read the names of the subsidiary companies, the companies with excessive sales peaks and significant net worth. He watched again for a reaction but caught nothing.

"Yes," said Spencer, "Companies with high projections, new markets opening up to them, companies with healthy sales orders on the table." He nodded slowly as he spoke. "I did my homework of course. I know I said earlier the information on the disk was all I based my decision on but I did check out the companies you have mentioned, verified the figures through the normal channels."

"Normal channels?" asked Clark raising his brows.

"Registered Company Accounts, securities, legalities, trade agreements, financial publications, sector forecast schedules, yada, yada, yada" replied Spencer.

Clark nodded. "So you invested your firm's money? But what I don't get is why? Your firm is not an investment firm. Have I got that right?"

Spencer sighed. "Yes. And why I invested I cannot answer. As experienced as I am at what I do perhaps I demonstrated a certain naivety in understanding the mechanics of my own firm. And I don't mean about the services we are registered to provide, I mean the internal reward culture. I suppose I thought if I could increase my fee revenue I could present a case to be brought into the Partnership. Perhaps I rationalised that increasing the firm's reserves equated to my increasing their fee deposits. It was no more than a moment of madness I can tell you. After I committed to it I immediately regretted it. But it was too late. I couldn't pull out. And then the money was gone. I thought if I could replenish what I lost I could cover my tracks somehow and move on; accept that any rise to Partnership would have to come another way. So I reinvested my own money in an attempt to generate enough to cover what I had lost. It was a second failed investment. And here we are. I need to reimburse the firm just to stand still." He looked at Clark," And Amy is my only hope."

Clark nodded again. It was the most he had heard Spencer talk. "So you trust your source and you trust your information?" he said.

Spencer looked at him. "Yes, I have said so. Why do you ask?"

Clark paused before reaching into his jacket pocket. He pulled out a business card and set it on the table in front of Spencer. He unfolded the printed photo of the two men in his parent's home and set it beside the card. Spencer's face drained. He looked from the card to the photo and to Clark, then back to the card again, moving only his eyes. Saliva began to drip from the corners of his mouth. "What's this?" he said pointing at the name of Detective Inspector Edward James of the Metropolitan Police Specialist and Economic Crime Command.

"Have you forgotten about the threats, the intimidation Spencer? Who are these men?" said Clark.

Spencer shuffled and shook his head. He took long breaths, held them and released them slowly. Clark glanced towards the foyer. The other man, the dishevelled man, was holding the beer bottle towards him and smiling. Clark continued to ignore him. "You okay Spencer?" he asked but received no answer. He added, "Leave it alone was the message Spencer. Leave what alone? Who are they and what do they want?"

Spencer shook his head again. "Nobody knows you have the disk Clark," he said quietly, avoiding the question Clark had asked and nodding towards the disk. Clark nodded and casually placed his hand over the disk, slipping it into his satchel. "So even if anyone knows we have spoken they will not know what we spoke of, and they will certainly not know what I gave you." He looked over his shoulder towards the foyer.

Clark nodded again and said, "As I asked you before Spencer, why did you give me the disk? You said it was all there if I looked for it? What's to look for? And why are you concerned about the police."

Spencer leaned forward. "Listen Clark," he said, "I trust my source, I have already told you that. I trust that my source gave me sound information. Or should I say information that he took to be sound."

The cogs were churning in Clark's head. "You have said you checked the information, did your homework as you put it."

"Yes, but who's to say a trail wasn't so well laid that any corroborating information was manipulated?"

Clark paused. "Are you saying that there is manipulation of records across a range of companies?" Clark stared at Spencer. "And how can one person infiltrate and manipulate a number of companies?"

"Who said anything about one person Clark?" said Spencer as he sat back.

Clark held up his hands. He recalled what McArdle had told him about City financiers organising indecorously around some shared purpose. He nodded. "But why, Spencer?" he asked, "And why you?"

Spencer shrugged. "Perhaps to destroy me, perhaps to destroy the firm," he said.

Clark dropped his head into his hands. The suited visitors to his parent's house had said Spencer's experience and capabilities were essential to the firm and that Amy should help him re-establish his credibility by bailing him out. This contradicted what Spencer was saying. Spencer was avoiding his questions about the police, and about the men in Belfast and Ballydorn. And Clark had yet to mention the men on the train. Spencer had placed his faith in a single source and yet he was unwilling to identify the source. If Spencer really thought the source had been manipulated then the natural course of action would be to question the source's source? And why were the partners of Rubenstein Roberts prepared to give Spencer a chance at redemption?

Spencer coughed drawing Clark from his thoughts. Clark nodded and dropped the business card, photo and notebook into his satchel and slid out of the bench seat, turning towards the foyer. He stopped abruptly, the tousled man having arrived at his shoulder.

"Hi Clark, the name's Ronald Hawk. I'm very pleased to meet you at last."

CHAPTER 11

Ronald Hawk. The name rang a bell. Of course; the friend that Amy mentioned Spencer met with regularly, the friend from another firm whom she had only met once.

Clark accepted his hand and nodded, Spencer still seated and glaring at Ronald.

"And how is the lovely Amy," Ronald asked continuing to smile. "You and she are very alike. I'm sure your parents are very proud. I've heard a lot about you. I hear you are a bit of an expert with computers?"

Clark nodded again and forced a smile.

"Listen Clark, we are just about to head out to a club. Why don't you join us?"

Spencer jumped from his seat. "No Ronald, I think not. Clark has more pressing things to do." He put his hand on Clark's arm and gently pushed him.

Clark stiffened and stared at Spencer. "Yes Ronald. That would be excellent," he said excusing himself and taking the lift to his room where he hid his satchel under the pillows of the bed. Back in the foyer he caught Spencer finger wagging and shouting at Ronald. Ronald ignored him.

"Right, let's go," Ronald said. "By the way Clark, you've already met Lance Oldfield?" Clark nodded. Lance returned the nod and walked out the door behind Spencer. Ronald put his arm around Clark's shoulder and smiled.

Ronald was about Clark's height, with dark brown hair that could do with a cut and a rugged face that could do with a shave. His eyes were a bright shade of blue and shone when he smiled, which he did often; charming, friendly and sociable. He engaged Clark in conversation about his job in computers and how he enjoyed freelancing. He asked Clark about his family and commented how lucky he was to be close with his sister. He said that he often wished he had made a greater effort with his own sister to stop their fighting like sworn enemies. His honesty and genuine interest drew warm responses from Clark. They laughed together when he mentioned football and began to banter Clark on his chosen team.

Ronald hailed a taxi, a familiar black hackney carriage, and climbed into the back giving their destination to the driver as he did so. Clark followed behind and glanced over his shoulder towards Spencer and Lance who stood stiffly against the wall of the hotel. Ronald called to them and they trundled slowly towards the cab, stepping laboriously inside taking up seats opposite, avoiding eye contact. Ronald nudged Clark and nodded towards them. Ronald and Clark both smiled.

It was a short journey, the cab travelling along Strand and past the West End theatres at Aldwych before making a left turn. A few minutes later and they were there. Although where they were exactly Clark had no idea. It didn't look like much of a club. They were in a small courtyard with cars parked all around. Behind was a Victorian terrace with ground floor shop fronts lit with bright neon flashing signs despite their being closed. Only one door was open, a single door beside a small window through which was a splintered wooden counter and a bored looking middle aged man behind it. There was no sign over the door.

Ronald led the way, Clark following, Spencer and Lance some distance after.

"My treat," said Ronald over his shoulder and walked towards the counter where he laughed with the middle aged man and handed over a fold of notes. "Jackets off," he called to Clark and nodded towards a half door on the wall beside where Clark stood, Spencer and Lance having stopped outside in the courtyard. Clark took off his jacket and moved towards the hatch. Spencer and Lance then followed. He handed his jacket to a haggard peroxide woman with dark roots and a contoured face heavily plastered with makeup. She wore a canary yellow halter top that hung low on her chest and failed in any attempt to keep her contained. A pair of tight leggings and scuffed shiny patent high heeled shoes did nothing to enhance her presentation. She handed Clark a stationery store cloakroom ticket in a manner that shouted she couldn't care less. He slid it into his rear pocket and stepped aside, to the top of a set of burgundy carpeted stairs that snaked into the basement, muffled music reverberating towards him. Spencer and Lance joined him in their shirt sleeves, and without ties which they had rolled into their jacket pockets. There was nothing to hide Spencer's paunch. He was sweating and panting, and continued to avoid Clark's eye. Lance was the youngest of the quartet, although not by much. Clark would have put him in his early thirties. He had rolled his shirt sleeves to above his elbows. He wore his shirt well, a well toned physique evident with buttons pulling tight across his chest. His arms and face were bronzed and glistening on the dim light. His hair was short and spiked, assisted by some product that equally shone in the light. His eyes were narrow. Clark had yet to see him smile.

"Right, let's go," said Ronald and led them down the stairs.

It didn't take Clark long to realise just what sort of club he was in. In front of him was a tall brunette with a tattooed shoulder wearing white high heeled shoes and little else. Her legs were long and sheathed in black self holding stockings. A small black G with a hint of lace matched a tight and meagre brazier. She smiled and led them to a table, or a row of small tables as it turned out. Clark sat against the near wall on a bench seat with Lance beside him, Spencer further along beside Lance. Ronald opted for a cheap looking wooden parlour chair opposite. He waved over a square jawed shaven headed man in black shiny polyester trousers and whispered in his ear. The man returned after a few seconds with four bottles of beer, the tops already pulled.

Clark didn't know what to think. Yes, he had heard about such clubs, he had seen them in the movies. He had an internet connection. But he had never been in one, Ireland not known for its promotion of such adult oriented venues. He shuffled in his seat, fighting hard to control his heartbeat and to stifle a reddening face. He looked at Ronald who smiled, winked and leaned forward shouting over the jungle beat bouncing from the speaker over Clark's head, "Don't worry, it's all taken care of."

Clark had no idea what he was talking about. He turned towards Spencer who was drumming out the jungle beat on his knees while nodding along in some sort of head dance, or ancient mating call. Clark shook his head; this was the man his sister, his beautiful, smart and successful sister had chosen to spend her life with. Lance was mirroring Spencer's head dance although his version more resembled a Trafalgar Square pigeon entertaining the tourists.

Clark looked around the club, which wasn't really much more than a room, a room with red papered walls and threadbare burgundy carpet. Small wooden bistro tables were lined against each wall with a couple of strays randomly dotted around the centre of the floor. Small woof and tweet speakers were periodically spaced along the wall at ceiling height. But there was no pole, no stage. Clark would have expected some form of central performance area, somewhere girls could dance for the entertainment of the clientele. At least that's what he had seen in the movies. He looked beyond Lance to a small raised horseshoe curtained area and wondered what it was for.

He turned back just as a body slid along the seat beside him. A hand was placed gently on his knee.

"Hi, my name is Lavinia," said a beautiful young girl with wide blue eyes and piano key teeth. Her skin was well tanned and her shoulder length hair was straight and shining. "What's your name," she asked in a slight accent, East European Clark guessed.

He forced a smile despite his discomfort. She was young, too young. She shouldn't be there. Then again, nor should he. "Clark," he said and dropped his head.

"And what do you do Clark?" she said.

She wanted conversation, which was something he didn't. He tried to move along the bench seat, to widen the space between them. But there was little room. "Computers," he said slowly.

"That's a nice accent. Where are you from?" She moved as close to him as she could, white fishnets pressing tight against his thigh. She placed an elbow on his shoulder and stared at him. He glanced down at the crucifix she wore around her neck and at the small white lingerie. She smelled good.

"Ireland," he said, "And you?"

"Latvia." She ran her free hand down his arm. "Would you like me to dance for you?"

He didn't, he really didn't. But then again something was telling him he should. And then he thought of Siobhan. "No thanks," he said. Lavinia smiled and slipped away from the bench.

There weren't many patrons in the club, other than themselves just a couple of twentysomethings in jeans and plaid shirts. It was early though. Clark imagined this to be the sort of place that would come alive much later, after pub closing time. He looked towards Ronald who nodded frantically towards the small horseshoe. Clark turned to see Lance sitting on a bench on the nearside wall, and Spencer sitting on a bench opposite. An attempt had been made to pull the curtain but Clark could see everything.

Lance had his hands on his knees and was staring at naked breasts swaying only inches in front of his face. The girl moved her hips from side to side along with the music and then slowly slipped her hands inside the waistband of her lacy shorts, rolling them over her hips and down bare legs. Lance smiled, the first time Clark had seen him smile. He lifted his hands from his knees and ran them up the back of the girl's legs, pulling her towards him. She resisted playfully and then dropped on his lap.

Clark shook his head. So this was not a pole dance club where you could drink and talk and chose to watch or ignore the stage. Not even a club where girls would provocatively dance and tantalise and titillate whilst maintaining some modesty. No this was a naked lap dance club. A no holds barred naked lap dance club.

He glanced towards Spencer and instantly regretted it. A tall large framed girl with shimmering ebony skin and bright yellow ringlet hair was sitting astride him, naked save for lilac stockings and shoes. She was writhing to the music as Spencer's hands wandered all over her. Clark had seen enough. His sister Amy deserved better than this. He shouldn't have come. He lifted his bottle and downed the beer before sliding out of the bench and leaving the club, Ronald smiling in his wake.

He decided to walk back to the hotel. Although not sure where he was exactly he remembered the cab turning left from Strand and then right into the courtyard. If he reversed the journey he would surely end up back to where he was familiar.

The walk was good, helping to clear his head. Although feeling remorse he rationalised he hadn't known where he was being taken to. And when he was there he left quickly. He thought of Lavinia, the beautiful young girl from Latvia. He thought of her vulnerability. And then he thought of the way he had looked at her, the way she had nearly enticed him. The remorse returned.

He turned his focus to Spencer. He thought of Amy saying she wanted to be sure before helping him. Clark was sure if she knew the disregard Spencer clearly had for her then the decision would be obvious. Yet he wanted to see this through. He had to find answers. He would deal eventually with Spencer's respect issues.

For now he had to consider what he had learned before they left for the club. He recalled Spencer's concern about his involving the police, and Spencer then seeming to guide him towards the possibility of some organised involvement. Clark had to meet with DI James, the business card in his satchel back at the hotel. He would call him as soon as he got back.

The satchel was where he had left it. He breathed a sigh of relief as he fished out the card and checked his watch. It was barely nine o'clock, not too late to call. And still plenty of time to do more research.

There was no answer when he called the landline number on the card. He contemplated leaving a message on the work answer phone but thought against it at the last moment when the call had clicked through to the answer service. He didn't know DI James, didn't know what to say. So he hung up. He thought then he would send a text message to the mobile number. That way the ball would be in DI James' court to reply.

A reply came back almost immediately. DI James suggested meeting at ten o'clock in Costa Coffee at Saint Paul's Cathedral. Clark sent back an acceptance. He had an idea where it was, not far from The Strand Palace Hotel.

He lay on the bed and began to flick through his notebook. He read again through the list of companies, but his mind kept wandering. One image kept returning, an image of a girl in virginal white pouting and flirting for attention. He closed his eyes and saw Lavinia calling out to him. He thought back to the question she had asked, and that he had so very nearly succumbed.

He needed to speak with Siobhan.

The phone rang a number of times before she answered, breathless. "Clark," she said, "How are you?"

He began to tell her all about his meeting with Spencer. She listened intently making intermittent noises, and asking relevant questions. Clark liked that about her. He was glad he had called. He was telling her about the meeting with DI James the following morning when there was a loud knock on the door.

"Hold on a minute," he said jumping off the bed, phone in hand.

He opened the door slowly and then froze.

There on the other side was Siobhan, beaming with her own phone to her ear.

CHAPTER 12

Clark awoke early to the thunderous sound of industrial vans and trucks rattling along Strand making hurried deliveries and collecting malodorous refuse. He stretched and rolled slowly onto his elbow, looking at Siobhan and smiling. She was sleeping soundly, hair tousled and uneven. She had kicked away the bedding and one leg had fallen over the side of the bed, the other was raised at the knee with her foot lying flat. He reached forward and gently touched her cheek. She purred and smiled through her sleep. His gaze fell down her neck to the Victoria's Secret floral Mayfair Slip that she had brought as a nightdress, its narrow string straps hanging loose from her shoulders, its short length having climbed to the top of her thighs.

She had come to London to surprise him, to comfort him after what had happened between them. She knew he had felt uncomfortable and she wanted to tell him she understood. She wanted to show him. He had told her where he would be staying so she had taken the flight after his. She had managed to sweet-talk his room number from the pleasant Italian receptionist while she was speaking with him on the phone. When he had seen her he had dropped his phone and pulled her into his arms. He had carried her to his bed. No words needed to be spoken. He knew how much he wanted her. She knew how much she wanted to be with him. They had hastily undressed and their bodies had melted together. They had bathed together. They had shared the bottle of wine she had brought. But most of all they had talked and laughed, eventually falling blissfully asleep in each other's arms.

The traffic buzz outside grew steadily louder as he watched her, the early morning commuters in cabs and cars eventually arriving to compete for the limited road space, horns blaring at the inconsiderate commercial vehicles, and at cyclists. He smiled again and bent to kiss her. She opened her eyes and stretched, a warm smile spreading across her face. She pushed him away and sat upright lifting the nightdress over her head.

It was after nine o'clock when they left the room, Thursday morning and Clark had the meeting with DI James. Siobhan said she could use the morning to catch up with some colleagues at Peterson's Global London office, which was somewhere around Embankment Place. Clark didn't know how long he would be with DI James so they arranged to meet at Victoria Station at two thirty.

As Clark was checking out of the hotel Isabella passed him an envelope with his name hand written on the front. He looked at her curiously as he accepted it. She smiled and shrugged before returning to her computer screen. Clark caught her glancing at him as he opened the envelope. Inside was a folded piece of paper with a phone number and a name. There were only two other words. *Call me*. He looked at Isabella and winked. She smiled back. Siobhan was sitting on a sofa in the foyer waiting for him. She turned to him and he waved, folding the note into his jacket pocket, the note from Ronald Hawk.

They said their farewells at the foot of the hotel steps. Clark held on to her for a long moment. He stood and watched as she walked towards Embankment, gliding elegantly in skinny jeans and suede knee boots. Over the shoulder of a matching suede safari jacket she carried a small Louis Vuitton overnight bag. In her other hand she swung a Chanel handbag. Clark smiled. Fifty yards later she turned and waved to him.

Clark started his walk in the opposite direction along Strand towards Saint Paul's Cathedral, his rucksack and satchel over one shoulder. He stopped for a moment at the side of the pavement and checked for anyone following. Satisfied all was clear he reflected there had not been any sense of threat since Brent and Wayne had left his parent's house two days before.

He moved on, passed the road from the previous night, the road of the club. He didn't look towards it, the guilt of his temptation erased. Siobhan's timing could not have been better. He had been thinking about her, wanting to show her and prove to himself how much she meant to him. And then she had arrived.

As he crossed the road he thought of Ronald and the note in his pocket, reflecting that Ronald was different from the others, in both appearance and demeanour. And that he had stood up to Spencer. Clark decided he would call Ronald after his meeting with DI James.

He continued along Strand passing the magnificent and imposing Royal Courts of Justice, the infamous Temple Church and onto Fleet Street with its long history of printing and publishing, its buildings and side alleys now home to barristers in abundance. He checked his watch as he crossed Ludgate Circus and onto Ludgate Hill. He was in good time. He could slow his pace and savour the striking architecture of the spires and dome of Saint Paul's ahead of him, the grand edifice that had stood proud since its rebirth following the Great Fire some three hundred and fifty years before, the grand edifice that had survived the Blitz as a morale beacon above the piles of surrounding rubble. He stopped and marvelled at the Cathedral entrance, the Great West Door, the extensive steps, the Corinthian columns and ornamental clock and bell towers, and of course Wren's iconic Saint Peter's Basilica inspired dome.

A few minutes later he was at the corner of Creed Lane and at Costa Coffee. He checked his watch again and stepped into the coffee house with no idea how to identify who he was looking for, but he needn't have worried. An arm rose from a small corner table and waved him over. He should have known the police would know him.

The man stood and held out his hand. Clark reciprocated and winced under the powerful handshake. The man was tall, about Clark's height, maybe a fraction more. Clark put him somewhere between his age and McArdle's, somewhere is his mid-forties. He stood poker straight with square shoulders. His grey sports coat was unbuttoned and revealed a flat stomach. He had a full head of fair hair with a touch of ginger at the sides and a thin well trimmed moustache resting on his lip. He reminded Clark of an RAF Squadron Leader from those war movies of the fifties.

"Clark," he said, "Good to meet you. DI McArdle speaks highly of you."

Clark nodded.

"It's James, DI James but please, call me Edward".

Clark nodded again and followed the policeman's lead in sitting. The detective had the prime seat in a corner facing the door, giving Clark no option but to sit facing him with his back to the door and to the rest of the patrons.

"McArdle says you can find your way around computers? Says you are invaluable to him? Maybe I could use a bit of you?"

Clark smiled at the flattery. "Not much computer work going on with what I'm involved in now," he said.

"Yes, of course, the task in hand. Let's order some coffee, some breakfast, before we start?"

Clark was famished. They had left the hotel without breakfast. They had been busy. "That would be good," he said, "Whatever you are having."

DI James called over a barista and ordered two Americanos and two breakfast rolls. Clark didn't think table service was a usual duty for the barista and assumed DI James was receiving some special attention. Maybe he was regular.

"So, fill me in," he said as they were waiting.

Clark started at the beginning, from Amy arriving on Sunday morning to his one day visit to London on Monday and his encounter on the train, to catching Brent and Wayne watching them in Belfast and then finding them waiting at their parent's house. He told him all that Spencer had said, and that Spencer had given him a disk. He didn't mention visiting any clubs.

Clark sat back and watched DI James reflect on all he had heard. The detective said nothing as he ran a hand repeatedly through his moustache. He nodded a couple of times and looked like he was about to speak. But he didn't.

Clark reached into his satchel and pulled out the printed photo of Brent and Wayne. He unfolded it and set it on the table. DI James looked at it briefly and then looked at Clark. He looked back at the photo.

"That's them?" he said slowly.

Clark nodded.

"Good work," said James nodding and folding the photo quickly as breakfast arrived.

"Do you know them?" asked Clark when the barista had left.

James handed the photo back to Clark. He looked at him and nodded slowly.

"Yes," he said, "I think I do." He pointed to the breakfast roll in front of Clark. "Let's eat first."

Clark was anxious to hear whatever it was James knew. But he was hungry and the roll with a mountain of bacon, egg and cheese oozing out its sides looked appealing. He lifted it in his hands and nodded across the table.

"You a family man?" asked the detective.

Clark shrugged.

DI James held up his left hand and wiggled his ring finger drawing attention to the gold band.

Clark smiled and nodded.

"Any kids?" asked James.

Clark shook his head as he bit into his roll ignoring the melted cheese as it ran on his chin.

"I've two girls," said James, "One just finished university, the other about to start. Hard work I can tell you. Bleed you dry but I'd have it no other way."

Clark smiled again and felt obliged to wipe his mouth with a napkin. He felt obliged too to say something although he did not know what. "Two girls?" he said eventually thinking it would be safe if he just repeated something he had heard.

DI James smiled. He had been given his cue and proceeded to recount stories of their upbringing, their schooling, their passage to adulthood, and the boyfriends. He beamed as he spoke, pride emanating from him. Clark had to admit it was heartening, infectious even.

"You married Clark?" he asked.

Clark shook his head.

"Girlfriend?"

Clark thought for a moment. He thought of Siobhan and the night they had just spent together. He thought of meeting her later and travelling home with her. He realised he was looking forward to it. He didn't shake his head, or nod. "Yes," he said proudly, "I do."

DI James smiled and nodded as if pleased that Clark, this man he didn't know, had found someone. Clark smiled back thinking he liked the man, hardly knew him, but liked him, thinking that perhaps he knew more about him after ten minutes than he knew about colleagues of months, if not years. He thought James and McArdle to be an odd couple, DI James seemingly an open book family man who kept himself in good shape, DI McArdle a man Clark didn't know anything about other than he was dishevelled and unfit. He didn't even know his first name. Clark smiled at his mental comparison. He laughed and DI James laughed with him.

"Your two guys," said James leaning forward and assuming a sudden serious air, "Brent Hynes and Wayne Demachi." He paused and Clark nodded. "And they were in Belfast you say? Followed your sister to your parents at Strangford Lough?"

Clark nodded again.

DI James let out a long sigh. He sat back in his chair and looked around the coffee shop. He sat for the best part of a minute and then leaned forward.

"An unusual departure," he said, "These guys tend to operate in and around the City. For them to travel is indeed a curiosity. How do you think they came to be in Belfast in the first place? Do you think they followed your sister over?"

Clark nodded. "Yes, Detective Inspector."

"Edward," said DI James, "The name's Edward."

Clark nodded again, "Amy came straight to Strangford Lough from the airport. I was already there and I'm certain it was their car I saw parked across a farm gate as I was leaving. At least I'm certain it was the same car that they were in when they later called on my parents."

"And when was that?"

Clark thought for a moment. "Late Tuesday afternoon," he said.

"So they were in Strangford Lough on Sunday morning and again on Tuesday afternoon? You would wonder what they were doing in between."

Clark nodded.

"And in that intervening period," said Edward, "You were in London and encountered another three guys?"

Clark nodded.

"Did you get a good look at them?"

Clark shook his head.

"Would you recognise them again?"

Clark thought for a moment and then shrugged.

"Okay," said Edward, "Leave it with me. I can see if I can pull out some facials. I'll talk to my City Police colleagues." He paused and ran his fingers through his hair. "More coffee?" he asked.

Clark shook his head. Edward held a finger up to the barista and pointed at his cup. "And the guys in London gave you a note telling you to leave it alone, the same message that was given to your sister the next day in Belfast?"

Clark nodded.

"Could be there was some communication between them," said James pensively, "Repeat the same message to give it some gravitas."

"Either that or it was predetermined," said Clark.

It was Edward's turn to nod. "Leave what alone?" he asked slowly.

Clark shrugged. "Everything? Stop interfering? Give Spencer the money and stop snooping? I really don't know." He looked over his shoulder and around the coffee shop which was has hemorrhaging its late breakfast crowd and beginning to receive the mid morning coffee brigade. It was busy, but not as busy as it had been when he first arrived. "Tell me about these guys, Brent and Wayne," he said.

Edward rubbed his chin and leaned forward, slowly shaking his head. "These guys belong to a small organisation, well structured and highly disciplined. We have no intelligence at all from members. Anything we do know is from their clients, if I can call them that, although some would say victims."

Clark nodded.

"There are a number of these organisations operating across the financial city. How many exactly I have no idea but I would guess single figures. Too many and they would start to cross each other's paths and get in each other's way. I have yet to hear anything about feuds."

Clark shook his head. He had many questions, and had no

structure to his thinking. "What exactly do they do? Why? Why threaten me? What are they called? How many are in the organisation?"

Edward shrugged. "I don't know what they call themselves, it's not like they leave calling cards or engage in graffiti artistry to mark out territory. This isn't an organisation involved in extortion, protection rackets, smuggling, or trafficking. This is not an organisation that will put a horse's head in your bed. This is a highbrow and, as I said, a well disciplined organisation, disciplined in the sense that that they submit to and follow their own rules and hierarchy, whatever that may be, but also disciplined in that I have yet to hear of any physical mutilations, or gun play. They resort to threats. Their clients, or victims, tend to play along, whether because of fear or because in some way they are in agreement with what the organisation stands for."

Clark sat back in his chair and thought for a moment. It was appearing that he and Amy were clients, as Edwards had put it, and had received a threat. But there was intimidation along with the threat. Brent was affable and authoritative, but he was accompanied by a larger man who deferred to him, a man Clark had taken to be some form of protector, or enforcer. And he recalled Brent moving his hand inside his jacket as if reaching for something. "And what does the organisation stand for?" he asked.

Edward sat back as his second cup of coffee arrived. He winked at the barista, a young slim man with the look of a student. He smiled back.

"Success," said Edward leaning forward again, "Continued success, more success, betterment. These guys are part of the city bonus culture. They have a good year and they get a good handshake. They like it. They get used to it. And then something threatens their potential, maybe a bad deal that blemishes their reputation. They can't afford a run of bad deals so they will try and make sure that doesn't happen."

"Like how?" asked Clark.

Edwards shrugged again. "Lots of ways," he said, "For example encouraging a lucrative sales order to be placed to boost a company's share price, or maybe ensure that a small company with potential sees the value in surrendering to an acquisition approach. I could go on Clark, but you get the idea."

Clark nodded. "When you say *encourage* and *ensure*, what you mean is put the pressure on, threat, intimidate?" he said.

Edward nodded.

"How do they organise?" asked Clark.

Edward took a long drink of his coffee, no cream but still managing to leave a froth deposit on his moustache. "As far as we can gather," he said, "it is a classic pyramid structure, no more than three tiers. I would say a strong head, two or three in the middle with, say, three or four working to each of the middle rankers. I don't think the organisation could function as cohesively and furtively as it does if there were many more than around a dozen members in all."

Clark sat back. After a moment he fished his notebook and pencil from his satchel and turned to a fresh page. "Right, let's humour each other," he said and drew a question mark on top of the page. "Let's assume this is the head." He smirked as he reflected on his initial impression of DI James and added, "Let's call him the Squadron Leader." He then drew three lines below, each with a question mark and each pointing upwards. "Let's assume three middle rankers and let's call them Lieutenants, or Flight Lieutenants to carry on the analogy." He then drew three more lines under each middle ranker, again with question marks. "And let's assume three guys working to each middle ranker. Let's call them the Pilots."

He had a diagram with thirteen question marks. He turned it around and showed it to Edward, who smiled and nodded. Clark unfolded the photo and placed it beside his chart. "Let's try and populate this diagram with what we know," he said pointing at the photo. "How do you know these two?"

"Good fortune, Clark, nothing more. An associate working across the road at the Stock Exchange was approached by two men a while back. They were looking for some inside intel and when they were told they were talking to the wrong man they produced some paparazzi style shots of his wife collecting his kids from school. He played along for a while dropping some insignificant facts and figures that they soon tired of. So they left him alone. But not until he had caught their pictures, a bit like the pictures you caught yourself." He nodded at Clark and took his turn to point at the photo, "Interestingly these guys seem to go by their real names. The names I have given you are the names they give to the Stock Exchange associate. And the names and mug shots checked out with the Driver and Vehicle Agency and the Identity and Passport Service.

"The same two guys also turned up in the offices of an import agency in the docks looking for contract details between a London based Chemical Company and its overseas suppliers. This was not something the import agent could provide but he was suspicious and reported it to us. His CCTV had captured the visit."

Clark nodded. "So these are two guys who seem to work as a team?" he said.

Edward nodded too.

There was something that the detective had said that made Clark pause. He flicked quickly through his notebook. "You mentioned a London based Chemical Company," he said, "That wouldn't be Thompson Braithwaite?"

Edward narrowed his eyes. After a moment he nodded. "Yes, he said, "That sounds familiar."

CHAPTER 13

Thompson Braithwaite, one of the two companies Spencer had invested in.

Clark flicked back to his chart. "Let's see if we can put the names of Brent and Wayne to this," he said. "Where do you think they sit?"

Edward shrugged. "An operational team," he said, "probably Pilots as you have suggested calling them."

Clark shook his head. "I don't know," he said, "Brent certainly seemed to have an upper hand. And Wayne seemed to follow his lead."

Edward nodded and was quiet for a second. "You have met them, go with your gut."

Clark wrote Brent's name over one of the middle question marks and added that of Wayne below as one of his team. He thought for a moment.

"Everything okay?" asked Edward.

Clark nodded and said slowly, "The three guys on the train?" He pointed at the chart.

Edward nodded. "Possibly," he said.

Clark waved his pencil. "What about the head, the Squadron Leader?" he asked, "Any ideas?"

Edward shook his head. He then pointed at the two names already on Clark's chart. "A bit of background from what was gathered after we did the Driver Licence and Passport checks on Hynes and Demachi, at least what I can recall.

"Brent Hynes is London born and bred, a good education at Winchester followed by a placement and promising career at LMN, the American Bank. No convictions. He has managed to keep his nose clean.

"The same cannot be said however for Wayne Demachi. He was born in Albania and came over with his parents at an early age. He had all his schooling in London and managed to secure a place London South Bank University. He started as a runner in LMN and worked his way up to Executive Assistant. That's no doubt where he met Brent Hynes. He's by no means a gifted banker but he would know his way around the financial system for sure. He would be able to talk the talk enough to convince his clients.

"Here's the thing, Clark. He's had three convictions for assault and battery, given probation but no jail time. You can ask the courts about that one. And despite the convictions he has held on to his job."

Clark looked from Edward to his chart.

"So I suppose what I am saying," continued Edward, "is to be careful. I'll do what I can to help. But there's only so much I can do. There's no evidence yet of a crime, threats yes, but no crime that would warrant compromising what intelligence is ongoing. So please Clark, don't wander into anything you're not sure of. "

Clark nodded. He would be careful, a warning he was becoming used to.

"Right," said Edward, "Before I go, tell me what else you've got."

Clark produced the disk from his satchel. "This is the data Spencer says influenced his decisions. He claims it he verified it all through what he called usual channels."

Edward looked at the disk and back to Clark. He sat back in his chair. "Manipulated data," he said under his breath.

Clark looked at him. That was the same expression Spencer had used, that his corroborating information could have been manipulated.

"That would be classic intervention by our friends," said Edward, "Manipulate data across a range of databases, and even produce supporting documents. Their client would have no idea and would act upon the information provided to them."

Clark shook his head, "But what was to be gained by encouraging Spencer to invest in the companies?"

Edward shrugged. "Maybe that was never the intention. Maybe Spencer was to use the information to advise others to invest, to encourage greater demand for a company's stock to raise its value?"

Clark nodded. "And maybe the information seemed too good to miss so he entered into his misguided personal investment strategy."

Edward smiled and shrugged. "Who give him the disk?"

Clark shook his head.

"Maybe if you can get me a copy I can have some of my guys look at it?" said Edward.

Clark screwed his face and shook his head again. "Thanks," he said, "But as it stands Spencer trusted the disk to me."

"No problem Clark, I understand." He then reached for Clark's notebook and began to flick at its pages, pausing at the table of companies, the parent and the subsidiary companies. After a moment he said, "The addresses of these companies are interesting."

Clark nodded. "I thought the same thing myself."

"Thompson Braithwaite and Wilson Group Headquarters aren't far from here. You might want to check them out. And interestingly the four subsidiary companies, as you have called them, are all in EC14. That's Canary Wharf. But even more interestingly is they all have offices very close together. All four companies seem to have a presence in Canada Square, indeed three in the same building. You might want to check that out too."

He gave Clark rough directions to the nearby offices and advised him to take a cab to Canary Wharf to avoid having to change underground stations, or taking the Docklands Light Railway which could take a while. This Clark appreciated as he didn't have much time, and in any case he would have chosen the cab over the prospect of another claustrophobic experience under London's ground. Edward recommended too that he cross the road from Costa Coffee to Patermaster Square for a look at the Stock Exchange building. Clark thanked him and stood, gathering his papers and disk.

"Be careful," said Edward again as he stood and offered his hand, a wide smile on his face, "Stay in touch. And look after that girl of yours."

Clark checked his watch as he ran across the road dodging the snaking line of red tourist buses and black hackney cabs. It was after eleven o'clock. He had three hours before he had to meet Siobhan at Victoria, three hours to explore London's Square Mile and Canary Wharf. And he had also to find time to contact Ronald Hawk. He needed to hurry.

He strode into Paternoster Square through the Temple Bar, a Portland stone archway that had once stood on Fleet Street, an arch with a colourful history, not least its displaying the heads of eighteenth century traitors from spikes atop the main arch. This was the sort of historical detail that Clark enjoyed, or at least would enjoy if only he had more time. The Square itself stood on the site of the medieval Paternoster Row, a procession route for the clergy of Saint Paul's, a space that was devastated during the Blitz and was rebuilt during the 1960s, only to be further redeveloped at the start of the twenty first century in its current impressive renaissance style. Opposite the Temple Bar stood the London Stock Exchange, a building combining the classical elegance of stone columns with a modern linear framework. Clark marvelled at the building, its lines and location befitting the significant financial institution within. He looked to the top of the Paternoster Column in the midst of the square, to the gold leaf copper urn. He turned to view the rest of the square, to the diversely styled buildings that housed the equally magnanimous financial beasts of Goldman Sachs and Merrill Lynch. This was the City of London, the Square Mile, one of the world's major financial centres. Clark found a certain absurdity with this concept of a city within a city, a city with its own independent Lord Mayor, an office separate from the wider reaching Mayor of London. He of course appreciated its origins, the City of London essentially the trading port that was the first century Roman settlement of Londinium.

He had to keep going, no time for nostalgia. He looked quickly again at his watch and stepped briskly through the Square, weaving through the hordes of tourists and suited workers, towards Cheapside and Bank junction and the offices of Thompson Braithwaite.

At Bank he turned left and walked along the side of The Bank of England onto Lothbury and to where he wanted to be, to the stunning period property that once housed the Headquarters of the National Westminster Bank. He walked slowly through the entrance looking in awe at the high ceiling held aloft by Portland stone columns, at the expansive Italian polished marble floor, black and white squares seemingly running in all directions yet at the same time running towards each other. Between the columns sat a long white counter, two figures sitting fervently scanning computer screens. Clark approached the counter slowly, taking on the look of a bewildered tourist, his satchel and rucksack hanging on his shoulder assisting the ruse.

"Hi," he said smiling to the pleasant round face that greeted him, chocolate brown skin and brilliant white teeth. "I was wondering where Thompson Braithwaite's offices are?"

"Yes Sir," said Darlene, the name plate on her desk and the name badge on her lapel giving her nowhere to hide, "Seventh floor suite, and with a roof terrace with lovely views across to the Cathedral. Nicest offices in the building, isn't that right Hector?" She looked across at her colleague, a beaming man with equally glowing skin.

"Sure is," he said, "Best place to sit for lunch, I can tell you. On a good day of course, and when no one is around," he added.

Clark allowed himself to laugh. "Yeah, I'm sure," he said.

"Are you looking for someone in particular? I can call up for you?" asked Darlene.

Clark thought quickly. "No. No thanks," he said, "It's just a friend used to work there and said I should check out the building if I was ever over here."

"No problem," she said and turned to Hector, "Keep an eye on things while I take this gentleman upstairs and show him what he's missing."

Hector laughed and winked and her.

Clark could feel the flush climb his neck. He fumbled a look at his watch. "No, it's okay," he said awkwardly, "I need to get going. But thanks anyway."

He turned and began to walk away. "Tell me this," he said turning back, "Is the building open at weekends?"

"Sure is," said Darlene, "Open every day, but I can't guarantee there will be anyone working weekends on the seventh floor."

"No problem," said Clark smiling as he ambled towards the door.

"Maybe see you over the weekend then?" called Darlene after him.

Clark waved over his shoulder.

Basinghall Street was next. He followed Lothbury to the west onto Gresham Street, passing Coleman Street before turning onto Basinghall. The buildings around him were functional, sprawling and tall and unlikely to win any architecture prizes. The Gherkin skyscraper looked down on him from only few streets away. That was more like it he thought, functional and tall but pleasing, not like the concrete and glass carbuncles before him.

He stopped and lifted the notebook from his satchel, checking first for the London headquarters address of Wilson Group and then checking the number on the soaring building beside him. He was close. Fifty yards later and he was there, at City House, a modern nine storey building with square lines of windows and stone, not unattractive but certainly not Lothbury.

He looked through the glass entrance doors. Unlike the deserted foyer of Lothbury there were scores of people milling, talking and laughing their way through an impressive modern atrium. Clark looked at his watch. Of course, lunch time. Colleagues were gathering in flocks to hit the restaurants and sandwich bars peppered around the locale.

He looked around and spotted a plaque embedded in the outside wall, eventually finding what he was looking for. Wilson Group occupied the third and fourth floors. He wanted to go in. But he didn't have time. He nodded and turned in search of a cab for Canary Wharf and the offices of the subsidiary companies.

And then he remembered the call he had to make. At the kerbside he dug out the note Isabella had given him at the hotel reception and dialled the number. "It's Clark Radcliffe," he said when Ronald answered the phone.

"Yes Clark," said Ronald. "Thanks for calling. Listen I just wanted to say sorry about last night. Maybe we can catch up for a chat? There is something I would like to tell you."

Clark sighed. He wasn't sure he wanted to spend any more of his time in the man's company. He had hoped the call would suffice. "It'll have to be at Victoria before I catch the two thirty train," he eventually said.

"No problem," said Ronald, "I'll see you two o'clock at the Cuisine Cafe on the concourse, by Bridge Place."

Clark looked at his watch. "See you then," he said and hung up.

The skyscrapers of Canary Wharf grew taller as the taxi worked its way alongside the river and into the docklands. This was London's second financial centre, redeveloped within the declined West India

Docks. The taxi left Clark off at Canada Square, the heart of the development. Clark handed over the meter amount and stared at the surrounding walls of glass as the cab pulled way. He looked left and right marvelling at the autumn sunlight reflecting off the banks of windows creating a sparkling aurora. And then he looked up. He cranked his neck further and further back until it could go no further. Only then could he see the top of the building before him, the tower stretching higher and higher into the sky finishing only when it reached its distinctive rooftop pyramid. This was undoubtedly the building he was looking for, one of Europe's tallest buildings. This was One Canada Square, E14, the building that housed the London offices of Santexon, Rancode Holdings and Yerco, the three subsidiary companies of Thompson Braithwaite.

Clark secured his rucksack and satchel over his shoulder and made his way towards the revolving entrance door set invitingly among a wall of polished steel and glistening glass. Inside the lobby he stopped, his mouth dropping at the expanse and the opulence, modern opulence, not refurbished historic opulence like at Lothbury. He'd seen such modern opulence before, the Burj in Dubai coming to mind, but this was different. This was a commercial building. These were offices where people came each day carrying briefcases, where people sat and shuffled paper and prodded buttons on keyboards. This was indeed something different.

He saw a long marble reception desk ahead and moved slowly towards it, taking in his surroundings, his head moving left and right, up and down.

"Good afternoon Sir," said a young man meticulously presented in a dark suit.

Clark nodded and stepped forward. "Do you have a directory of the building?" he asked.

"Certainly Sir. Can I ask if you are enquiring about anything in particular?" the man replied with a smile, but did not move.

Clark smiled. "Of course," he said. "A friend works here with

Yerco. I just wondered where I might find him." Clark thought he would try the friend routine again. It had worked before at Lothbury.

The man nodded and smiled. "Twenty third floor," he said. They have their own reception just beyond the lift lobby. Would you like me to ring ahead?"

"No thanks," said Clark looking at his watch and thinking quickly, "I don't have time now. But maybe I'll come back." He turned to walk away. He was happy enough. At least he knew on what floor to find one of the companies, and he knew he could access its own reception directly. Maybe from there he could find his way to the other companies.

"Excuse me Sir," called the man from behind him. Clark turned and the man handed him a brochure, a glossy brochure with a photograph of the building on the front. "Our directory Sir," he added.

Clark smiled and thanked him. He left the building and found a bench on the plaza outside where he sat and looked again up and down the building before opening the brochure. He drew breath as he read about the ninety thousand square feet of Italian and Guatemalan marble in the lobby, three thousand nine hundred and sixty windows, and four thousand three hundred and eighty eight stairs. He laughed when he read that the building was designed to sway nearly fourteen inches in strong winds.

He flicked on through the brochure until he found what he was hoping for, a list of all the companies occupying the building's fifty floors. He found Yerco easily enough as he knew to look to the listing for the twenty third floor. He eventually found Santexon, fifteenth floor, and Rancode Holdings on the thirty third. He was about to close up the brochure when he instinctively glanced across all the company names.

That was when he saw something unexpected.

On the thirty ninth floor was a listing for Green Crab Commodities, the subsidiary company to Wilson Group. Clark pulled his notebook form his satchel. He had recorded Green Crab Commodities as having a UK address at Twenty Five Canada Square, a different building completely. This was something he would have to clarify. But more importantly, it put all the subsidiary companies highlighted in Spencer's disk as having a presence in one building.

He looked at his watch and stood. It was approaching one thirty and he had to get back to Victoria to meet with Ronald, and eventually Siobhan. He turned and walked along South Colonnade towards Canary Wharf Underground Station thinking it would be the best place to find a cab. He was thinking too he would have to come back to Canada Square when he had more time, he would have to come back and get into the building, to speak with people, to try and find out if and how each of the companies were connected.

And he would have to come back soon. But he had to get back to Belfast that afternoon. He had to go to the Slieve Donard to check on Amy and on his mum and dad. He had to get to Chesterton and Williamson the next day to check on Jimmy and Annabel. And he had arranged to meet with Jackson the following night, Friday night. He had asked at Lothbury if the building was open at weekends. He wondered then if the other companies would operate at weekends, if the buildings would be open. He knew the London Stock Exchange operated Monday to Friday but somehow he thought the international manufacturing and supply companies would be seven day operations.

He wondered if he could come back to London on Saturday.

And then out of the shadows came a figure, a figure that stood directly in front of him; a figure that he recognised. His heart skipped but he kept going, standing straight and confident as he approached the squat but well dressed bull dog that was Wayne Demachi.

CHAPTER 14

"Hi Clark, a word?" Wayne said and pointed back towards the shadow of the building. Clark nodded and followed. He checked left and right, and over his shoulder. "It's okay, I'm alone," said Wayne.

Clark nodded again.

"I've been watching you. You have been a busy man Clark. But tell me, what are you up to?"

Clark said nothing as he tried to quickly put the pieces together. Wayne had been following him, but had stayed hidden. Before, on the train and in Belfast the tail had made itself known, had given a warning to leave it alone. But now the tail was in the shadows, only now revealing itself. Why? And the tail was now one strong, not two or even three as it had been. Again, why? And why had Wayne asked him what he was up to?

Clark shrugged.

It was Wayne's turn to look left and right and over his shoulder. He moved closer to Clark and lowered his voice.

"Who's your muscle, Clark?" he said.

Clark looked at him.

"What's your connection, Clark?" he said with a twitch, sweat developing on his brow.

And then Clark realised. He smiled as he remembered the encounter at his parent's house, when he was flanked by Vince and Ryan. Wayne and his compatriots were concerned. There was something about Clark that they suspected they didn't know. They were thinking he too was organised but did not know how, or to what. That was why the explicit tail had dropped off, and that was why Wayne Demachi had been charged with following him, to stay hidden, to find out where he was going, and if the opportunity presented itself, and it was safe to do so, to talk with him.

"I have my agenda," said Clark confidently and then added, "We have our agenda."

Wayne nodded. "Does Spencer know?"

Clark didn't know what he was referring to but said, "Yes, Spencer knows. Spencer knows what I am capable of."

Wayne nodded and leaned forward, "Okay Clark. As we have said before you should leave it alone. We don't want any... let us say complications, any unfortunate incidents?"

Clark smiled. "No Wayne, indeed we do not. And perhaps you and your friends might want to remember that." He then stepped to the side and brushed past the short man.

Clark sat in the back of the taxi cab feeling he had just won the round, but wondering what might come next.

Ronald Hawk was waiting for him at a table outside Cuisine Cafe, the table tight against the cafe's canvas barrier that served to demarcate the allotted space on Victoria train station's concourse, a space that was undeniably popular affording as it did a perfect vantage point to watch the confused wanderings of the station's eclectic mix of passengers.

"Clark, good to see you," said Ronald, a broad grin across his face. He stood and grabbed Clark's hand firmly, placing his other hand on Clark's forearm. "Sorry again about last night, clearly not your bag."

Clark nodded and sat on the seat opposite, a paper cup of coffee awaiting him. Ronald sported a well cut navy suit and what looked like a college tie, striped but its origin Clark could not determine. Despite the chic attire he still looked decidedly rumpled, a few too many creases in the jacket and a shirt collar that appeared a bit on the loose side. The knot on the tie could have been tighter. His hair was ruffled and overdue a trim. He was unshaven. But he continued to radiate a warm glow, a wide infectious smile and a sparkle from his deep blue eyes.

"Let me cut to the chase," said Ronald. "Spencer is a good bloke. He is good at what he does, finds leads, and follows leads. Tenacious you could say. He has a reputation among the industry as a well informed and reliable analyst and adviser."

Clark stared and said nothing.

"He has his ways," Ronald continued, "methodical and diligent. He gets results. Colleagues come to him for advice, and not just from within his own firm but from across the industry. Like me for example, I don't work with Spencer, never have, but we will often meet to discuss the markets."

Clark sighed. "You said you would cut to the chase," he said looking at his watch.

"Yes, of course." Ronald reached across the table and touched Clark gently on the arm. He looked around him and smiled again. "He made a mistake. A monumental mistake I grant you. He is a good friend. He has been a good friend to me over many years. Your sister will tell you. He is a gentleman, unorthodox perhaps on occasion, but his heart is in the right place. He thinks a lot of Amy you know. Maybe he doesn't always show it."

"Ronald," Clark interrupted, "In case you have forgotten I was there last night. It didn't look to me like he had respect for anybody, let alone my sister."

Ronald held up both hands and laughed loudly. "Clark," he said through his laughter, "Forget about last night. Such nights are... like tradition. We need to let our hair down and that is how we do it. There is nothing meant by it."

Clark shook and head and looked away. He couldn't believe what he was hearing, this justification for obscene gratification; for abuse. He thought of Lavinia and her vulnerability; middle aged men ogling and pawing while those they said they cared about were at home, oblivious. Clark pushed his chair back and stood.

"Goodbye Ronald," he said.

Ronald jumped from his seat. "Please Clark sit, at least for a minute." He ran fingers crudely through his hair leaving it in standing like an eighties' glam rocker's perm. He beamed an exaggerated grin. Clark smiled despite himself. He nodded and sat.

"As I was saying," said Ronald, "Amy means a lot to Spencer. He speaks often of her when we are together, and always complimentary. He often tells me how she is his professional compass, a knowledgeable sounding board, capable and very smart. Maybe she doesn't realise it, but her words of encouragement and advice do not go unheeded. Spencer respects her intervention."

Clark smiled and nodded. She was indeed knowledgeable, capable and smart. But she was also very wealthy. "Where are you going with this?" he asked Ronald curtly.

Ronald grimaced and looked around the cafe. "You got me Clark. He might not be able to express himself as well as he might, but he needs her."

"Needs her how, Ronald?"

He opened his hands across the table and nodded. "He cannot function without her."

"He needs her money, is that it? Is that what you are trying to say? Or are you trying to give some sloppy sentimental parable about compatibility so Amy feels guilty if she doesn't help him?" said Clark sitting forcibly back in his chair.

Ronald smiled and nodded slowly. "Yes," he said, "Amy can provide a lifeline for him, of that there is no doubt. But Clark, they are a couple. They should be there for each other. They should help each other..."

Clark had heard enough. He stood abruptly for a second time. "Is that what you think Ronald? That they are a couple? That they should be there for each other? That they should help each other? Is that what Spencer thinks? Why does he not tell her himself? Why are you here telling me this? Why is Spencer dismissive and condescending to me, her brother, if she means so much to him? Why is Spencer an enigma to my family if he sees himself as part of this great couple who should help each other no matter what?

"And why Ronald, does he molest young defenceless girls when Amy is not with him?" Clark's face was red with rage. "And one more thing Ronald," he said drawing a deep breath, "What is all this to you?"

Ronald stood and smiled, offering his hand across the table. Clark looked at the hand and back to Ronald's face. He was conscious of other eyes around him glancing in their direction, curious no doubt as to why these two men kept standing and sitting. He accepted the hand.

"So tell me Clark," said Ronald, "How are things going with the police back in Belfast? I believe you consult to them through one of your associate firms, Chesterton and Williamson? Is that right?"

Clark shook his head. "Yes," he said, "It's going well." Ronald had done it again. He had mellowed Clark with his smile and deflection, and his unusual appearance; his tie fallen to mid chest, two shirt buttons fallen open to reveal grey and black tangled tufts, and the hair on his head taken on a life of its own.

"Spencer and I are good friends," said Ronald, "It's no more or no less than that. I know what he can be like, how he might be perceived. But I can assure you he is like that with everyone. I suppose I am used to it and accept him as he is, take no offence. It is just the way he is. He's the same with Lance, a good young man, but maybe a bit too impressionable for my liking.

"Maybe Clark, after a while you can come to see that too, to see that he is, if nothing else, consistent. He means well. He is a good man, a loyal man. And Clark, as I said, forget about last night, at the club. To Spencer, in fact to all of us, it is just a bit of harmless fun. No one needs to know anything about it."

Clark assumed the last line was a message; don't tell Amy. He didn't know if he could oblige. But he nodded. He was done with Ronald, whose objective was clearly to persuade Clark to in turn persuade Amy to help Spencer, to help his great friend. But why there was such loyalty? He sighed and looked around the café, eventually looking over his shoulder toward the station entrance at Bridge Place. Something caught his eye. He made a double take.

Siobhan was standing face to face with a tall man in a camel cashmere coat and college scarf, not quite the attire required given the mild weather. He was laughing. He wrapped both arms around her. The two of them embraced. She broke away and stood on her toes and they kissed. Siobhan then walked towards the entrance to the Gatwick Express, the man following her with his eyes. Siobhan stopped and turned towards the man and waved. The man waved back and then left the station.

Clark nodded again at Ronald and bent to lift his satchel and rucksack from the floor. He walked towards Siobhan without saying another word.

CHAPTER 15

Siobhan smiled warmly as he approached but it was a smile he could not return. She opened her arms to him but he stopped short. She looked at him. He looked away.

"Are you okay?" she asked.

He nodded but didn't answer. He walked towards the train and she followed. She sat opposite him, staring. He ignored her. The train pulled away from the platform. Who was the man she was with? Why had he held her? Why had she raised herself to kiss him? And not the air kiss or the kiss on the cheek you would expect from family, friends, or colleagues. No, this was a full kiss. Why had the man watched her walk away? And why did she turn and wave?

He managed to look at her but it was her turn to look away, arms folded tight. He could ask her for answers to his questions, but he didn't want to. Was he afraid of the answer? Was saying nothing the best way of dealing with it? She was beautiful, both in body and person. This he kept telling himself. There must be an explanation. He thought of the previous night, of Lavinia at the club and the guilt he had felt. Was his not telling her about Lavinia any different from her not telling him about the man at the station? He debated it in his head, eventually arriving at an answer. One cancelled the other.

"I missed you," he said turning round to look at her.

She held his eye and then slowly unfolded her arms. The corners of her mouth began to rise. She nodded and reached forward to hold his hand in both of hers. She caressed his fingers gently. Clark swallowed hoping the tears would not come.

They sat side by side on the plane, each with a flight sized bottle of red wine and comfortable with each other's silence. Eventually Siobhan placed her hand on Clark's leg. She moved closer to him and rested her head on his shoulder. He kissed the top of her head.

"How was your day?" he asked softly.

"Very busy," she said. "I really don't know where it went. I just called into Petersons to say hello and the next thing I was invited to a meeting, something about data transfer security. Not quite my thing but I think I was able to contribute something. And that was it, straight back to the train station and now on the plane."

No mention of anybody else. Clark tried not to dwell on it. He ran his fingers through her hair.

"How did you get on?" she asked nestling closer.

He told her some of what had happened since they had parted that morning, about meeting DI James for breakfast but not about organised gangs of financiers. He told her about going to Lothbury and One Canada Square but did not tell her he was inside. He did not tell her either about meeting Wayne Demachi or Ronald Hawk.

"One Canada Square?" she said, "Canary Wharf? I spent some time there you know, a while back. Thirtieth floor I think it was."

He looked at her but said nothing.

"Are you still cooking tonight?" she then asked.

Of course, he had forgotten. He had told her on the phone a couple of days before to come to his house when he got back from London. But that was before she had surprised him at the hotel. He smiled as he recalled the unhurried and tender night they had spent together. "What about a night out instead?" he said.

"Sure," she purred and placed a hand on his chest, "Where?"

"The Slieve Donard?"

She bolted upright. "You mean where your family are staying?"

He nodded.

"But I've never met them."

He shrugged. "And maybe stay over at mine afterwards?"

She fell against his chest, smiling. "If you are sure that is what you want," she whispered.

He smiled too and kissed the top of her head again, certain that he was indeed what he wanted.

They left in separate taxis from Belfast City Airport, Siobhan home to Kerrsland Drive and Clark to Ethel Street. They had to freshen up for dinner, and Siobhan had to organise another overnight bag. Clark had to tidy the house.

It was after six o'clock when he arrived home. A quick wipe around the kitchen and a straightening of cushions would have to do. And then it was off to his study, the small second bedroom that also served as his gym. He pulled his bench away from the wall and began to push his free weights. He worked himself hard, the strength for extra reps coming from his recalling that he was apparently connected, that he had muscle. He laughed.

Forty five minutes later and he was showered, dressed and in his Toyota on route to collect Siobhan. He had sent Amy a text saying he would be at the Slieve Donard later. He did not mention bringing Siobhan.

Clark rang Siobhan's doorbell and waited. A few moments later the door opened, as did his mouth. She was clearly aiming to make an impression. Her hair was shining and had been frizzled away from her face, eye shadow and lip gloss augmenting her natural features, pearl earrings and matching pearl necklace setting off the bare neckline of her short sleeved black tight fitting Raffia dress that fell to her knees. Her legs were bare down to a pair of Jimmy Choo

Dawn sandals. Over one her arm she carried a Vivienne Westwood weave cardigan and her Chanel handbag, in the other she carried the Louis Vuitton overnight bag.

"Will I do?" she asked.

Clark smiled and shook his head. He stepped towards her and kissed her forehead not wishing to trouble the lip gloss. "You're beautiful," he muttered under his breath. "Thank you for doing this." But she couldn't hear him.

Dusk was falling as they approached the Slieve Donard Hotel. The Mountains of Mourne rose up before them to meet the darkening clouds, their slopes quite literally sweeping down to the sea. It was a sight to behold. Clark glanced at Siobhan as she sat cross-legged on the passenger seat beside him. Yes, he thought, truly a sight to behold.

Clark parked the car and helped Siobhan from her seat. They stood and looked at the grand facade of the old nineteenth century railway hotel, the red brick and grey slate turrets peppering the skyline. The waves crashed on to the rocks behind them, very close behind them, the hotel having an enviable position on the shoreline.

Clark reached for Siobhan's hand and they walked together across the car park and through the hotel reception towards the bar from where he intended to call his sister. But she was already there, sitting with their mother and father beside her. She waved. His father waved too. But his mother looked away.

"Hi everyone," said Clark gently pushing Siobhan in front of him, "This is Siobhan."

Siobhan smiled. "Hi. Lovely to meet you all," she said.

It was Clark's father who responded first. "And it's lovely to meet you," he said. He began to rise.

"Oh please, don't get up," said Siobhan and stepped towards him to shake his hand. "I've heard so much about you. How is your recovery?"

"Very well thanks," he said smiling broadly.

Amy gave Siobhan the once over. She too eventually managed a smile and nodded.

"You're late," said Amy to Clark, "We were waiting for you for dinner. I have a table organised in the Oak restaurant." She looked at Siobhan. "I suppose I'll have to arrange an extra seat."

Clark squeezed Siobhan's hand.

Amy moved away and their mum followed. Their dad nodded and smiled again at Siobhan, raising a hand to Clark's shoulder. He squeezed and nodded again.

They were seated at a large round table in the restaurant; the room to themselves save for a couple in the corner staring continuously into each other's eyes. It was midweek and it was late, not surprising therefore it was quiet. The advantage of course was they were afforded the full attention of the staff. Menus and wine lists were handed to them by a middle aged woman in a grey suit. Some sort of manageress or maitre d thought Clark, her grace and authority positioning her somewhere beyond a paid by the hour waitress. Clark nodded to her as he accepted the menu. He sat facing into the restaurant with his back to the bank of windows and mahogany clad pillars, Siobhan at his one side and Amy at his other. His father sat beside Siobhan leaving his mother between her husband and her daughter, and essentially sitting opposite Clark. She focused her attention on the windows.

"How are you Mum?" said Clark.

"Fine," she said without looking at him. Amy nudged him under the table and shook her head. He nodded. He had lived with his mother's anger for years, and had accepted it was not always unjustified given his own attitude towards his parents when he had left home to the student life in the city, effectively cutting his parents out of his life. But he thought things were improving. He had been making an effort lately, albeit with more tangible success with his father. He still had a way to go.

He heard laughter from beside him and turned to see his father with his head back guffawing and Siobhan with her hand on his arm laughing along. Clark smiled. She too was making an effort, and an impression. He smiled.

"Enjoying your stay Mum?" he said thinking he would give it another try.

"Not as much as home," she replied with a scowl but at least looking at him.

Clark nodded. So that's it he thought. She blames me for her being here, for being evicted from her home. Even though it was Amy who had led the men to her house, and I am helping. He shrugged and looked to Amy who rolled her eyes.

"Good news," he said, "The coast is clear. You can go home."

Amy stared. "What happened, Clark?" she said slowly, "Is everybody all right?"

Clark laughed. "Yes, everything's fine. Suffice to say the threat appears to be no more." He nodded and raised his eyebrows, a signal to Amy that he would tell her later. She returned the nod and placed her hand on his knee.

"About time," said their mum.

"Well, what do you make of Siobhan, Mum?" Clark asked not only in a further attempt to engage her, but because he wanted her opinion and if he was truthful, her approval.

"A bit younger than I would have thought," was all she said.

Clark sighed and went back to the menu.

They enjoyed a hearty meal of sirloin and lamb cutlets, all beautifully prepared and presented. The service was second to none, the grey suited women giving them her undivided attention. Clark spent the entire time talking to Amy about where he had been in London, all he seen in the short time he was there. Well, not quite everything. The club story could wait. He tried on more than one occasion to draw Siobhan into the conversation but she was too engrossed in sharing tales and laughter with his father to pay him any attention. His mother ate in silence.

At coffee Clark interrupted Siobhan and whispered that he and Amy were going to the bar to talk. Siobhan squeezed his thigh and leaned towards him seeking his lips. He obliged, albeit awkwardly.

"Well, how was he?" asked Amy when they found a comfortable and secluded corner table, Clark with a small bottle of sparkling water, Amy with another glass of Merlot.

Clark laughed. "Spencer certainly is something else," he said.

"As difficult as ever, huh?"

Clark shook his head. "Difficult yes; aloof and inhospitable."

Amy nodded. "I know what he's like."

Clark raised his eyebrows. "Do you?"

She looked at him. "What do you mean?"

He shook his head. Now was not the time.

"Nothing," he said. He told Amy about meeting with Spencer at the hotel bar and that he had brought Lance and Ronald with him. He told her about Spencer refusing to say who had been his source but had insisted he had corroborated the information on the disk. He told her about Spencer denying he knew the two men who had followed her and that he had been nervous when the Police had been mentioned. And he told her Spencer had insisted that Amy was his only hope.

Amy listened intently, nodding periodically but saying nothing.

Clark excused himself and walked to the bar, coming back with a pen and a blank page from an order pad. He told Amy about his meeting with DI James and began to redraw the chart for the organisation. He wrote the names of Brent as a middle ranker and Wayne as one of his team, or 'pilot' as he had taken to refer to the team members as. He noted that the three men he had met on the train were possibly involved as another unit.

Amy stared at the chart shaking her head.

"I met Wayne again," said Clark.

She lifted her head. "The short guy at Mum and Dad's house?"

Clark nodded and told her what DI James had said, that Wayne had some previous convictions and was most likely involved for his ability to intimidate. He told her again he felt the likelihood of Brent and Wayne coming back to Belfast to be slim. He told her Wayne had thought he was involved in some organisation and that he had played on it. He felt that gave him an advantage, at least for a short while until someone found out otherwise.

That made Amy smile. "Don Clarkeone," she said adding, "But be careful. Don't let it get out of control."

Clark nodded. He would not get carried away. He told Amy about meeting Ronald and his glowing testimony of Spencer. "There are a lot of people Amy who are very interested in advising that you help Spencer," he said and glanced at the chart.

She looked at him and then down at the chart. "What are you saying Clark? Are you suggesting that Spencer is in some way involved in this?"

Clark shrugged. "Maybe more than involved," he said and pointed to the question mark at the top of the chart.

Amy sat back in her chair and laughed aloud. The barman looked over but quickly returned to his wine glass polishing. She put both hands over her face and shook her head. After a moment she leaned forward and placed her elbows on the table. "Have you any idea how ridiculous you sound," she said.

"Amy, you asked for my help remember?"

"Yes", she said, "Help me by checking why Spencer did what he did. Help me by checking if it would be prudent for me to cash in and invest in his future, in our future Clark. I did not expect you to concoct some scenario that included Spencer as some sort of Mafioso."

"Amy," he said, "You asked me to investigate. Yes, this might be a scenario that is fantastical but it still one that I must consider."

She looked at him and said nothing. She looked down at the scribbled chart and then back to Clark. She nodded. And then began to cry.

He leaned forward and held both her hands in his.

"I miss him," she said.

Clark nodded. He knew Spencer was far from perfect but they must have had their good times. It was the good times she undoubtedly remembered. Maybe she did know there were things he got up to, places he went. Maybe for her that was okay. "I'm sure you miss him," he said softly, "But let me find out what I can." He paused for a moment. "And let me ask you this... Will you accept what I find?"

She looked at him and wiped the tears away. She sighed and nodded slowly.

"Have you had a look at the documents on the disk?" he asked.

She shook her head.

Clark stared and sighed. "You haven't spoken yet with Siobhan," he said changing the subject.

She smiled. "She's very... glamorous, Clark."

He laughed. "What are you saying? What could she possibly see in me?"

She shook her head and laughed. "And young. Seriously Clark, I hope she is good for you."

Clark smiled. He nodded." Yes," he said, "Yes she is." After a moment, "Amy, there's more I could be doing in London. I need to be in work tomorrow and in Belfast tomorrow night, but after that ..."

Amy nodded. "Leave it with me," she said, "I'll organise a flight on Saturday. A couple of nights in the same hotel okay?"

Clark nodded. They left the bar to rejoin their parents, and to rescue Siobhan.

Siobhan sat in the passenger seat of Clark's Toyota on the journey home relaying the many stories his father had shared with her. She'd had a good night, had enjoyed his company. Clark had to admit his dad was an interesting character, a very clever man, a retired academic with a sharp wit and an interest in many things. She had thought Clark's mother was a pleasant woman too but Clark suspected she was being polite given he hadn't witnessed any communication between the two. Amy had sat beside Siobhan when she and Clark had returned from the bar and had struck up conversation, conversation peppered with many laughs. Clark had no idea what they talked about but guessed he would have featured prominently. It had heartened him when Amy and Siobhan had embraced before they departed. His father had been the gentleman and shook her hand. His mother had nodded and forced a smile. His mother and father had agreed to check out of the Slieve Donard the following morning and head home to Ballydorn. Amy would stay with them at least for the weekend, until Clark had finished whatever it was he was planning to do in London.

He parked on the road outside his house and opened the passenger door for Siobhan, watching as she slipped gracefully out of the car, the shortness of her dress not hindering her. As she stood Clark leaned forwards and kissed her, a planned short kiss developing into a long lingering one. He slid his hands down her back and pulled her tight towards him. "Thank you," he whispered in her ear before breaking away and reaching into the back of the car for her bag, her overnight bag.

He was awakened the next morning by the sound of running water and melodious tones flowing from the bathroom. He smiled and turned to check the bedside clock. Seven o'clock on Friday morning. He thought about getting to Chesterton and Williamson, to check on his two charges. He was however brought quickly back to the present as Siobhan stepped into the bedroom, her hair encased in a towel in some miraculous way that only women seemed to know. She wore nothing else. She leaned towards him and they kissed gently. He began to pull her towards him but she resisted. She shook her head playfully. "Later," she whispered.

Clark made breakfast. Nothing fancy, just coffee, boiled eggs and well done toast. It hadn't taken him long to shower and dress in his usual smart casual work attire. He was happy, and relaxed. So different from the few mornings earlier when he had awoken in Siobhan's house disorientated and confused. He had thought he had lost her then. But she had understood. She had surprised him in London. She had played a blinder with his family. And she had spent the night with him, at his house and at his pace. He bent and kissed her neck as she sat at the table with her coffee. She turned and smiled and drew his lips to hers.

"Don't forget we're out tonight with Jackson and Tracey," he said.

"Yeah, I'm looking forward to meeting Tracey," she said smiling.

Clark laughed. "You'll get on like a house on fire," an image of Tracey filling his mind. He then looked at her, at how she had somehow managed to produce a creaseless tailored black trouser suit from her small overnight bag. He looked to her black red soled Louboutins with a four inch heel. He lifted his phone and ordered a taxi. She wasn't dressed for the bus.

They sat side by side in the rear of the taxi, Siobhan turning to face Clark. "Thanks for last night," she said slowly, "for everything. It meant a lot to me." And to me too, thought Clark. She held his eye. "Maybe later we can have a talk. There is something I need to tell you."

Clark looked away, an image of the man at Victoria station coming back to him.

CHAPTER 16

Clark was first to alight the taxi, Siobhan having further to go to reach Peterson's offices by the River Lagan. He watched the car pull away and tried to focus his mind on the day ahead, on Fabian, Penny, Jimmy and Annabel.

The lift carried him quickly to the sixteenth floor of Windsor House. He recalled the first time he had been in the building many years before, and had travelled twenty three levels to the top floor for a meeting with some public sector company, he couldn't remember which. But he did remember the nose bleed. He remembered looking out the window across the city towards the docks and the iconic bright yellow cranes at Harland and Wolff shipyard, the birthplace of the ill-fated Titanic. He remembered looking down towards the road in front and his head spinning. And then the nose bleed came. That was back when Windsor House was Belfast's tallest building, an accolade now held by the Obel Tower, a residential skyscraper of subtle curves and walls of dazzling glass. He often wondered how his head and nose would manage wakening up in the dizzy heights of its rooftop penthouse.

He shuffled towards his desk and removed his laptop from his satchel, glancing at Jimmy as the machine powered up. Jimmy stared at some printed document on his desk. Clark smirked and shook his head. He looked across to Deanna. She sensed his glance and raised her head. Her eyes lit and she smiled warmly. Clark smiled in reply and nodded.

"Hi," she said softly, leaning towards him keeping her body low, the angle forcing her generous chest upwards, forwards and barely contained. "How was London?"

"Good," replied Clark.

She pointed surreptitiously towards Jimmy."He's been quiet," she whispered, "And busy."

Clark nodded and smiled. He turned back towards his laptop. He had messages to check, and a data investigation report to finalise and sign off. After an hour he lifted his head and looked again at Jimmy. "The meeting room Jimmy. Bring the laptop," he said as he pushed away from his desk and moved to the small glass fronted cubicle. Jimmy took his time.

"What did you find?" said Clark when Jimmy had eventually sat opposite him, the laptop from McArdle sitting between them.

"Nothing," he said curtly, arms folded.

"Nothing?" repeated Clark nodding slowly. "There is always something."

Jimmy jumped and leaned across the desk, hands either side of the laptop. "Look," he snapped, "I didn't know what to look for. You took off and left me with no instruction. And then you give me a trainee to work with, a trainee who asked questions I could not answer. You made me a fool Radcliffe."

Clark smiled. Jimmy was concerned about the dent to his ego, hoping no doubt to impress Annabel but apparently unable to offer anything but the routine and obvious, probably nothing more than she could have found herself.

"You wanted this Jimmy, remember. You offered yourself as

having some sort of competence," said Clark slowly. "Looks like I will have to treat you and Annabel the same. Start with the basics. Treat you as two beginners."

Jimmy stormed out the door and back to his desk.

Clark charged up McArdle's laptop and set to work, alone, the way he liked it. He had asked Jimmy to analyse the building firm's data and to write a report of his findings, anything at all he could find about payments for labour and supplies. Jimmy hadn't shown any signs of having produced a report. Clark set about creating one himself. It didn't take him long to have a skeleton outline of his initial findings, explicit entries on spreadsheets of payments made to suppliers that he married across to a set of cost tables detailing each of the company's registered suppliers. The two sets of documents did not tally. This was basic stuff. This was just comparing onscreen data. He glanced up through the glass wall to Jimmy. He shook his head.

Returning to the laptop he began to search beyond the obvious, for any cross referenced files and documents, for any data transfer trails, and for any fragments of deleted data. This was the time consuming bit. This was when it could take hours to find very little, if anything. But this was the bit Clark liked, meticulous investigation and scrutiny where the discovery of a smallest fragment of data could lead to something bigger. Find the fragment and submerse yourself in the mind of the data author, follow the logic, develop the scenarios and test what and who might benefit. This was not something that could be readily taught to another.

He didn't see her coming, wasn't even aware she was standing over him until the sweet perfumed aroma reached him. He looked up, startled. She stood so close her hip brushed his elbow. "He wouldn't let me even look at it," said Annabel pointing at the screen.

Clark looked at her, at her eyes as they began to moisten. She rested a hand on his shoulder and for some reason he lifted his own hand and placed it on hers. He smiled and nodded. He squeezed her hand and pointed towards the chair at the end of the table, the chair furthest away from the door, and a chair from which Jimmy could not see her.

She pulled the chair away from the table and turned it towards Clark, still out of sight from the main office. She sat slowly and crossed one leg over the other, the black skirt rising further than she should have imagined, a hint of smooth bronzed flesh displayed above the stocking top. She made no attempt to straighten her skirt. A white blouse was buttoned high but pulled tight across her chest, the buttons straining to fulfil their function.

"I wanted to look at the computer, to see if I could find anything but he just…," she said quietly and then burst into tears. Clark reached into his pocket for his handkerchief, a cloth handkerchief he always carried and was thankful it was unused, still ironed and folded. He reached it to her.

"What is it Annabel?" he said softly.

She looked at him and managed a smile, her makeup somehow managing to survive the tears. "He just… wanted me to sit beside him and…"

"And what Annabel?" said Clark struggling to keep his voice calm.

She began to sniffle again. "He just stared…"

"Right, enough," Clark said and pushed his chair back, his focus and attention now fully on Jimmy.

"No Clark, it's okay," she said quickly and leaned forward enough to rest a hand on his arm. "He just made me feel uncomfortable."

"Annabel," said Clark, "If he made you feel uncomfortable then it is serious. This is a workplace. He has no right."

Clark looked at Jimmy and back to her. He nodded, deciding he would deal with it another time. "Are you sure you are okay?" he asked.

She nodded.

He smiled. "Right then, slide back behind the table" He moved his chair beside hers, close but not too close. He moved the laptop across the table, away from eyes in the main office. No one could see them unless they came tight against the glass or right into the office. Clark opened the spreadsheet listing all the building firm's suppliers. "I want you to tell me what you see," he said.

She looked at him and her face lit up. She turned back to the computer and began to navigate around the spreadsheet with some speed and dexterity, and with some confidence. Clark watched her. Her face furrowed, her lips tightened, her eyes narrowed. She pointed at the screen and then ran her hand over her face. She began to tap the screen. She ran both her hands through her hair. Her fingers danced again over the keyboard. Clark nodded and smirked. He pushed his chair back slowly and slipped out of the room leaving her concentrating and content.

Penny Critchlow was sitting at his desk talking with Deanna and Jimmy. The conversation stopped when Clark approached. Deanna smiled. Penny and Jimmy looked at him.

"Have a good day away yesterday?" asked Penny eventually.

Clark nodded. He stared at Jimmy.

"We need a chat," said Penny managing a smile.

"Yes we do," said Clark and turned towards the foyer doors leaving them to their conversation. Behind him he distinctly heard Penny and Jimmy laughing.

He left Winsor House and crossed Bedford Street to the small coffee shop opposite. It was nearly lunchtime. Ordering a chicken sandwich and large coffee he sat at a small bistro table by the window and thought back to Fabian saying Jimmy had particular aptitude for computers. He thought back too to Penny saying that Jimmy had skills and aptitude that could be developed to help in computer analysis. Quite frankly Clark had not seen any such competence or aptitude, and certainly had not seen any pertinent productivity. He wondered what Fabian and Penny had based their assessment on. Was it aspiration, and if so was it theirs or his? He thought back to Penny saying Annabel was unknown to her other than she was an accountancy trainee who had demonstrated potential as an analyst and had expressed an interest in working in consultancy. Clark however had heard differently from Fabian, information that he had been told only he was party to. He thought of the passion and desire in Annabel's eyes when he had let her loose on the laptop. He had been impressed with the comfort she demonstrated in navigating the spreadsheet. This was a natural passion and desire. She clearly had competence and aptitude, the two unfounded qualities conferred on Jimmy. Clark thought then of the way Penny and Jimmy had laughed together at his desk, friendly, relaxed laughter.

An hour later and Clark was back at Chesterton and Williamson. There was no one else at his bank of three desks, all out to lunch no doubt. The door to the meeting room was closed. Clark walked over and peered through glass to the chair at the end of the table. And there was Annabel with her head in her hands staring at the screen, her long golden hair pulled back tight from her face and tied behind in a tail. She wore glasses, subtle frameless glasses, the first time Clark had seen her wearing them. She looked up and smiled. Clark smiled and stepped back to the door. He opened it a crack and slid his head through.

"Well?" he said.

"Payment schedules and supplier registers don't match," she said without lifting her eyes from the screen.

"What?" said Clark and walked over to look over her shoulder.

She had two screen windows open, the spreadsheet that Clark had given her and the company register that she would have had to identify herself. She was comparing and contrasting the data in each. Clark looked at her. She looked up at him and smiled and pointed at the screen. Clark shook his head. She had carried out exactly the same process he had and had drawn the same conclusion. He dropped into the seat beside her, keeping his distance. "Whoa," he said, "I'm impressed."

She turned towards him and pulled the tied hair away from her neck with one hand, and caressed her neck with her other. She winked and smiled. "You'd be surprised what I can do Clark." She dropped her hand from her neck to his knee. He didn't react, other than a nod and a smile.

"I'm glad you're impressed, I really am," she said moving her hand slightly, upwards. He still didn't move. "I know what I can do. I just need to be given the chance." She winked.

Clark nodded again thinking to what Fabian had confided in him, that she was smart but lacked confidence. He had given her a chance with the computer, a chance to show what she could do. And she had delivered, impressing him with her mind, with her potential. Maybe this was what she meant when she said she knew what she could do. Maybe it wasn't always innuendo and flirtation. Then again, maybe it was.

"Yes," said Clark slowly, "I think I'd like to see more of what you can do." He thought of what he had asked Jimmy to do, what Jimmy hadn't done. "Annabel, could you write up a report on what you have found? Just basic memo format will do."

She beamed. "No problem," and turned back to the computer, her fingers rapidly finding the keys without need to look at the keyboard. Clark laughed quietly and shook his head as he left the meeting room.

Clark re-read his computer audit report and made a few changes, satisfied it was ready to pass to Fabian. He knew he was to report to Penny in the new regime but the audit report had been commissioned in the old. So it would be to Fabian he would deliver it. Aware of Jimmy and Deanna returning from lunch he read the report yet again, unnecessarily he knew but anything to keep him focused away from his colleagues.

After an hour he heard his name called and looked up to see Annabel beckoning him. Deanna looked up towards Annabel and then at Clark. Jimmy looked over his shoulder and then he too looked at Clark. Clark glared back and after a moment he turned towards Deanna and smiled before stepping towards the meeting room.

"We're not networked in here," said Annabel, "and I have no other computer so I have just handwritten the memo." She pointed at a lined foolscap file pad.

Clark sat on her seat, and she on his. He read intently. Every word was neatly written and perfectly crafted, the art of the pen still with her. She moved close and watched him as he read. Her turned and looked at her, her face only inches from his. "This is excellent. You have captured all the main points and have applied all the right terminology. It's succinct, accurate and well structured. Well done," he said.

She sat back and folded her arms, the golden hair still tied back. Her eyes and cheeks had lost their painted glow, the lips were pale. The skirt was pulled low. She smiled; a natural smile.

Clark looked at his watch. "You came up with this in one hour? I think you have earned the right to break for lunch." He smiled and nodded.

She shook her head. "Not when there is work to do."

Clark shook his head, still smiling. "Right," he said, "Watch closely and I'll give you a quick lesson on hard drive data searching."

She placed both elbows on the table, one touching Clark's arm as he began to show her basic search and explore functions on the computer, how to find file fragments and how to interrogate the system's registry. This was some of what he had spent the morning doing, and with some success. He showed her what he had found and she asked many questions. She said she would like to explore the computer further and would add the findings to her report.

"I want to show you something else," he said. "Bring in my Dell and satchel from my desk if you don't mind."

She stood and moved towards the door only to stop dead after a few steps. She turned and looked at Clark, her face pale. And then Clark realised. Jimmy was sat with his back to her. Clark quickly saw this as an opportunity.

"Annabel," he said, "You have just proven to me you have ten times the competence he has, ten times the ability. Walk out there with your head held high."

She looked at him and smiled. "Thank you," she mouthed.

Clark moved McArdle's computer to the side and keyed the password into his own Dell, the satchel Annabel had retrieved at his feet. She sat close beside him. He accessed one of his diagnostic data programs and gave her a quick run through its function and capabilities. He explained he would need to connect the two computers to allow the diagnostic to run on the actual data, informing there were many ways this could be done, transfer the program on disk or electronically, or by networking both computers.

She was intrigued, fascinated and again asked many questions. There was however little more Clark could do then to demonstrate. He didn't want to actually transfer his programs in the office, preferring the sanctuary and security of his own home. These were his programs, some of which he had modified himself and he didn't want to compromise access to them. Annabel looked disappointed.

An idea then struck Clark. The disk Spencer had given him. He could run the disk through his Dell and let her see how the diagnostic tools worked. She didn't need to know anything about the content or the detail, all she needed to see was the program's capability. He glanced up at the glass wall just as Jimmy stepped away. He shook his head, no idea how long Jimmy had been standing there. He looked then at Annabel but she was staring at his Dell, too engrossed to have noticed Jimmy.

Clark reached into his satchel for the disk.

He froze.

The disk was gone.

He thought back to when he had last seen it. He recalled it in his hand the day before when with DI James. He recalled putting it in his satchel and he'd had his satchel with him ever since. Except, he remembered, when he was at the Slieve Donard. He'd left it at home.

But there was no sign that anyone had been in the house, and he was sure the satchel was exactly where he had left it. No, he was certain that nothing had happened to the disk at Ethel Street. He thought back to where he had been after he left the coffee house at Saint Paul's. He thought about meeting Wayne Demachi and wondered if that could have been a distraction, if someone had picked his bag as he spoke with Wayne. He thought then of meeting with Ronald Hawk. He remembered placing the satchel on the ground beneath his seat. Could that meeting have been a distraction? He thought about having had the satchel with him all day at Chesterton and Williamson, on the floor under his desk.

Then his heart skipped. He had left it under his desk when out for lunch, and it was out of sight when he was in the meeting room. He cursed himself for having been so careless.

"Is everything all right?" Annabel asked.

"Yes," said Clark slowly, "It's just... I was going to show you something... but I must have... left it at home."

She placed her hand again in his knee. "Don't worry, you can show me another time."

He nodded and managed a smile. He shut down his Dell and pulled McArdle's laptop towards her. "Take another look at this. I need to go and see Fabian, and then I need to get home to get ready for a night out," he said.

She squeezed his knee and then moved her hand back to the table. "Thanks for everything Clark," she said. "And good luck with Fabian."

He looked at her and detected a smirk. He wondered if she knew that he knew about Uncle Fabian. Somehow he suspected she did. He smiled and nodded.

"Going anywhere nice tonight?" she asked as he stood.

"Just to the Cloth Ear with some friends," he said and dropped the Dell into his satchel, putting it over his shoulder and walking towards Fabian's office.

He hadn't long to wait for an audience with Fabian. Charlotte, his secretary had tried to put him off saying Fabian didn't want to be disturbed. But Clark encouraged her to announce he wanted to speak on a personal family matter. Two minutes later and he and Fabian were sitting at his small conference table.

"Well?" said Fabian, unusually genial.

Clark told him about Jimmy not delivering and how impressed he had been with Annabel's enthusiasm and ability. He told him that Jimmy had not given her any opportunity and felt a misogynistic attitude was a factor. Clark added that he had his doubts if Jimmy did indeed have competence or aptitude for the analytical computer work.

Fabian drew a deep breath and shook his head. He told Clark that while he had reviewed much of Jimmy's work and had been impressed with his commitment and attention to detail, it had been Penny who had promoted his desire to expand his skills to include the computer and police work.

Clark told Fabian how Annabel, when given the chance, had almost instantly recognised the financial irregularities. He told him how he had praised her for her work and how she responded to the praise.

Fabian smiled. "That's exactly what she needs," he said, "I knew I was making the right decision entrusting her to you."

Clark told Fabian he didn't want Jimmy to have anything more to do with the computer analysis work. He'd had his chance.

Fabian told Clark to leave it with him.

Clark then told Fabian Annabel should be kept away from Jimmy.

Fabian nodded.

Clark was however concerned he was going to London the next day and would be away from the office on Monday. He told Fabian he didn't want to lose the momentum with Annabel. She had ability, ability that could progress McArdle's computer over the weekend if she had some guidance. But he would not be there to provide it. A thought then came to him. He smiled as he suggested introducing Annabel to DC Campbell, McArdle's colleague.

Fabian thought that an excellent idea.

Clark dug into his pocket for his mobile phone to make the call. There was a message on the small screen, a message that he had missed from earlier. Amy had confirmed his trip to London for the next day, Saturday. The flight was leaving at ten o'clock in the morning and returning on the last flight on Monday evening. He was booked again into The Strand Palace Hotel. He sent Amy a quick reply acknowledging the message and wishing her and their parents well on their return home to Ballydorn.

And then he called McArdle. It was four o'clock in the afternoon and the detective was at his desk, answering after one ring and asking Clark about his last trip to London and if he had met with DI James. But there was only so much Clark could say in front of Fabian. He told McArdle he would meet up with him soon to talk through the detail. He then told him he was going back to London the next day for some follow up and that he and his colleagues in Chesterton and Williamson had made some progress on the laptop. He explained that one colleague, Annabel to be specific, had made huge strides in identifying irregularities and he didn't want to lose momentum. He explained he wasn't yet confident that the police laptop be entrusted to a trainee in his absence and asked if DC Campbell could be available to supervise.

McArdle laughed. "Rest assured Clark, Campbell in on his way. Be careful over in the City. " And then he hung up.

Clark nodded towards Fabian. "It's good," he said.

And then Fabian stood and extended his hand. "Many thanks, Clark. I really appreciate it." He nodded over his shoulder towards the main office and Jimmy, and towards Penny Critchlow's cellular office. "Leave them to me," he said.

Clark nodded and left Fabian's office, satchel over his shoulder. He brushed past Charlotte's desk and marched towards the glass walled meeting room, turning his head slightly to see Deanna form a deft smile and raise her fingers in a subtle wave. He nodded back. Jimmy ignored him. Annabel was staring at the laptop screen, nodding and making notes in her file pad. Clark watched for a moment from the doorway and smiled. She lifted her head after a few moments and her face beamed. Clark stepped into the room and told her he was heading away for a couple of days but he had been so impressed with her progress that he wanted to introduce her personally to one of his police contacts, and that perhaps she could continue with her work over the weekend. She frowned, but only for a second.

"Thank you Clark," she said softly.

"No, thank you Annabel," he said in return.

And then in came DC Campbell, tall and as smart as he could be in his chain store suit and polyester tie. His face sported a five o'clock shadow, but his hair was tidy, spiked and shining from some supermarket gel product. Clark had no idea how old he was but he had often guessed he was probably a few years younger than he. He thought too the detective must have been very close by to have arrived so soon.

Clark nodded and shook his hand. Clark had worked closely with DC Campbell in the past but they had rarely spoken. He was a quiet and methodical, not unlike himself in many ways Clark had often thought. He introduced Campbell to Annabel. She stood and walked towards him, hand extended. Campbell smiled as he received her hand. Clark thought it might be the first time he had seen him smile.

Clark nodded and left them in the meeting room. As he closed the door he looked towards his desk. Deanna repeated the dainty wave. Jimmy had spun in his chair and was staring at Clark, a blank cold expression on his face.

CHAPTER 17

Clark and Siobhan arrived at the Cloth Ear, a thriving bar adjoined to the Merchant Hotel in Belfast's Cathedral Quarter. The Merchant was the place to be seen, a place of opulence and wealth. And a place filled with glamour. Clark liked the Merchant. He liked being at the Merchant with Siobhan. She was made for the Merchant he thought, with her beauty and her stature. Clark held tight to her hand as they squeezed through the crowd by the door, a crowd effectively blocking their entrance while simultaneously polluting the air with their nicotine exhales. He remained patient however. This was the way it was with social prosperity, and it was a prosperity that he relished. He enjoyed his city and its nightlife. Crowds were something that came with the territory.

Jackson and Tracey were already seated at a corner table, holding two extra seats. The table was well away from the bar affording at least some respite from the throng and the noise. Jackson rose and shook Clark's hand. He leaned his tall gangly frame across the table and greeted Siobhan with a peck on the cheek. He introduced her to Tracey. Tracey smiled and turned to look out the window. Clark let it pass and offered to buy a round, the girls agreeing on a bottle of wine and he and Jackson opting for their usual bottled beer.

Clark made his way to the bar and stood amongst the rows of revellers waiting to catch the eye of a bartender. He had the feeling it could be a long wait. He glanced over his shoulder towards their table, but it couldn't be seen from where he stood. He inched towards the bar increasingly feeling he was too old for this waiting and jockeying just to buy a drink, a drink he could readily pull from his own kitchen fridge. His age paranoia was not helped by his being surrounded by clientele he surmised to be half his age. As if he didn't feel conscious enough when out with Siobhan, a decade his junior. To pass the time he began to count the optics behind the bar, drifting into some sense of reverie.

A body closed in behind him but he paid no attention, engrossed as he was in his bottle count. Feeling a hand reach around his waist he turned sharply and found himself looking at Tracey. She smiled as she placed her other hand around his waist and pulled herself tight into him. She buried her head into his shoulder. Clark glanced again towards their table. Still he couldn't see it, the growing mass providing additional camouflage.

"I've missed you Clark," said Tracey, her lips brushing his neck. He made no attempt to loosen her grip from his waist. Nor did he say anything. He moved her round in front of him, or at least as best he could in the crowd. He held both her hands in his and looked at her. She smiled again. Clark smiled. He looked to her striking bright red hair, short and spiked, distinctive and appealing. He looked to her dark eyes, long lashes and expertly applied makeup, perhaps too much for some but stunning nonetheless. He looked to the dark red lips and comely smile. He glanced down the slim athletic body, its contours evident in a tight black vest top and leggings, set off with a deep brown leather belt and half length brown leather boots. She looked well. Clark had always thought she looked well. And she was the same age as him.

He nodded. "Things are good with me and Siobhan," he said, "And you mean the world to Jackson."

Tracey nodded too, slowly and pensively. "I know," she said wrapping both her arms around his waist again and dropping her head onto his chest. Clark ordered their drinks and Tracey helped him carry them back to their table.

"Well Siobhan, I've heard a lot about you," said Tracey brightly and leaning across the table, the two girls clinking glasses. And that was all it took for them to engage in full on conversation, mostly one way from Tracey it had to be said. Clark smiled. He rested his hand on Siobhan's knee, and he winked at Tracey.

Clark and Jackson caught up on their respective work gossip, football banter and general nonsensical beer talk. He laughed plenty. He had missed these times. It was good to have Jackson back. He was building up to telling him about Amy and his parents having stayed in the Slieve Donard Hotel and about Spencer in London when Jackson touched him on the arm and nodded towards the bar. "Don't look now," he said in a hushed voiced, "But there's a girl staring at you."

Clark smiled. Just more banter. He stole a furtive glance, and then did a double take. Annabel waved at him, leaning with her back against the bar, one leg cocked in a pair of bright red satin hot pants and knee high white patent go-go boots. Her shoulders and arms were bare in a white crop bralet save for the golden hair flowing over them. Gone was the Versace and Gucci work attire. Clark shook his head. "No," he said slowly to no one in particular as he stood and walked towards her.

She moved her knee to the side as he approached allowing him to stand closer. She flicked the hair from her face. Clark glanced to his left and his right. All eyes were on him, or more specifically, on her. He didn't dare look over his shoulder towards his friends.

"Hi," she said.

Clark nodded as she slipped her forefinger between two of his shirt buttons. Clark stepped back. "Please Annabel, stop it."

She looked at him for a long moment and slowly dropped her hands. Her face darkened as her eyes wetted. "I'm sorry Clark," she said softly and ran towards the restroom. Clark stared after her before turning and walking back to his corner table. Jackson raised his hand to receive a high five but Clark shook his head. Jackson quickly dropped his hand.

"Care to explain?" said Siobhan with narrow eyes. Clark grimaced and looked at her. He shrugged. And then she laughed. "I'm only joking," she said, "Young students going all dopey eyed over my Clark? I would be disappointed if they weren't." She leaned towards him and planted a firm kiss on his cheek. He blushed and glanced at Tracey who stared, not laughing.

After a moment the two girls resumed their conversation, Jackson taking the opportunity to question Clark about his encounter at the bar. Clark was relieved Siobhan had given him an opening; able to brush the question away saying she was indeed one of the student trainees in the firm. He kept half and eye in the direction of the restroom. Although difficult to see through the crowd some ten minutes later he caught a glimpse of the red satin shorts. She was with a group of people, her back to him with a phone to her ear. She didn't turn around. After a moment she headed towards the door, held open by a man in a suit. The man turned and looked instinctively around the room. Clark stared as DC Campbell followed her outside.

With the girls still talking Clark told Jackson all about London, the meetings with Spencer, the men on the train and the men in Belfast, the confrontation at his parents' house with his neighbours by his side, his sister and parents leaving their home, and his meeting with DI James. He told him about his whistle stop tour around the City and Canary Wharf and of his conversation with Wayne Demachi. He even told him about the club and the subsequent meeting with Ronald Hawk. He told him too about the disk, the disk that was missing.

"I'm heading back over tomorrow morning," said Clark.

Jackson ran fingers through thick hair and stretched long lanky legs in front. He turned and looked at Tracey and then at Siobhan. He rubbed his hands over his face. "Will you be okay?"

Clark nodded. He knew Jackson was concerned. Ever since he had known him Jackson had been there for him. He glanced at Tracey and grimaced as he remembered how he had once almost betrayed Jackson's friendship. Tracey turned and caught his eye. She smiled and continued with her talking to Siobhan.

Jackson sat forward in his chair, taking a long drink from his beer bottle. "We never did get away to celebrate our engagement you know." He glanced at Tracey and then back to Clark. "Why don't we all go, the four of us? You can do what you have to and I'll be there if you need me. The girls can shop." He nodded towards Siobhan and laughed. "It looks like they will have no problem getting along. And we can all get together in the evening?"

Clark stared back. He looked at Siobhan and at Tracey. He nodded. "Yes Jackson," he said, "Good idea."

And so the next half hour was spent making arrangements. Jackson had no problem taking a day's leave from work on Monday, and nor had Siobhan. Tracey was a hairdresser and the salon did not open Mondays. She had already taken a day's holiday the next day as a precaution should she have to recover from her night out, not relishing attempting one hundred pound haircuts and colours with shaky hands and a throbbing head.

Clark phoned Amy, who was back in Ballydorn with their parents contently tucked up their own bed, and asked if she could work some magic with the airline and the hotel. And work some magic she did. She called back after ten minutes with additional flights arranged to correspond with his. But she had cancelled the hotel, instead booking them into two double Superior rooms at the Grange Hotel Saint Paul's, not only a hotel perfectly located for where Clark wanted and needed to be, but a hotel where they could pamper themselves in its Health Club and Ajala spa.

The excitement mounted and everyone quickly finished their drinks and stood to leave. They had to get ready. Their taxis departed after arranging to meet the next morning in the foyer at Belfast City Airport.

Back in Ethel Street Clark folded a range of clothes for all eventualities. He checked his satchel to make sure there was nothing else missing. His notebook was still tucked tight behind his Dell. He made a photocopy on his all-in-one printer of the print out of disk documents and slipped them into his satchel. He hid the other copy under the mattress of his bed. After a quick workout he slipped into bed with muscles pumping.

Saturday morning and they gathered at the entrance to the City Airport bookshop. Clark greeted Siobhan warmly, holding her tight and planting a long lingering kiss. He shook hands with Jackson and nodded at Tracey. She smiled and winked. Clark smiled to himself and shook his head.

"Right, let's get these bags in the hold," said Jackson and led the way towards the check-in and bag drop.

The flight was on time. Clark sat beside Siobhan with Jackson and Tracey behind giggling and fooling like love struck teenagers. Clark rolled his eyes and Siobhan laughed, squeezing his knee. He looked at her and thought ahead to the weekend in a luxury spa hotel in London. He thought of her long dark hair and flawless skin, her curves and exquisite presence, her intuitive mind and understanding persona. But yet it was an image of Tracey that was on his mind.

After collecting their bags from the carousel they made their way to the Gatwick Express to Victoria Station. There had been some debate about which underground line to take but Clark had insisted on a taxi, having had enough of the underground for one week. He marched defiantly towards the taxi rank leaving the rest no option but to follow.

It was after one o'clock when they pulled up outside the hotel. "Yes," said Tracey stamping her feet on the floor of the cab and waving her fists like a child who had just received the best birthday present ever.

Clark smiled and was first out of the taxi, holding the door open for Siobhan. She threw both arms around his neck. "Let's make this special," she said. Clark smiled again and led the way into reception.

Clark and Jackson moved towards the check-in desk leaving the girls standing open mouthed at the luxurious red and brown velvet seats and the glass walls stretching beyond six storeys into a glass ceiling. They were in luck. Their rooms were ready despite their arrival before the preferred check-in time, two rooms on the sixth floor close by but not beside. Clark suspected this suited everyone.

The rooms were indeed superior, a large bed draped in a lavish bed throw and festooned with pillows and cushions. A matching sofa sat in front of a full length window with a striking view of the dome of Saint Paul's, a view that Siobhan stood in awe of. After a moment she moved to the bed and waited for Clark to finish checking out the bathroom. "Later," he said laughing. She feigned disappointment and winked. Clark grabbed his satchel and left the hotel, Siobhan having arranged to meet with Jackson and Tracey to explore the area, to visit Saint Paul's and Blackfriars.

He made his way to Lothbury and the offices of Thompson Braithwaite.

CHAPTER 18

Darlene was sitting at the reception behind her computer, alone, no sign of Hector although Clark suspected he, or someone else would be on duty somewhere. He didn't think one person would be left as a sole gatekeeper.

"Well, hello there," said Darlene with a wide, warm smile when Clark approached her. "That's my day made."

Clark laughed, managing to hide any embarrassment. "Hi Darlene," he said. "Is anyone in on the seventh floor today?"

"Not today pet. You still looking to see where your friend used to work?" she said surprising him with the extent she remembered the detail of his previous visit. He nodded, cringing at how pathetic a reason to access a building it sounded. But she didn't seem to notice, or care. "Just hang in there. I need to wait for my partner to come back from lunch and I can take you up. Can't have you wandering around on your own now, can we?" she said. "And I can't leave this desk unattended."

Clark nodded and began to pace around the vast marble floor, counting the black and white inlays to pass the time. He hadn't long to wait as it turned out. Another woman appeared out of nowhere to sit beside Darlene.

"Glad you're back Marge," he heard Darlene say to the slim middle aged woman with shoulder length yellow hair and roots of a different colour. "I need to take this gentleman up to the seventh floor."

Marge smiled at Clark as Darlene began the process of extracting herself from behind the desk. She was round and heavy, her uniform clinging. Wheezing she wobbled towards him, leaving him guilty at having forced her from the comfort of her seat. "Follow me," she said and led him slowly towards the lift.

At the seventh floor the bell chimed and the door opened onto a grand marble archway and a set of monumental glass panelled doors. Darlene lifted a mammoth set of keys from her waist band, a set of keys Clark had not even noticed. She opened the door and stepped inside holding Clark back as she fiddled with the small numbers on the alarm keypad.

"Come on ahead pet," she eventually called over her shoulder.

It certainly was a grand reception area, an oak horseshoe counter set between two marble Corinthian columns. Black leather sofas set in pairs with a magazine table between were peppered throughout the space. A corridor ran from each side of the reception counter. Darlene led Clark to the back of the counter, behind what he discovered was a partial and ornamental wall, to large glass doors that led onto the roof terrace. Darlene opened the doors and led the way. Clark moved to the side railing and marvelled at the view across the city to the dome of Saint Paul's. He smiled and looked at Darlene who was holding out her arm like a tour guide. She was grinning broadly. "Well," she said, "What do you think?"

"Stunning," said Clark quietly.

"I can't show you around any of the offices, but you can look around the reception area if you want."

Clark nodded. "Thanks," he said but wasn't sure what it would achieve. He looked again towards Saint Paul's before turning towards the office space, spotting a corporate magazine and brochure carousel in the corner of the reception. He walked briskly towards it leaving Darlene to lock the roof terrace doors and fall into one of the sofas. He began working his way through the magazines.

He flicked at brochures and publicity flyers, business plans and annual reports not seeing anything of particular interest, until he came across a montage of photos from the Company's annual conference. One photo in particular caught his attention, a photo of three men. He checked the names included below the picture. He narrowed his eyes as he read the names of Jewell Wooten and Colby Hayward, two names that looked familiar. He sat on the nearest sofa and set the brochure on the small table before opening his satchel and pulling out his notebook.

J Wooten and C Hayward, the two names he had found when analysing the data on the Spencer's disk, the two names that had created the documents influencing the decision to invest. And in the middle of the picture was a dishevelled man with tousled hair and a lopsided tie. It was a man Clark certainly recognised. Ronald Hawk, the caption further informing he was Chief Executive of Hawkson Investment Funds.

Clark looked again at the pictures of Wooten and Hayward, more closely this time. He couldn't be certain but there was something about them, something vaguely familiar. He thought back to the three men in suits who had sat with him on the Gatwick Express train, the three men who had passed him the note. He knew he hadn't been able to recall anything about them when DI James had asked, but something was clicking in his mind. He nodded as he thought he had just identified two of those three men.

He dropped the brochures into his satchel and nodded at Darlene. He had found something. Thanking her for her time and ignoring her small talk in the lift he began to think through what he had seen. He waved at Marge before striding outside and leaning his back against

171

the nearest wall.

So Ronald Hawk was Chief Executive of an investment company. And he was linked with two men who had developed spreadsheet data that had been passed to Spencer, data that may have been manipulated according to DI James. Spencer would not reveal his sources, who had given him the investment advice and the disk. To Clark however it was looking very likely that the source was Ronald Hawk.

He wanted to get to Canada Square at Canary Wharf. He wanted to get to the reception of Yerco, to see if he could find any other piece of the jigsaw.

The sun was lost behind the towering buildings as Clark stepped from the cab. He raised his collar against the cooling air and walked towards the entrance of One Canada Square. Moving through the revolving doors and into the commodious lobby he passed the marble reception desk where he had asked for the building's directory. There were pockets of people milling around the various corners and crannies of the lobby, not many but enough to signify there was indeed weekend activity in the building. He turned and stepped into one of the open lifts and pushed the button for the twenty third floor.

The lift opened onto a small hexagonal shaped lobby with doors leading down corridors in all directions. In front was a brass nameplate with a list of company names accompanied by arrows. The arrow for Yerco pointed straight ahead though a single oak door with frosted glass panels at each side. Clark duly followed into a reception that was little more than an antique effect Edwardian pedestal desk with a pair of matching bookcases behind. The bookcases seemed to be used more as shelving for framed photographs and certificates than for books. Sitting behind the desk was a young woman, looking smart, officious and welcoming. She smiled as Clark approached and sat upright in her chair, whatever chore she was administering to on the computer screen at the corner of the desk no longer of interest.

"Hello," she said, "Welcome to Yerco Limited. How may I help you?"

Clark smiled at the insincerity of the delivery, despite the welcoming appearance. He wondered if she had any substantive role in the organisation other than trotting out the same old line of greeting. He wondered too how many visitors she would be required to greet. He suspected not many given the scale of the reception area.

"Hi. My name is Clark Radcliffe," he said smiling and deciding on the charm offensive. "And what's your name?"

"Sarah," she said and flicked a stray strand on auburn hair away from her face. She took off her narrow framed glasses and smiled. She slowly slipped one of the legs of her glasses into her mouth and bit down gently. Clark deduced she was fighting to hold back a giggle.

"Hi Sarah, hopefully you can help me," he said removing his satchel from his shoulder and starting into the cover story he had quickly developed as the lift ascended. "I'm a student studying the Meat and Poultry industry and specifically the role of multi-national corporations in shaping the global food chain."

Her face took on an ashen shade as a look of panic filled her eyes.

"Have you worked here long?" he said.

She set her glasses on the desk and shook her head, lips pursed tight.

Clark lowered his head. "Do you work here at all?" he asked quietly.

She shook her head.

"So you're just covering for someone?"

"Yeah," she said, "I come in some Saturdays and just sit here in case someone comes in. But no one ever does. My dad works here and comes in on weekends to catch up on some stuff he says he hasn't time to do through the week. He likes me to sit here and watch the door, answer the phone if it rings or greet any visitors. But as I say I don't really get any, at least not until now."

"Ah," said Clark, "and what do you normally do?"

"I'm a student too," she said, "at college doing childcare. Do you want me to call my dad for you?"

"No, no. No need to disturb anyone. All I need is some general information on the company, something I can use in my analysis. Is there anything here that might be of some use to me?"

She looked at him blankly. "What about the Website?"

Good answer Clark thought. "Tried that," he said quickly, "But sometimes companies have brochures, publicity documents that sort of thing that are not always on websites. I just thought I would check."

She shrugged and stood, smiling as she brushed passed him towards a grey four drawer metal filing cabinet in the corner of the room. Clark followed her and tried to keep his eyes high, well above the short tight skirt that just about covered her.

"Have a look in here," she said opening the top drawer, "I'm not sure what you'll find."

"Thanks," he said and began to rummage, Sarah standing beside him with an elbow on top of the cabinet and a hand massaging her hair. Clark wasn't sure if she was watching what he looking for or if she was looking at him. He tried to ignore her.

He pulled two glossy booklets, what seemed to be a history of the company and another that seemed to be tables of figures and forecasts. "Okay if I take these?" he asked.

She shrugged. "I suppose."

He dropped them in his satchel. "There are another couple of companies I'd like to check out while I am here," he said and then rhymed off the first that came to mind, even though he knew it wasn't a food company and therefore not in keeping with his cover story. He didn't think she'd notice. "Santexon is one, on the fifteenth floor I think. Do you know if all companies have folk in on Saturdays?"

"I don't know," she said, "but my dad says it can be as busy in the building some weekends as through the week."

"Thanks," said Clark and put his satchel over his shoulder. "Thanks for all your help. And good luck with the childcare." He walked towards the door, and then turned back towards her as he thought of something. "Tell me this," he said, "Who's your dad?"

"Tyrone Oldfield," she said, "He's the Finance Director."

Clark nodded. "Thanks again," he said and began to turn the handle of the door. He stopped and stared at the glass panels. "Oldfield," he said slowly turning again towards Sarah, "Anything to Lance Oldfield?"

She smiled. "Yes, Lance is my dad's younger brother. Closer in age to me than to him as it turns out. Why, do you know him?"

"Just someone I have come across," he said and nodded. He left the offices of Yerco Limited thinking about its Finance Director and his brother who just happened to be Spencer's protégé.

Exiting the lift on the fifteenth floor Clark arrived in a lobby almost identical to the twenty third. He looked at the brass company nameplate, locating Santexon Corporation to the left though a set of double wooden swing doors. He paused for a moment and pulled from his satchel the brochures he had lifted at Yerco. He flicked at photographs finding a group picture of the senior management team, identifying the Finance Director as the tall broad shouldered and bald headed man to the right of the Chief Executive. Clark shook his head, disappointed. He didn't recognise him, nor did he recognise anyone else from the picture.

"Can I help you Sir?" came a voice from behind.

He turned to face a short man with a full head of grey hair coiffed at the front in some retro style of years gone by. He wore a dark blue woollen coat emblazoned with gold braiding and a brass name badge, the appearance of some form of doorman, porter, or concierge. Or perhaps a security person dressed to look more like a commissionaire.

"Oh, hi," said Clark, "Just looking for Santexon Corporation."

"And you have business there?"

Clark held up the Yerco brochures. "A mature student researching mergers and acquisitions," he said, "Gathering up corporate documents."

The man gave him a quizzical look. He nodded. "Very good Sir, follow me." He led Clark through the double swing doors to a large well lit inner foyer with a wall of windows affording views across the Wharf's forest of buildings. A long straight reception desk of glass and steel lay ahead but with no one behind it. "Wait here." The man disappeared leaving Clark standing alone in the middle of the space. Spotting a photo board display in the corner to the right of the desk he walked towards it and perused many pictures from what was labelled 'The Spring Conference.'

"Hello Sir. How may I help you?" said a low husky voice.

He spun to meet a middle aged woman with a broad smile and wide eyes. She was slightly shorter than him but her confident stance made her appear taller. She was impeccably dressed in a black trouser and jacket suit, the cut and trim of Dior not lost on Clark. She held out her hand. "Marybeth Reid," she said.

Clark nodded and reached to shake her hand. He recognised her from the pictures on the board he had just been looking at, but he had no idea of her position. He imagined however it to be something of authority. "Clark Radcliffe," he said, noticing the short blue coated commissionaire man standing in the corner watching, arms folded.

"I believe you are a student?" she said.

Clark nodded.

"What college are you with?"

Clark grimaced. This was going to be harder than he thought. "Cranfield," he said quickly, the first college that came to mind that he knew had a school of management.

"Yes, a good school. I know many of the lecturing staff there. I have even been invited on occasion to deliver guest lectures. You are a bit far away from Cranfield today Clark?"

"I know," he said, his hands beginning to sweat, "Enjoying a weekend in London with friends and thought I would do a bit of research while I had a moment."

"And why might I ask this company in particular?"

Clark had to think quickly. He pulled his satchel in front of him and lifted the brochures from Yerco, holding them so she could not see the company name. "Going around the building gathering up as much as I can," he said, "You just happen to be next on my list."

"So you have a list?"

Clark grimaced again, digging himself further into a hole. "Not per se," he said, "just a mental note of commodity companies who may be targets for merger or acquisition."

"And why do you feel this company may be a target for merger or acquisition?"

It was time to go.

"Thank you for your time," he said and turned towards the door. He glanced to his left and saw the coiffed commissionaire smirking.

He pressed the ground floor button in the lift and dropped his eyes to the floor, annoyed at not having planned his quest more carefully. But then he began to smile, thinking maybe it wasn't a wasted journey after all as he asked himself why the woman was so inquisitive, and why was the little man with the quiff was watching and smirking.

The doors opened on the ground floor and Clark slowly lifted his head, suddenly finding himself face to face with someone he knew.

"Hello Clark," said Ronald Hawk grinning. He stepped backwards and Clark followed him into the foyer. The doors snapped closed. Ronald slipped his hand into his jacket pocket and pulled out a small plastic case, one that looked distinctly familiar.

"Look what someone sent me Clark," he said turning and walking away towards the revolving doors laughing, waving the disk over his shoulder.

CHAPTER 19

Clark needed to think. He moved towards a sofa in the far corner of the foyer, well away from the reception area and the bank of lifts. He tried to piece it together. He had found a connection between Ronald Hawk, Jewell Wooten and Colby Hayward, authors of documents on the disk that had influenced Spencer's investment decisions, a disk that apparently no one knew Clark had. Yet it was now in the hands of Ronald. Clark thought back to the meeting earlier in the week at Victoria Station and surmised again that there may have been the opportunity for Ronald to lift it from his satchel. But no, while there had been much standing up and sitting down, much pointing and posturing, the satchel was always at his feet. There was no way Ronald could have accessed it, never mind fish around in search of anything specific. And what was it Ronald had just said? '*Look what someone sent me.*' He had said *sent* not *gave*.

Clark lifted his notebook and looked to the chart he had drawn with DI James, the chart with a three tier organisation, with a leader, with lieutenants and with operational teams. He had the name of Brent Hynes as a lieutenant and Wayne Demachi as one of his team alongside two question marks. Clark thought about the names of Jewell Wooten and Colby Hayward. He thought about the message on the train. He recalled it had not been them who had spoken, or who had actually handed over the message. That had been someone else, someone who left the train first and who they had followed. He considered them a team, but to a different lieutenant. He wrote the names of Jewell Wooten and Colby Hayward under a lieutenant question mark and stared at the chart. He had something, although realised it was still not much; possibly two units, one with Brent and Wayne, and one with Jewell and Colby. But there were still a lot of blanks. And what about Lance Oldfield and Ronald Hawk? As for Spencer, he just didn't know.

He thought about Ronald waiting for the lift doors to open. How had Ronald known he was there? Was he followed? It was possible. He then thought about the offices of Yerco and Santexon. He had introduced himself to Sarah and to Marybeth. Were they expecting him? Could Sarah or Marybeth have called Ronald? Possible again he thought. But how could Ronald have arrived at Canary Wharf so soon, especially if it had been Marybeth who called him as Clark had left her only minutes before? Unless, of course, he was already there.

Clark reflected on Wayne Demachi's question of his having some form of connection. He wondered if he still had that advantage. He looked at his watch. The afternoon was disappearing. Siobhan, Jackson and Tracey would be back from wherever it was they were going, expecting him to join them. But there was something else he wanted to do. His friends could wait. He called the number for Detective Inspector Edward James.

"I'm a bit out of the City now," said DI James, "Let's say twenty minutes, same place as before?"

"No problem," said Clark and hung up, the same place as before being Costa Coffee on Ludgate Hill, not far from the Grange Hotel. He was moving in the right direction, at least geographically.

Clark was first to arrive and ordered two Americanos. He couldn't remember what the detective had ordered before but thought a simple shot of espresso with hot water would be a safe bet. The same table was free and Clark took the seat with a view towards the door. Not long after DI James arrived, throwing the door open and shouting greetings at all the staff, referring to most by their first names. Clark stood and held out his hand. Ignoring the hand the big man came round to the side of the table and grabbed Clark in a bear hug. "Good to see you Clark," he said, "How's that woman of yours?"

Clark pulled away, lips tight and cheeks reddening. "Good," he said before falling into his chair.

"Glad to hear it Clark. You know if you look after your woman she will look after you." He held up his ring finger and began to turn his wedding band. "Always there for me you know."

Clark smiled as the barista brought the coffees to the table.

"Right, fill me Clark," said DI James lifting the mug to his lips.

Clark told him what had happened since they had last spoken, about the visits to the offices, and about the disk. He showed him the chart in his notebook, the chart that had additional names.

DI James nodded. "I have some mug shots for you to look at," he said and delved into the inside pocket of his sports coat. "I pulled these from the database at the Metropolitan and City Police joint task force on organised financial crime."

Clark looked at him, certain this was the first he had heard mention of the existence of such a task force. DI James shrugged and fanned the pictures across the table. Clark worked his way through them, slowly and methodically. There were about a dozen in total, some better pictures than others, some clear close up head shots and others blurred distance shots.

"Who are these people Detective?" he asked.

"It's Edward. These are suspected associates of Brent Hynes and Wayne Demachi. People suspected of involvement in exerting financial influence, if you know what I mean."

"People in the organisation?" said Clark quietly.

Edward nodded.

Clark took his time, eventually sliding two pictures out of the fan. "I think these two are Jewell Wooten and Colby Hayward," he said thinking back to the picture at Lothbury.

Edward nodded again and held the two pictures to the side.

Clark continued looking through the fan, stopping abruptly when he arrived at a shot of a well toned physique. He looked at it carefully and then looked at Edward. The policeman was watching him. Clark slid the picture towards him. "Lance Oldfield," he said.

Another nod.

Clark examined the rest of the pictures and shook his head, concluding they were either faces he didn't recognise or were too grainy and blurred. He straightened the photos into a neat stack.

"Take another look," said DI James slowly.

Clark stared at him and then back to the photos. He fanned them out again and began to leaf through them, one hazy picture after the next. There was one he kept going back to. He slid it out of the fan and lifted it towards his face, squinting. He held it far away from his face and stared. He set it back on the table and stared again.

He looked at Edward. "Not a great picture." he said. "It doesn't do her justice."

Edward nodded.

Clark tapped his finger on the photo. "Marybeth Reid?"

Edward smiled. "I was hoping you would pick that one out. She is indeed a person of interest. A person of some power it would seem in a world of male dominance. Not one to mess with by all accounts."

Clark laughed nervously. "And I just walked straight into her office." He thought for a moment. "There was a man," he said, "A short man with an Elvis hair thing going on, dressed as a commissionaire, or a porter or something. He brought her to me and then stood leering. Could he be involved?"

Edward nodded. "Possibly some form of guard. They don't all have to be financial activists, although that would be the norm. Think of Wayne Demachi, a thug on one level but still financially competent. In this case maybe she feels she needs some form of watcher. Particularly, as I have said, as she is operating in a man's world." Edward pointed at the fan of pictures. "Take one more look Clark."

With a heavy sigh Clark gathered the photos into a stack and looked at each one again in turn. He eventually set a couple to the side, misty shots of sort stocky men. He couldn't be certain but one of the shots looked to be of a man with grey hair, a man standing with his back to a concrete wall. He looked closer. Maybe there was just a hint of an outline of some raised platform of curls. "I'm not sure," he said, but this could be him.

"Good work," said Edward. "Dressed as a Las Vegas commissionaire you say?"

Clark nodded.

"Right, shouldn't be hard to spot. I'll put someone on him at Canada Square." Edward sorted the pictures onto two piles and slipped them back into his pocket. "I think we have another couple of folk to add to your chart," he said, "the woman as another lieutenant and Elvis as one of her team?"

Clark nodded and added the names of Marybeth and Elvis. The chart was starting to fill. He had three teams with names for two of the lieutenants. He had one named operational team member in each unit with a named lieutenant, and the names for two team members in the other. He thought for a moment, recalling he had earlier identified the picture of Spencer's protégé Lance Oldfield from the mug shots. But Lance was not on the chart. He dabbed his finger on the page. "Let's put Lance Oldfield in here," he said pointing at Marybeth's cell, thinking that as he had identified a link to Lance at One Canada Square then he would associate him with the other two people he had come across there. It was no more scientific than that.

Edward nodded.

"And what about Ronald Hawk?" asked Clark.

Edward looked at him and then at the chart. He allowed his finger to hover over the page and let it fall slowly to the top of the page. "What about here?" he said, "Fancy him as the leader?"

Clark stared at Edward as he thought through all his interactions with Ronald, the way he spoke with people, the response and authority he seemed to garner despite his demeanour. Maybe he didn't need presentation, maybe his authority was established. Or maybe the garb was a distraction. "Yes," said Clark, "I can't disagree."

He jotted the name, but added another smaller question mark. He sat back and stared at the chart, his mind processing all before him. Something was forming, something he was about to add to his notebook when he felt a vibration in his pocket. He shrugged towards Edward and dug out his phone, his sister's name on the screen.

"Clark," she said, her voice high and breathless, "There's something wrong. It's Spencer."

CHAPTER 20

"Slow down Amy. What is it?" he said as calmly as he could.

"He's not answering his phone. I've been trying him all day. It's not like him. I think something might have happened Clark."

"Take a deep breath Amy. Maybe his phone is dead. Have you tried him at home, at the office?"

"Yes Clark," she snapped, "Of course I have. I called his office and spoke with Leona, his secretary. She said he was due to call in today but he didn't appear. I have been calling his mobile all day. It rings but there is no answer. I called the house and again no answer."

"Leona, his secretary?" said Clark raising his eyebrows to Edward, "First I have heard mention of a secretary?"

Amy sighed. "Not really his," she said, "More of an assistant to a number of the analysts at Rubenstein Roberts. It's no big deal Clark, just a woman who answers the phone and takes messages."

"Okay," said Clark. "What do you want me to do?"

"Is everything okay there with you? Have you found anything?"

"It's still work in progress, Amy. What do you want me to do about Spencer?" he asked again.

She paused for a moment, took a deep breath. "I'm worried," she said, "What with everything going on. I just... I just hope nothing has happened to him." She began to sob.

Clark shrugged again towards Edward. "Amy, are you all right?"

"Clark, could you call over to the house and check for me?"

He rolled his eyes. "Amy I have no idea where your house is. I have never been, remember."

"I know. Sorry."

"What about your friend, the neighbour?"

"You mean Natasha? She's away to the Bahamas to be with her husband. He's working there for a while."

Clark sighed. "Okay, give me the address."

Amy promised to send a text and rang off. Clark stood and offered his hand to Edward. "Need to go," he said, "Sister is worried about Spencer."

Edward took his hand but held on. "We might be onto something here Clark. Be careful."

Clark had never been to Greenwich. In fact he knew little about it other than the Meridian Line ran through it, the line regarded as separating east from west just as the Equator separated north from south. He knew too it was the line that determined the earth's system of time zones. Amy had told him he could get to Greenwich on the Dockland's Light Railway or he could take a regular train from Charing Cross, Waterloo or London Bridge. He chose a taxi.

The journey didn't take as long as he thought, the taxi passing though Blackwall Tunnel and arriving at Greenwich's Hyde Vale after twenty minutes. Clark was surprised when the cab stopped outside the house. He checked the number on the door with the number on the text message. He wasn't sure what he was expecting but thought with all her career success, and with Spencer as a city analyst, that the house would have some form of grand entrance gates and a tree lined avenue leading towards a double fronted gentleman's residence. The house he sat outside was a large terraced Edwardian town house with a small yard and steps to a bright red door. The only parking available was on street.

"Cost some money, these houses," said the taxi driver, "No change out of a million, maybe more." He pointed at Amy's house. And with that Clark got his answer. It clearly was a grand house, just not in the style he was expecting.

The front door of the house opened just as Clark was stepping from the taxi. He dropped back into the seat. A woman came out and stood on the top step, a tall and slim middle aged woman in a dark trouser suit and hair tied back in a tight ponytail, an unusual style for a woman her age Clark thought. She looked left and right and turned back towards the door. Spencer stood in the doorway in his suit trousers and dress shirt unbuttoned to his chest, his face red and beaming. The woman leaned towards him and met his lips. He put both arms around her and pulled her close. They kissed again. Eventually she backed down the steps waving at Spencer as she did so. Spencer waved in return, mouthing kisses. At the roadside the woman moved towards a small black sports car and opened the door from where she waved one last time before speeding off. Spencer waved her out of sight and then reversed back into the hallway.

That was when he saw Clark.

"The Grange Hotel at Saint Paul's," Clark said quickly to the taxi driver. He had seen all he needed to see. Amy had been concerned about Spencer. She had asked Clark to check on him in case he was in some kind of trouble. Some trouble, thought Clark. He thought not only about what he had just seen but reminded himself about the club. He thought yet again about what sort of man Spencer appeared to be, and how he was treating Amy. He could not shield her any longer. She had to know. She had to know he was not worth spending time with. She had to know he was not worthy of her fortune.

But there were still questions he had to find answers to.

It was nearing six o'clock when the taxi turned the corner towards the hotel. Clark smiled at a couple embracing by the doors, a smile that quickly disappeared as he realised it was not just any young couple. He stared at Siobhan and the man from Victoria Station.

"Keep going," he barked at the taxi driver, who sighed and did as asked. Rounding the corner Clark spotted The Centre Page bar. He paid his fare and pushed into the tavern finding an empty stool by the wall. "Bottle of Corona," he said tersely to the young barman and threw a note on the table. "Keep the change," he added.

What's going on, he thought. What's Siobhan doing? He felt his eyes well. He tried to swallow, a pained sharpness shooting through his bone dry throat. He raised hands to his face and hid behind them. He thought again about the night in the club, the night he met Lavinia. He thought about how he could so easily have let himself go. But he didn't. He'd fought it. He'd fought it because he could not shake Siobhan from his mind. He'd fought it because the feelings for Siobhan were so strong. And then he thought of her with the man outside the hotel. He choked back the bottle of beer. He would have to face her. And then out of nowhere, and not for the first time, an image of Tracey came to his mind.

He wanted another drink. He nodded at the barman and repeated the process with the banknote when he remembered he should call Amy. She had asked him to check on Spencer which he had done. He supposed the next course of action would be to tell her what he had found. But what in fact had he seen; a woman kissing Spencer as she left the house? She could have been anyone, a visiting relative, a studious, grateful and over friendly colleague even. He suspected however he was clutching at straws. He knew what he had seen, the dishevelled clothing and the tousled and hurriedly tied back hair, the fawning, the waving and the blowing of kisses. It was what it was. There was no denying it. But did he want to be the bearer of bad news to his sister over the phone while she was caring for their parents? He thought not. He decided to gloss it for now.

He rang her number.

"Well Clark?" she said anxiously.

"It's all right Amy. I saw him. He's fine."

"Oh, thank goodness," she said somehow managing a long exhale at the same time. "What did he say? What's wrong with his phones?"

Clark closed his eyes and sighed. "I didn't speak to him Amy. I..."

"What do you mean you didn't speak with him? For goodness sake Clark can you do nothing right? A simple instruction, a simple request and you can't even manage that..."

"Amy," he said interrupting but keeping his voice low, slow and calm. He wasn't going to let her rile him, not now, maybe never again. He reminded himself he was in London to help her. "Amy," he repeated, "You asked me to check on him, which is what I did. Are you going to listen to what I have to say?"

There was silence.

"I took a taxi to your house and as it was pulling up I saw Spencer. It looked like he had just come out of the house. He was talking with some people at the top of your steps. There seemed to be laughter and handshakes. It looked important. And Amy, to be honest I didn't want to get involved, what with everything going on. As far as I could see Spencer was fine. He didn't look to be any trouble or difficulty. I can only suppose that whatever he was doing was so important he didn't want to be disturbed with phone calls."

And that was the story Clark told. Not the truth but then again not a full fabrication. The truth was buried in there somewhere. Probably the only falsities were the reference to some people on the door step rather than one person, or more specifically a woman, a tall slim woman, and the reference to handshakes rather than embraces.

"Okay Clark. Sorry. I understand. Thanks for doing what you did. So can you tell me anything about how you are getting on?" she said sounding somewhat more at ease.

"There's a lot happening here Amy. But I can't talk now," he said and rang off. He finished the beer and walked briskly back towards the hotel, Amy and Spencer pushed to the back of his mind as he thought again of Siobhan and the man.

He let himself into his room. Siobhan had showered and was in the midst of drying her hair, wrapped only in a hotel monogrammed bathrobe. He moved behind her, breathing heavily. He wanted to say something, but couldn't. She rolled her head towards him. He placed both hands on her shoulders and began to gently massage.

"How was your day?" she asked.

"Okay," he replied, "And you?"

"Good. I met an old friend for coffee."

He rocked backwards and closed his eyes. "Who was that?" he said slowly.

She turned towards the mirror and began to play with her hair. "Just someone I used to work with," she said.

Clark said nothing. He thought again about asking her outright. But he didn't. "What's happening tonight?" he asked instead.

"We are all meeting in the bar at half seven. We'll either eat in the hotel or head out somewhere nearby," she said.

"Fine by me," he said and stepped into the bathroom to shower, leaving Siobhan to finish with her hair.

"I'll meet you in the bar," he said after dressing quickly in his chinos and blue shirt and pulling on his brown college jacket. He left the room without waiting for an answer.

Jackson and Tracey were already in Silk's Cocktail Bar, sitting on bright crimson seats set around a low dark wood table, their faces glowing in the soft seductive lighting. "Drink?" said Jackson as Clark approached.

Clark nodded and Jackson stepped towards the bar. Clark sat opposite Tracey and stared at his feet.

"Everything okay Clark?" Tracey asked.

He looked at her and forced a smile.

"Where's Siobhan?" she asked softly, leaning towards him.

He tried to retain his smile but struggled. He looked away and blinked hard. He swallowed and ran his hands over his face. Tracey reached and gently touched his knee. "Clark?" He put his hand on top of hers and squeezed. She put her other hand on top of his and began to caress slowly. He looked at her. "It's okay Clark," she said, "Everything will be okay."

She sat back as Jackson arrived with two bottles of beer and a glass of wine. "Well, what did you do to today?" he said.

Clark shrugged and shook his head. A lot had happened and he didn't know where to start, or even if he wanted to. "I'll tell you later," he said.

"We were all at Saint Paul's," said Jackson with a smile.

Clark took a long drink from his bottle and nodded, suspecting Jackson was going to tell him all about it. He glanced at Tracey who was still watching him. She had not spoken since Jackson had returned, which was unlike her.

"A great place," continued Jackson and went into lengthy detail about the history and architecture as if Clark himself had never been. As interested as he was Clark switched off and stared at a spot on the wall somewhere over Jackson's shoulder, occasionally nodding to give an appearance of attention.

That was until Jackson said, "Siobhan took off after a while. I don't know where she went. She said something about meeting someone she used to work with. We haven't seen her since, have we Tracey?" He turned towards Tracey who shook her head but still said nothing.

"Is she back yet?" Jackson asked seemingly only realising Clark had arrived alone in the bar.

Clark nodded. "She'll be down in a minute." He glanced again at Tracey who tilted her head to the side and smiled.

"Oh look, here she comes now," said Jackson glancing over Clark's shoulder towards the lobby at the sound of clicking heels, "And looking as stunning as ever." He stood and stepped around Clark's seat to greet her. Clark didn't move.

Siobhan sat on the seat beside Clark and leaned towards him. He turned and met her lips, cold and uncommitted. He could not however bring his eyes to meet hers. "Is everything okay Clark? Did something happen today?" she asked softly.

"Everything's fine," he said.

"Are you sure? You seem a bit... distant?"

He looked at her and glanced towards Tracey, Jackson oblivious and babbling about his hunger and options for dinner. No one was listening.

Tracey came to the rescue. "Jackson, come with me," she said and stood nodding towards the lobby, "I've left something in the room." She moved around the table brushing past Clark as she did so, letting her hand drop to his shoulder.

"What's going on Clark?" asked Siobhan when they were alone.

He looked at her. Earlier in the hotel room he had wanted to ask her. But he didn't. He couldn't. But it was eating him. His breathing was irregular. His brain was pulsating. He couldn't focus. He had to do something. He had the say something. He opened his mouth to speak but nothing came out. Siobhan held his gaze, her own eyes beginning to well. She nodded a gentle and silent encouragement.

"You went off today," he eventually said.

"Yes, and?"

He drew a deep breath and closed his eyes. "I saw you outside with someone, with a man. You and he were..."

"Clark, what are you talking about?"

He opened his eyes slowly and held up his hand. "And I saw you at the train station the other day, with the same man."

She lowered her head and moved away from him. "Thomas? You saw me with Thomas?"

"I don't know, Siobhan, who it was."

"Clark, listen to me," she said sharply, "I already told you up in the room I met a friend for coffee. For your information Thomas is someone I used to work with. He's engaged, getting married next year, and in case you have forgotten I am with you. What is this, jealousy? I never put you as the controlling type Clark."

Clark's head was spinning. He looked away. He didn't want to control anyone anymore than he wanted to be controlled himself. He had seen Siobhan with another man and he began to fear the worst, began to think there was someone else, that it was not he she wanted. Was that insecurity? Was it jealously? He didn't know. He had never before worried about how or what a girlfriend thought of him. Maybe this was why it was different with Siobhan. "I'm sorry," he said, "I suppose I thought… It's just that you..."

"Clark," she said softly and leaned towards him again, "I studied here remember. I worked over here. For goodness sake I have worked all over the world. You remember Qatar? I know people. I know lots of people. But Clark, it's you I am with. It is you I want to be with. Believe me Clark, I... I..."

She put her hand on his leg and rested her head on his shoulder. He stared at the wall, eventually turning and dropping his head to rest on hers. He blinked heavily to clear his eyes, lifting his arm and wrapping it around her shoulder pulling her tighter into him. "I know," he said, "I know."

She looked up at him and smiled, "You know what they say's the best part of breaking up?"

He laughed.

Five minutes later they were standing hand in hand in the foyer waiting for Jackson and Tracey. They had agreed they would eat wherever Jackson wanted. They were more interested in getting back to their room.

CHAPTER 21

They ate their way through a mountainous Italian meal in a chain restaurant close to the hotel. The bread, olives, pasta, chicken and rigatoni all flowed, as did the wine and conversation. Tracey had earlier found a moment while Siobhan and Jackson were checking on table availability to ask Clark how he was. He had thanked her for her subtlety at the bar. "No problem. Anytime," she had said and raised herself on her toes and kissed him gently, an action from which he did not flinch.

Over coffee the girls began to discuss the latest fashion in handbags and shoes. Clark tried to stay with them but quickly lost interest. As much as he appreciated style and trends there was only so much debate he could endure. Jackson however could endure none of it. He was an own-brand department store kind of guy. He liberated Clark from the conversation. "What happened in the City today?" he asked.

Clark told him everything, about Lothbury, and about One Canada Square. He told him about Marybeth and Ronald. And he told him about the disk. Jackson asked many questions, many pertinent questions and at one stage asked if he could see Clark's notes, see the chart he was building with DI James. He asked Clark what his plans were for the following day, on Sunday, and offered to go along. Clark looked at him, eventually nodding. "There is one place I'd like us to try and get into tomorrow," he said.

Jackson smiled, nodded, and waited.

"City House at Basinghall, the headquarters of Wilson Group," said Clark, "I only got as far as the front door on Thursday."

Jackson nodded again.

"And I wouldn't mind having another go at One Canada Square, to try and find something about Rancode Holdings and Green Crab Commodities."

Jackson ran his hand across his chin. "Remind me again who they are?" he said.

Clark leaned closer and lowered his voice, "Rancode are a munitions company, one of three companies highlighted by Thompson Braithwaite for possible takeover. According to the information on the disk they had recently posted an exceptional sales peak. And Green Crab Commodities are a gold company, part of Wilson Group. They posted sales figures way in excess of any other of Wilson's subsidiaries." Clark looked over his shoulder and then back towards Jackson. "What is of particular interest," he added quietly, "is Green Crab's registered UK correspondence address is not One Canada Square. But they have an office there, a presence of some sort, a presence in the same building as all the other subsidiary companies Spencer received information about."

"The other companies?" asked Jackson.

"Yerco and Santexon, the two companies whose Canary Wharf headquarters I was in today."

Jackson nodded again. "Do you have the data from the disk with you?" he asked.

Clark nodded slowly. "Yes, a hard copy in my satchel."

"Good," said Jackson. "I'd like a look."

It was Clark's turn to smile. While Jackson also worked with computers he had spent his entire career in banking. He understood financial records. "I'm thinking tomorrow morning of doing a bit of online research before heading to Basinghall," said Clark. "I want to try and find out some more about Yerco and Santexon, see if I can dig up any blurb that might be useful. Why don't you come to my room after breakfast and you can look at the disk data while I check online? We can send the girls window shopping in Knightsbridge?"

"Yeah," said Jackson laughing, "Sound like a plan."

They re-joined the conversation with Siobhan and Tracey, Jackson eventually suggesting that he spend the next day with Clark and the girls spend the day shopping.

"Funny you should say that," said Siobhan, "Tracey and I were just saying we should pamper ourselves tomorrow in the hotel spa. Maybe we could organise an early morning spa treatment, a lazy breakfast, a swim, a long walk, a champagne lunch, a bit of afternoon shopping?"

Tracey smiled and nodded.

With the wine bottles drained and the coffee cold Jackson said, "A nightcap back at Silk's?" Clark set has hand on Siobhan's knee and shrugged when she turned. She nodded. A nightcap it was then, so much for an early night.

Clark and Jackson stood at the bar waiting on four mojitos. They'd had a brief conversation whether the barman preferred to be called a mixologist, a term that seemed to be gaining acceptance. The barman's brusque retort was either a sign that he disagreed or that he had been asked the question so many times he didn't care to answer.

"Everything good with you and Siobhan?" asked Jackson and nodded in her direction. Clark smiled as he followed Jacksons's gaze to her long dark hair turning in curls away from her face, a face naturally radiant enhanced by only the lightest of makeup. She crossed her legs and the Marc Jacobs perforated lace dress rose to her knees. She rolled her hanging foot in circles, a foot displaying a Pied à

Terre Roman Sandal. She turned towards him and smiled through thick ruby red glossed lips. She waved. He nodded in reply.

"Yeah, everything's good," said Clark.

"You still on for best man?" asked Jackson.

Clark looked at him, colour draining from his face. He had forgotten. Jackson had asked him to be best man at his wedding to Tracey, a wedding that was somewhere on the horizon with definite plans yet to be made despite their engagement. He glanced towards Tracey, tall slim Tracey with her short red hair and tight figure-hugging leggings and vest. He looked from Tracey to Siobhan and then back to Tracey. "No problem," he said, "But sure you're in no hurry."

They sat together and sipped their drinks over multifaceted and instantly forgettable conversation, Clark and Siobhan the first to finish and make a move. Jackson stood and shook Clark's hand. "See you in the morning," he said. Tracey rose and leaned towards him. She wrapped both arms around his shoulders and held him tight. "Good luck," she whispered and winked as he stepped back.

"We've an early start in the morning," said Siobhan when they arrived in their room. "We could only get spa appointment first thing."

Clark laughed. "No problem. Just don't wake me when you leave."

She too laughed and fell into his arms, the momentum pushing them backwards onto the bed. "Remember I said before I had something to tell you?" she said.

"Not now," he said softly and pulled her into him.

He awoke as bright sunlight beamed across his face. He had no idea what time it was, but he was alone. Siobhan must have gone to her early morning spa. He stretched and smiled as he recalled the tenderness and passion of the night, the recent doubt and pain forgotten. He turned and looked at her side of the bed, the empty side. He reached across. He thought of his living alone, of his reluctance to share his house with anyone. He smiled. That was before Siobhan.

A key card click in the door startled him. He quickly turned towards the window and feigned sleep, silently chastising himself for not hanging the Do Not Disturb sign to the door, the maids no doubt in the midst of their rounds. The door opened slowly and he heard a low whisper, barely audible, "Clark?"

He didn't answer. He heard the door close and he smiled to himself, continuing his sleeping pretence, lying statue still in the foetal position, the bedding pulled tight around him and eyes held shut. He heard the rustle of clothing as it slipped over skin and fell to the floor. He smiled again as a weight fell in behind him. He felt the warmth as legs spooned behind his. His breathing deepened as a hand dropped over his arm and began gently caressing his chest. Teeth began to pull gently on his earlobe. He turned.

Tracey put her fingers to his lips. She lifted her finger and dropped her head to meet his lips. The kiss was brief but tasted good. He pulled her towards him and kissed her deeply. She moved closer, kicking the bedding away as the sun continued to rise, illuminating them as one.

"Tracey, what was that?" he said quietly as he fought to regain his breathing.

"Something we wanted," she said slowly.

He looked towards the door.

"Don't worry," she said, "She won't be back for a while. She's having another spa treatment. She asked me to come up and tell you."

Clark nodded, noting that Tracey could not bring herself to mention Siobhan's name. She was right. It was something he'd wanted, something he had wanted for some time, something he had been fighting against, at least up until that point. He thought about last night with Siobhan, about what he had been thinking earlier about their compatibility, their passion, even about sharing his house. And then he thought about Tracey, about how natural and fulfilling their brief encounter had just been. And yet he felt little guilt, unlike before at the club.

"Perhaps I could go?" Tracey said breathlessly.

Clark nodded. He watched her as she dressed. And she watched him as he watched her, both smiling.

"I'll leave her key back to her," said Tracey as she left.

Clark showered and made his way to the hotel's Novello Restaurant for breakfast. Jackson was already there, alone. "Morning Clark," he said warmly, "We'll need some fuel in our stomachs before we get going."

Clark nodded.

"Tracey said for us to go ahead with breakfast. The girls will eat later."

Clark nodded again and sat opposite Jackson, relieved he do not have to face Siobhan, or Tracey. They filled their plates at the continental buffet and set to work with their cutlery. There was little conversation as they ate, and for that Clark was grateful. At least until Jackson said, "Here they come now."

Clark turned to see Siobhan and Tracey stride towards them, both showered and dressed for their day on the town. They were both smiling broadly. Clark grimaced as he stood but was saved as Jackson intercepted Tracey. Siobhan came towards him and stretched to kiss him. He held her tight and glanced towards Tracey. But she had her back to him.

"Thank you Clark," said Siobhan, "Thank you for everything. Thank you for last night and thank you for this morning. The spa was luscious. I feel so invigorated." She kissed him again. He nodded and said nothing.

"I think Tracey and I will skip breakfast, save ourselves for our champagne lunch." She reached into her bag and sighed. "Oh no," she said, "I must have left my purse in the room." She turned and headed towards the lift. Jackson called after her. "Siobhan, wait up, I've to get something from my room too." And the two of them disappeared, leaving Clark and Tracey together.

He looked at her, and she looked at him. She smiled and shrugged. He could do nothing else but the same. He stepped towards her keeping his hands in his pockets. "Why?" was all he could say.

Still smiling and shrugging she said, "I don't know. But it sure felt good."

Clark nodded. "I can't deny that," he said. "But... Siobhan... Jackson?"

"Clark," she said, "As strange as this may seem, I love Jackson. I want to spend the rest of my life with him."

Clark looked at her. "What are you saying?"

She held up her hand. "Please Clark, let me finish."

He drew a deep breath and nodded.

"As I was saying I love being with Jackson. I love the conversations we have. I love cooking for him. I love our days away and our nights out."

"But?" said Clark.

She shook her head. "There is no but, Clark. I love Jackson. I love everything about him, and... I also have feelings for you. I like being around you Clark. I like the way you look, the way you dress, the way you smell. I like your confidence. I see you with Siobhan and I feel my heart sink. Then I look at Jackson and it rises again. Why is that Clark?"

He shook his head.

"Who makes the rules Clark? Who said we can only have feelings for one person? Who said spending ninety percent of your life with one person and ten percent with another is betrayal?"

Clark looked at her.

"Do you love Siobhan?" she asked.

Eventually he nodded. "Yes," he said slowly, "I think I do."

Tracey leaned towards him and said softly, "So what do you think happened between us?"

He shook his head. He couldn't answer.

"Maybe you think like I do? Maybe you love one but have feelings for another, feelings that you cannot resist, feelings that you wish you did not have to deny or suppress?"

"Are you saying we keep going? Have some sort of affair?" he said slowly.

"No Clark. That sounds too mechanical. That's not what I want. I love Jackson. And you have said you love Siobhan. Let's follow the paths we have chosen. You and I are friends, and hopefully always will be. We know how we feel about each other. Let's just live our lives as we want. Whatever happens happens."

He nodded as they embraced, holding on to each other for a long moment. And then she broke away and disappeared into the foyer to wait for Siobhan.

CHAPTER 22

Clark sat in his room at the small dressing table, laptop balanced beside the hairdryer and bottles of cosmetics. Jackson lay on the bed flicking between the printout from Spencer's disk, the brochures from Thompson Braithwaite and Yerco and Clark's notebook.

Clark started with an online search for Thompson Braithwaite hoping to find some link to the other companies or images that he could check for a familiar face. He had already carried out a basic online search back in Belfast but this was more focused. He was however having little success, finding nothing other than a standard website with basic corporate information that appeared to be a rehash of the information in the brochures. It appeared to Clark as if the company was obliged to have a web presence but did not see the merits in maintaining it. An image search brought up only the same pictures from the brochures. He checked them all. He lifted the Annual Report brochure off the bed and flicked until he found the pictures of the conference. He checked all the pictures in the brochure with the ones on the screen.

They were all there, except for one.

The picture of Jewell Wooten and Colby Hayward was missing, the picture with Ronald Hawk in its midst.

He tried the website for Yerco but again found very little. He was less surprised however as he had already drawn a conclusion that Yerco was trying to keep its overheads to a minimum, hence the small simple office in One Canada Square and Sarah the student, Sarah the Finance Director's daughter, manning the reception.

He was more hopeful however about Santexon, the oil exploration and mining company. Their larger plusher office gave the impression of a company who wanted to impress, who wanted to receive potential clients and promote the business. They were a company who felt it necessary to employ the services of a commissionaire, a doorman, a security man or whatever it was the quiff did. They were a company therefore that should embrace the web in reaching out, in maximising its potential.

And he was right, up to a point.

The Santexon website had page after page, link after link of facts and figures, gross figures and net figures, locations and destinations. But there was no organisation chart or names of senior or key staff. He looked for reference to The Spring Conference, the display montage he had seen in foyer. He found no reference on the web, no photos, nothing. There were however picture galleries galore of sand and of machinery, of spectacular sunrises and sunsets. But there were no pictures of corporate or management personnel. He thought that odd.

The only Santexon name he had was Marybeth Reid. He fed it into the search engine and waited. A string of hits appeared before him and he began to read his way down them, stopping on the second page. There was the name of Marybeth Reid highlighted under the heading and website link to Cranfield University. She had said she guest lectured there, after he had made up on the spot that he had been a student. He clicked on the link and worked his way around the university's homepage, checking for profiles of professors and lecturers. He found lists of staff accompanied by short career paragraphs and small pen pictures, but none for guest lecturers. He clicked on the link to the Business School and moved around its numerous dropdown menus, eventually pausing when he reached an Events page. There he found a series of group photographs. One was titled *Investment Strategies – The future in Oil* and there in the centre of a hoard of posing students was Marybeth Reid, upright, confident and assured in a thin striped business suit and jacket.

He enlarged the photo just to make sure. It was undoubtedly her. He checked the wording below and received confirmation, although it read that she was from Aztec Enterprises and not Santexon Corporation. He then noticed the date. It wasn't a recent picture, the event having taken place some years earlier, any regular refreshing of the Business School's Website clearly not yet having reached its events page. He looked along the rows of smiling faces, the gaunt faces of the students. Some looked bored, others looked tired and hungry. He smiled as he recalled his own days in university back in Belfast, the numerous lectures and events he had attended, but most of all he recalled the end of the lectures and events, when it was time for refreshment at the student's union. He turned and glanced at Jackson as he recalled the many beers they had both put away together back in their student days.

Clark looked back at the photo. He looked again at the rows of students, working his way from the top to the bottom.

And then he stopped.

Standing directly behind Marybeth was a face he recognised, younger but unmistakable. He drew a deep breath as he then realised how the disk had found its way from his satchel to Ronald Hawk.

He told Jackson who spun his feet to the floor and sat up on the bed. He nodded. "Well spotted," he said adding, "And I've found very little, other than confirming what you have already found, that the figures on the disk printout do seem a bit convenient."

"Exactly," said Clark, "And if we can see that why did Spencer the city analyst fall for them?"

Jackson shrugged. "Maybe he really did carry out deep background validation checks and was satisfied?"

Clark nodded.

Jackson looked at the pile of documents and then back towards Clark. "You noted in your book that the scanned documents seemed to be taken from a brochure of some sort. I haven't seen those tables in any of the brochures we have."

Clark nodded.

"And why exactly did Spencer's Thompson Braithwaite and Wilson investments fail?" said Jackson.

Clark shrugged and shook his head.

"Maybe it was never anything to do with the other companies, the subsidiaries?" said Jackson.

Clark looked at him, nodding slowly. Yes," he said, "maybe Thompson's and Wilson's were going to fail anyway."

Jackson smiled. "And someone encouraged Spencer to invest in them to resurrect confidence in the market?"

It was Clark's turn to smile. Jackson lifted the disk printout from the bed. "Maybe we need to look at their stock performance."

Clark nodded. "So if it was about the parent companies then the subsidiaries were merely pawns?

Jackson shrugged.

"Right, let's go," said Clark, "Let's check out the other subsidiaries before hitting Wilson's headquarters." He dropped his laptop, the brochures, the printout and his notebook into the satchel and marched from the room, Jackson close behind.

A taxi was waiting at Godliman Street as they left the hotel. Twenty minutes later they were at Canada Square, Jackson staring upwards in awe at the building before him. Clark led the way into the foyer and made straight for the lift having memorised the floor numbers. He knew Rancode Holdings, the munitions firm, was on the thirty third floor and that Green Crab Commodities, the gold company, was on the thirty ninth floor. He hoped he could gain some sort of access even though it was a Sunday. There certainly was a hive of activity around the ground floor foyer he had noted, the day of rest apparently not respected to the same extent in London as in Ireland.

He opted to try Rancode Holdings first, the lift door opening on the thirty third floor onto a grand foyer of reproduced Corinthian columns and with a momentous central ceiling chandelier hanging over a circular marble counter. It was certainly different to the other foyers Clark had seen in the building. There were corridors leading to the left and to the right, corridors that were barricaded by thick wooden double doors. Luminous keypads sent an ominous glow towards the foyer, a glow that announced no-go. The foyer was deserted. Clark walked slowly towards the central counter and leaned over to check for any signs of activity. Jackson stood silently by his side, hands in pockets.

"Doesn't look very promising," said Jackson.

Clark nodded but said nothing. He spotted a button on the counter, a button that asked to be pressed if attention was sought. Clark pressed it not knowing if there would be any response.

"Can I help you?" asked an immediate voice.

Clark looked over his shoulder, Jackson spun around. There was no one there.

"Can I help you?" the voice said again.

Clark turned back towards the counter and leaned across again, identifying what looked like a speaker. "Hello?" he said and turned to Jackson who shrugged.

"Can I help you?" the voice asked for a third time, a male voice Clark finally registered.

"Yes," said Clark thinking quickly, "Just looking for some information."

"On?"

"Just general information on Rancode Holdings. We're students," he said and then cringed thinking the voice likely had a camera feed somewhere and was at that moment looking suspiciously at two middle aged men asking for pamphlets to help them finish a homework. "Mature students" he added quickly.

Silence from the speaker. Clark turned and looked at Jackson whose head hung low as he kicked air with his feet.

"I'll be right with you," the voice said.

The double wooden doors to their left opened with a slow and determined whir, a final thud and hydraulic whoosh signifying the action complete. A man stepped through and came towards them, a man well into his sixties wearing casual corduroys, open necked shirt and a warm smile.

"Gabriel Kennedy," he said extending his hand to Clark, "Operation's Manager. You're in luck, there's not always someone about on a Sunday. We share this floor with another company." He pointed to the other set of double doors on the right. "There's definitely no one in there today. Now, how did you say I could help you?"

Clark took his hand. "Clark Radcliffe," he said, "and this is Jackson Morrow." He nodded towards Jackson who extended his hand but said nothing. "As I said, we are students, studying at Cranfield Business School looking at the development of the mixed economy and specifically the role of private sector suppliers." He was proud of the cover story and hoped the man would buy it. He had stuck with the Cranfield link for consistency.

Gabriel Kennedy nodded, the smile never leaving his face. "And your studies have brought you to Rancode?" he said.

"Yes," said Clark, "Well, it's not that we were sent here. We did our own research and came to London to check out a few companies. We thought a munitions company would have some level of contract with the government, supplying the armed forces, that sort of thing."

Gabriel nodded. "Yes," he said, "Did you try our website for information?"

Clark was glad he had done just that earlier in the morning. "Indeed," he said, "But not much there. I guessed you can't give too much away on the public web given the security implications of what you do?" Clark made that last bit up as he was talking.

Gabriel nodded again. "Very true, we can't be too careful. Now what can I tell you that would be helpful to your studies?"

"I was thinking there might be something you could give me, something to take away, maybe a strategic plan, an annual report, or publicity and promotion material?"

"Sure," the man said, "I think I can do that." He disappeared back down the corridor and returned with what looked like a promotion pack, a glossy folder that appeared filled with leaflets and booklets. "I think you'll find all you need in there."

"Thanks," said Clark and shook his hand again.

"What other companies are you interested in?" the man then asked.

"Yerco," said Clark absently mentioning the first company that came to mind. The man's unremitting smile quickly disappeared. He nodded and walked once again down the corridor, this time stopping to enter a code into the key pad. The doors began their slow mechanical closing routine behind him.

"Let's go," said Clark to Jackson, slipping the folder into his satchel and walking towards the lift.

The thirty ninth floor was different again. The lift opened onto a narrow foyer with three corridors, one ahead and one each to the left and right. Each corridor had door after door lined along its walls, each door with an equal distance between.

"Looks like one size fits all cellular offices," said Clark.

"The Canary Wharf equivalent of drop boxes," said Jackson, the first time he had spoken in a while.

Clark nodded slowly. Green Crab Commodities had a registered UK address at Twenty Five Canada Square and yet had a presence in

One Canada Square. Maybe that was it, he thought, some companies felt a presence in One Canada Square boosted their profile, maybe even allowed them to physically network on occasion. And that was what this floor was, somewhere companies could retain a small office to hold meetings, maybe even outpost someone. He glanced at the direction plaque in front and his eyes were immediately drawn to number twenty one and the name of Green Crab Commodities. An arrow pointed to the right. "This way," he said and led the way down the long narrow corridor.

Number twenty one was locked. It was a plain solid oak door with two small brass plates screwed to its midst, the one at the top showing the number, the second one giving the company name. And that was it. Green Crab Commodities located in One Canada Square behind a door into a room that could be no bigger than a standard hotel room. Clark moved along the corridor trying the next few doors, thinking he could ask when there might be someone in number twenty one. All the doors were locked, handles turning but the key latches holding firm in their couplings. He turned and shrugged at Jackson who had waited outside Green Crab Commodities. He thought he would try one more door. He walked further along the corridor, and then suddenly stopped. He dropped his satchel on the floor and nodded Jackson towards him.

He said nothing as he stared at number twenty six and the name of Hawkson Investment Funds inscribed underneath.

Ronald Hawk was Chief Executive of Hawkson Investment Funds.

CHAPTER 23

"Well?" asked Jackson as they stood outside at the edge of Canada Square awaiting a taxi. Clark said nothing as small nuggets of disparate information continued to swirl around and come together in his head.

Jackson shrugged. "This Ronald Hawk chap seems to be everywhere. He's with Spencer, he's in photographs, and he has an office in the same building as all the subsidiary companies. And then there's the disk." He blew out a long breath.

Clark nodded. "Let' see what we can find at Basinghall," he said as a cab pulled up at the kerbside.

City House in Basinghall Street was quieter than it had been when Clark last visited, the time he looked through the glass doors at hoards of offices workers gathering for lunch, the time he had read the outside plaque that told him Wilson Group's headquarters were on the third and fourth floors.

Clark tried one of two large glass doors, sighing in relief as it opened smoothly into the bright cavernous atrium. He stepped inside and with Jackson following close behind they made for the central reception counter even though they couldn't see anyone sitting behind it. A few feet short they were intercepted by a tall slim man in blue overalls pulling an industrial floor polisher. "How do," said the man, "Not much life about here today."

Clark nodded and smiled. "Hello," he said, "I take it with the front doors open the building is open today?"

The man stopped and glanced briefly at the door. "Yes and no," he said, "Open because a few people are about upstairs but they should have locked the door again."

Clark got a sense that the man didn't want to be bothered with a couple of interlopers. He was there to clean, plain and simple. Security and access were not his responsibility. He thought he would chance his arm. "Anybody in at Wilson's?" he asked.

The man looked at him blankly.

"Third and fourth floors?" said Clark.

The man shrugged.

Clark pulled one of the brochures from his satchel and held it up. "Just need one or two of these. We're doing a bit of research?"

"From Wilson's?" the man said.

Clark nodded.

The man paused and looked around the empty atrium. "Okay, I suppose. C'mon and I'll take you, anything to break the boredom." He dropped the handles of his floor polisher and led the way towards a service staircase behind the counter where they climbed to the third floor, the man wheezing but otherwise silent. Eventually they arrived in a small but ornate reception area, two large leather sofas sitting perpendicular around a low table scattered with trade magazines and advertising flyers. Behind was the reception desk, little more than an antique executive bureau. There was no sign of life, an eerie silence filling the air with the only smell that of potted plants and furniture polish.

"Help yourself," the man said quietly, his voice amplifying through the stillness. He pointed over Clark's shoulder towards an antique library bookcase that matched the desk. Clark nodded and turned towards the bookcase. Jackson had beaten him to it.

"I'd best get back," the man said. "Just come down the stairs when you have finished. I don't think you'll get lost. As far as I know everywhere else is locked."

"Thanks. Will do," said Clark and Jackson in unison.

The bookcase was filled with generic hard backed corporate reference books, company specific reports, and framed photographs. Clark wasn't sure if the bookcase was for display only, the books and reports carefully stacked in order of size. He noticed however there was more than one copy of some of the reports indicating they were most likely for distribution. He lifted Wilson Group's Five Year Strategic Plan, a weighty report that gave historic success stories along with the forward look. This included market analysis and growth forecasts.

"Bingo," said Clark and handed the report to Jackson who nodded and began to flick through its pages. Clark began to look at the framed photographs, mainly portrait shots of well groomed individuals, both male and female. Clark assumed them to be Company Executives. He looked carefully but there was no one he recognised. He moved along the bookcase not wanting to miss any of the photos. At the end was a group picture, maybe two dozen sharp suited men and women standing in a pose on a set of steps somewhere. Many of the faces matched those of the portraits.

But one face did not.

One face in the middle of group was very familiar, the beaming smile and tousled hair standing out. "Let me see that report," he said to Jackson, holding out his hand. He turned to the page with details of the Board and Executive team. And there was the name of Ronald Hawk listed as a Non- Executive Director of Wilson Group.

"So it looks like Ronald Hawk has a connection to both of the parent companies and each of the four subsidiaries" said Jackson looking over Clark's shoulder.

Clark nodded slowly. "On the Board at Wilson Group and he pops up at Thompson Braithwaite's annual conference, sandwiched between two employees who just happen to be the authors of documents on his disk."

"So it looks pretty certain he had a strong hand in developing the disk and passing it to Spencer. Not that we needed much corroboration given he blatantly waved the disk in your face," said Jackson.

Clark nodded again and stared into the distance.

Jackson nodded too. "I wonder how the girls are getting on?" he asked changing the subject.

Clark glared at him, his train of thought disrupted with images of Siobhan, and Tracey. He looked quickly away.

"You okay," said Jackson.

"Sure," said Clark, his back turned, "Come to the sofa and let's check through some of this stuff we have." He lifted the brochures and reports from his satchel and set them on the magazine table, dropping the satchel on the floor and kicking it underneath. He picked a brochure at random and began flicking through its pages, his mind drifting somewhere between the complications he had allowed to develop in his personal life and the complications of the investigation. He tried to steer his thoughts towards the latter.

"I think I'll stretch my legs," said Jackson, "Maybe try and find a vending machine. You want anything?"

Clark shook his head.

"Back in a minute," said Jackson disappearing into the stairwell.

Clark looked at what he had, the brochures from Thompson's, Yerco, and Rancode. He looked at the hefty report he had just lifted at Wilson's. He thought too about the frosty reception at Santexon when he left empty handed and the locked door at Green Crab. He dropped his head into his hands and tried to make some sense of the common denominator in it all, Ronald Hawk. He tried to imagine how Ronald would have done it. He thought he might have an answer, something evolving around loyalty and authority, power and control of a number of people from a wide network. And then he said it aloud, "A leader."

He jumped as a rumble and clatter cut through the stillness. A door behind him opened and he turned as a shadowy figure emerged and stayed in the darkened doorway.

"Hello Clark," a deep raspy accented voice said. Clark stood and walked towards the dimness, squinting as he moved. The figure stepped forward. Another figure emerged from behind and the two stood side by side, two squat figures in dark casual clothes, the only lustre coming from their wide smiles. Clark stopped in recognition, his heart skipping as he looked first from the bulldog that was Wayne Demachi to the coiffed reinforcement that was Elvis the doorman.

The two men continued to smile as they stood shoulder to shoulder with arms folded, no further words spoken. Clark rocked back and forth on his heels as he processed what was going on, what his next move should be. He didn't hear the shuffle behind him until it was too late. All he felt was the sharp pain shooting from the crown of his head down his neck to his shoulders.

He fell to his knees.

CHAPTER 24

It was the smell that stirred him, the dank musty smell of cold, damp clothes. He tried to focus his eyes but could see only dark blurred shadows. He listened but could hear only the drone of a motor. He tried to think what had happened. He remembered the two men at Wilson's reception, he remembered their grins, and he remembered their arms defiantly folded. The pain in his head reminded him of what had come next, the shuffle from behind and then blackness.

He tried to lift his head and quickly gave up as the pain shot across his forehead and down behind his eyes. He winced and drew a sharp breath as he raised a hand to check for cuts, letting out a low whine as he felt a lump at the base of his crown. But there was no bleeding. Nor could he feel anything that could have been dried blood matted in his hair. He was satisfied the skin had not broken and for that at least he was grateful.

He dropped his hands to his sides and felt rumpled blankets, deducing he was laying on a bed somewhere, the fusty smell no doubt emanating from the bedding. He listened again to the drone and tried to place it. It sounded like a boiler, a heating system. But the air was damp and cold. The bedclothes were stale and the air was fetid, but yet a boiler burned? He thought he must be somewhere that had lain unused for some time. Wherever he was someone had just reignited the heating.

He tried to move his head from left to right, but with limited success. A roll of his eyes allowed him to determine an outline of walls close by. He then rolled his eyes forward over his nose to decipher a chink of light, a crack of light high up on the wall in front. It was the faint light from the other side of an ill-fitting door. He was in a room, a small room that appeared to contain little more than a bed.

The pain shot again through his body and he closed his eyes tight, clenching his teeth. His head fell to the side and he drifted back to sleep.

"Good morning Clark," he heard a voice say as he awoke for a second time, a low, gentle and well spoken voice. There was a tunnel of brightness in the room, a brightness that drew his attention towards the door. The door was open wide against its frame with the piercing light thrown from a naked electric light bulb swinging from the ceiling beyond it. He lifted his hands to his eyes and rubbed, surprised at the relative ease at which he managed it. He felt his head. The lump was still there but there was no pain, his body seemingly having transcended some miraculous self healing process.

He looked towards the voice, to the shadow of a tall broad shouldered man standing back from the light.

"Good morning," the man said again, "I trust you are feeling considerably better." He stretched forward and reached out his hand, holding on to Clark's hand. "We haven't met," he said. "My name is Tyrone Oldfield."

Clark closed his eyes tight. He thought for a moment. Tyrone Oldfield, the Finance Director of Yerco Limited. Tyrone Oldfield, the father of Sarah the childcare student. Tyrone Oldfield, the brother of Lance Oldfield, Spencer's protégé.

"I am sorry. This was not meant to happen," Tyrone said. "Check on him, see what he up to, bring him to me, is what I asked. I assumed it all would have been done amicably. Rest assured I will be having words."

Clark sighed and caught a shimmer of light reflecting off the man's hairless head as he stepped back into the shadows.

"You are in no danger. You will be looked after, but alas I cannot let you go. We have, let us say, some loose ends to tidy up. How are you feeling?"

Clark swung his legs into the floor and sat upright on the bed, feeling surprisingly strong. He glanced at the open door and for a moment contemplated running. But he didn't know how he would feel if he stood, and he didn't know who else might be in the place. "Where am I?" he asked.

"An apartment," Tyrone said, "An apartment overlooking the river. Nice views of Tower Bridge too, but unfortunately the windows are boarded. It's a place I've kept for some time and am only now getting round to the renovations. It will be something to behold when it is finished."

Clark nodded as he rolled his head in circles, stretching his neck and shoulder muscles. He looked again at Tyrone trying to see his face, his features, to check for any recognition. But all he could make out was his height, his width and his shiny head.

"You said Good Morning," said Clark slowly. "How long was I sleeping?"

Tyrone looked at his watch. "It's now seven o'clock," he said, "You arrived here yesterday around noon. You have been sleeping more or less ever since."

Clark dropped his head in his hands. Seven o'clock, he thought? Monday morning? What about Siobhan, and Tracey? What about Jackson? "My friends?" he said as he looked towards Tyrone.

He detected a shake of the head and a shrug. "I know of nobody only you," said Tyrone quietly.

Clark sighed and allowed himself to relax; recognising that Tyrone and his colleagues had no interest in anyone other than him. His friends would be okay, even if they were beside themselves with worry.

"I believe you have been showing some interest in my company?" said Tyrone.

Clark shrugged. "And what company would that be?" he asked striving to present a level of confidence. Although he couldn't see it he detected a smile.

"Yerco," the man said evenly. "We are in the meat and poultry business."

Clark nodded. "I am interested in many companies, especially ones with particularly healthy net worth that may interest a conglomerate, let us say in a takeover or merger?"

Tyrone laughed. "I'll send in some breakfast. Make yourself as comfortable as you can." He pointed towards the corner of the room. "There's a small en-suite bathroom over there, a bit dark I'm afraid but functional." He walked towards the doorway and turned back towards Clark, the light behind allowing a clear view of his round bald head and neatly trimmed beard that might have been grown in compensation. His eyes were wide and warm. He smiled and nodded at Clark before pulling the door behind him.

Clark stood, remaining still for a moment. He felt steady enough on his feet and moved slowly in the direction of the bathroom, small, heavy but determined steps. Cold water on his face and through his hair and he was revived, hungry but revived. The pain was certainly gone. He drew long deep breaths as he made his way back to the bed and sat with elbows on his knees staring into the dark space. He had to think. He was certain he had his strength, but what was he going to do? He thought about Tyrone Oldfield and what he had said. He reflected that he had in fact said very little, but he had sounded almost remorseful, regretful, but regretful for what? For Clark's injury? For his kidnap, his imprisonment? Or something else?

There was a rattle as the door opened throwing light again into the room. Clark squinted towards the opening as a figure glided through, a different figure than before.

"Breakfast Clark," said Lance Oldfield, the first time Clark could recall having heard him speak. And it was the first Clark had seen him since the club, since he was sitting in the booth opposite Spencer pawing and groping naked gyrating girls, the disgust from that episode still resonating with Clark.

Lance set a polystyrene container on the bed and a cardboard cup on the floor. "Coffee and a bacon roll," he said sneering. Clark looked at him. The sneer spread further across his face. "How's the head?" he asked and then laughed. Clark couldn't recall having heard him laugh before. He could feel his stomach tighten. "Maybe I should have hit you harder?" Lance said.

Clark's fists balled and he jumped to his feet, knocking over the coffee. Lance stepped back laughing loudly. "Not a good idea Clark," came a loud shout from over Lance's shoulder. Clark glanced towards the door as Wayne Demachi stepped into the room. "Lester," Wayne shouted and the short man with the quiff arrived at his side. "Take it easy Clark," Wayne said, "You're on your own now remember. No muscle now."

Clark relaxed and stepped back. Lance laughed and stepped forward, stopping inches from Clark's face. Clark could hear his breathing, could smell the sour breath over his cologne and hair product. Lance laughed again. "You are a bit of a pain Clark, or should I say were a pain." He leaned further forward, his shoulders back and shirt pulled tight across his chest. His face was an inch away, his smell unbearable.

Clark clenched his teeth and dropped his head fast and hard, not flinching as he connected with the soft nose cartridge. Lance screamed and fell backwards holding his face. Wayne and Lester reacted instantly, running forward and jumping over the wailing Lance, tackling Clark onto the bed. Clark mustered all the strength he could but struggled against their weight. He was quickly overpowered and restrained. He braced himself for what might come next, the kicks, and the blows.

"What's going on here," shouted a voice from the doorway. Wayne and Lester moved hastily back as Tyrone Oldfield came back into the room. They bowed their heads and stood either side of the open door.

"Get up," Tyrone snapped at Lance, his younger brother.

Lance sniffled as he clambered unsteadily to his feet, both hands over his face, thick red blood oozing through his fingers. Tyrone shook his head. "Get out," he said firmly. "And you too," he shouted towards the two stocky men at the doorway.

Tyrone and Clark were alone, the door still open and the light streaming in.

"I must apologise for Lance," said Tyrone. "You probably gave him no more than he deserved."

Clark sat up on the bed with feet on the ground. His polystyrene breakfast had survived and sat undisturbed at the foot of the bed. He ignored it. He closed his eyes tight and ran fingers through his hair. A few deep breaths and he relaxed. He nodded.

Tyrone pulled a chair from the shadows and sat facing Clark. "He always was a bit headstrong," he said seemingly aiming to provide an explanation even though Clark didn't care for one. "I thought I was doing the right thing bringing him in."

Clark was then interested. "Bringing him in?" he said staring at Tyrone, now able to see his face clearly.

Tyrone paused, eventually smiling and showing small but gleaming teeth. He nodded. "You were right when you said you were interested in many companies," he said. "I have been speaking with a few acquaintances. It seems you are a student?"

Clark shrugged.

Tyrone laughed. "Writing an essay or an exposé?"

Clark shrugged again.

"I believe you met with Marybeth Reid at Santexon, a formidable woman indeed, very capable, self assured and dogmatic when it comes to business. She certainly is an asset."

An asset thought Clark, but to who, or what?

"I believe too you have met Gabriel Kennedy at Rancode? He does a sterling job in developing market share for them. And of course you made a few enquiries at my company, at Yerco."

Clark shrugged. He could do little else. He wanted to listen. Tyrone seemed to be outlining some connection between the companies; a connection Clark knew was there from the disk.

"Sarah told me she had a visitor yesterday," continued Tyrone, "She was quite excited. You were her only caller and hence she remembered all about your visit, what you said you were there for and what information you left with. She spoke well of you. In fact she spoke a lot about you. I think you might have made an impression." He laughed. "I think she is one I will have to keep an eye on."

Clark managed a smile.

"Anyway," said Tyrone, "why, I ask, would you be so interested in Yerco, Santexon and Rancode?"

And others thought Clark but said nothing.

"Do you think the companies are connected? Is that your angle?"

Clark shrugged. "I don't know. Are they?"

Tyrone stared at him. It was Clark who broke first.

"Spencer Livingstone," he said.

Tyrone maintained the stare and eventually nodded.

"How does this all link back to him?" asked Clark. "It was my offering to help Spencer that brought me into this. He asked my sister to bail him out financially after he made bad decisions. But then again you know all that."

Tyrone nodded slowly, the permanent smile on his face. "Why do you say that, Clark?"

"The organisation." he said, "Sending your colleagues to Belfast to put some pressure on my sister."

Tyrone tilted his head back and laughed. "The organisation?" he said quietly. "Please tell me more."

Clark paused as he pictured in his mind the chart he had pencilled in his notebook. He thought about the three cells with their lieutenants. He thought about Brent Hynes, the man who had been in Belfast and in his parent's house with Wayne. He thought about Marybeth Reid, the assertive and powerful woman who needed a minder. And he thought about Ronald Hawk.

He thought too about Tyrone Oldfield, the man sitting before him, the man who commanded respect, who had authority. He thought about Wayne and Lester bowing their heads to him. He thought about Lance, his brother, scurrying sheepishly away. And he thought about what Tyrone had said about Lance, about bringing him in. Clark looked at him, the assured yet cheerful demeanour. He didn't need aggression. He had influence without it, in many ways similar traits to Ronald Hawk. But who was the greater influence? Who had the greater authority and power? Who was the leader?

"Your organisation," said Clark, "Your select band of City financiers working together for their own and collective interests, their own betterment and advancement."

Tyrone leaned forward. "Keep talking. This is interesting."

"What's your structure?"

"You tell me."

Clark looked at him. He decided to reveal his hand. Although a hypothesis it was one he felt had some grounding. Now was a chance to test it.

"A pyramid," he said, "A three tier structure, a leader at the top and a number of cells underneath each independently controlled by a lieutenant. I would guess three cells, each with around three operatives. Anymore and control would be lost."

Clark sat back and looked at Tyrone who hadn't moved, the smile fixed. Eventually he nodded slowly. "And who might be in this structure?" he asked softly.

Clark leaned towards him. "One leader and three lieutenants, for which I have four names" he said. "Brent Hynes, Marybeth Reid, Ronald Hawk and Tyrone Oldfield. Hynes and Reid I have as lieutenants. Ronald Hawk I had as the leader. But that was until I met you."

Tyrone nodded. The smile grew and he broke into laughter. "I am flattered," he said and looked over his shoulder. He leaned closer to Clark who too moved further forward. "I like you Clark Radcliffe," said Tyrone, "You have tenacity, resolve, a certain determination, and an undoubted analytical mind. You are good. You have found pieces and you are trying to make something of them. I commend you for that. But I must tell you anything I might be involved in would not be as sophisticated as you suggest. A regimental hierarchy? I don't think so."

Clark nodded. It wasn't an admission but then again it wasn't denial. And why was he being told anything at all?

"So how do you ensure control, and what are your communication channels if you have no system?" he asked somewhat hopefully.

Tyrone sighed and looked again over his shoulder. He lowered his voice to a level that was barely audible. "Everything needs a system," he said, "Without a system there is no boundary, no structure. We all need a system to manage our behaviours, to manage our connectivity. So yes, there are rules. Orders and instructions need to be given, and they need to be followed. But there are no cells, as you put it. And yes, like all structures an ultimate decision maker is necessary, someone who can cut through any indecision and give direction."

He laughed and scratched his head with one hand while he ran his fingertips through his short beard with the other. "And yes, you are right again. Any directive needs to be controlled and managed, but we are not lieutenants."

He continued to laugh.

Clark nodded. He was getting somewhere, having just heard what was as good as an admission that Tyrone was one of the middle tier. And he did not deny any of the others. Did that mean Ronald Hawk was the leader, the director, the decision maker, the controller? He thought he would probe further.

"I have Jewell Wooten, Colby Hayward, Wayne, Lester and Lance as operatives. And I assume Gabriel Kennedy fits in there somewhere?" he said and waited on a reaction.

Tyrone nodded. "Yes," he said "Good guys generally. And I must apologise again for the actions of my brother."

Clark nodded again.

"But not operatives. More like ambitious novices, granted of varying ages and degrees of experience, but novices nonetheless. Keen to impress, to make a name for themselves, to not only survive in this cutthroat world of ours, but to prosper. We make sure they are nurtured. We develop their confidence. We put them in places where they can learn the game and also support the greater good."

"The greater good?" asked Clark.

"Corporate survival," said Tyrone, "Corporate financial survival in this Global market we find ourselves in. Collectivism is the only way to prosper. It's a huge pond out there with no room for little fish. Only the whales can survive. That is what we are about. We make sure the fish can survive as whales, swimming together as a shoal.

"But believe me Clark when I say this, we exist as a group to stay above the law. Where there are legal corporate advantages in our doing what we do we will certainly exploit them. We are not a group to fear. If our businesses survive we are succeeding. If our members' careers develop so be it. If our pockets get fuller as a result, again so be it. It wasn't us who created the free market Clark. We just happen to work within it."

This is it Clark thought, the ultimate admission, the confession. It was all coming together just as he had foreseen. But Tyrone was painting a glossy picture, a picture that his group had to exist to ensure the survival of smaller companies in the global market. Maybe he was right. Maybe there were numerous such networks around the City, maybe even around the world. Maybe they were necessary, essential even.

There were still a number of answers Clark wanted while the man was talking. "If you are so peaceful in your objectives, why the muscle?" he asked deliberately using Wayne's terminology.

Tyrone sighed and shook his head. He looked away towards the wall. "Wayne does a good job at the bank, working with Brent. He may not be the sharpest tool in the box but he did manage an education at the London South Bank University, something he puts to good use. He might even achieve more if he applied himself. He is a good guy to have on board." Tyrone's voice began to quiver. "Lester however is the exception in our group. He has no academic background and contributes nothing to us corporately or financially. But Marybeth likes him. She can trust him and is safe in the knowledge he is always there to look out for her." His voice began to trail off. "So he is part of the team, although with limited benefit to the rest of us." He dropped his head into his hands and stared at the floor.

Clark nodded. It wasn't much of an answer. He didn't acknowledge physical threat, other than to say Lester looked out for Marybeth. But what did that mean? How far would he go to protect her? And he appeared to promote Wayne's corporate contribution rather than his physical one. An air of remorse however was not lost on Clark. He decided to move on. "Three guys came to me on the train last week and gave me a note. Two were Wooten and Colby. Who was the other?"

Tyrone lifted his head and looked at Clark, his eyes hollow and sombre. "I don't know. That was all Brent's doing. But I would guess it was Alvin Summers. Alvin works with Jewell and is never too far away from him."

He paused and looked yet again over his shoulder towards the door before adding, "There are a few others that work with us Clark but I must say you have your finger on the pulse. You have discovered the nucleus. I am impressed."

There was a whole other line of questioning Clark wanted to get to, questions that had been earlier deflected, questions about the companies and their connections, questions about the parent companies and each of the subsidiaries. What were they trying achieve exactly? And what was Spencer's role in it all? Why was there so much initial effort expended in persuading Clark to leave it alone?

But first he wanted to know more about Ronald Hawk.

CHAPTER 25

"How do you know Ronald?" he asked.

Tyrone looked at him, the smile long gone and his eyes downcast. "Ronald is a good man, a successful and influential man," he eventually said, his voice unsteady. "We've been… acquaintances for some time. Ronald was an adviser who guided me through my personal investment options. He was very successful in what he did, always knowing what, when and where to invest."

"Hawkson Investment Funds?" said Clark.

Tyrone nodded. "Yes, that's him. He has a very infectious personality and I warmed to him very quickly."

It was Clark's turn to nod.

"Maybe too quickly," continued Tyrone. "I brought him onboard, introduced him to my colleagues, my network. And in he came, smooching around everyone, befriending them, advising them, worming into their businesses."

Clark nodded again, encouraging the man to continue.

"He gained their affection and eventually their trust. They began to respond to his requests without question. They began to listen to him above everyone else." Tyrone sighed heavily. "And so began the exploitation."

Clark stared at him. "How so?" he asked softly, breaking Tyrone from a trance.

Tyrone nodded slowly. "He began to encourage our people to feed him information, information that he exploited for his own advantage. When challenged he would always find a way to talk himself out of it, always come up with some reason or justification, and always in a way that would leave no one feeling they had done anything wrong. Ronald Hawk is the classic manipulator." Tyrone looked away and rubbed his face, exhaling yet another long, deep sigh.

"You said you brought him onboard?" said Clark.

Tyrone looked at him. "Yes," he said slowly, "I brought him into the group. I introduced him to everyone. And how did he repay me? He overthrew me. He gained the trust, the support, the favour of all and before long it was he they looked to, and not me. We were in danger of collapsing. We could not survive a power struggle. So I stood down. I let him assume the position at the top of the network."

Tyrone looked towards the floor and shook his head. "And he has let the group become what it has. He has taken it to where it is…"

He lifted his head and looked directly at Clark. "Clark," he said, "He has taken the group in a direction I did not envisage. He has taken it in a direction I do not like, in a direction I do not approve."

Clark's mind was turning. He nodded slowly. It was indeed coming together. Ronald Hawk had ousted Tyrone Oldfield as the leader. He thought he understood why Tyrone was opening to him. It was confession, atonement and regret for what had happened.

"What about Spencer Livingstone?" Clark asked.

Tyrone ran fingers across his beard. "That was all Ronald's doing. Spencer Livingstone is an innocent party, guilty only of allowing himself to be won over and influenced. It seems Ronald befriended Spencer and gained his trust before encouraging him to invest in a couple of companies, a couple of companies that he and others in our group have an interest in. But he used our people on the inside. He used them to manufacture exaggerated financial data that he then presented to Spencer. He even provided due diligence cover. In short he used our guys for his own selfish purpose, and our guys got in so deep that they became part of it. They had to protect themselves as well as him."

Clark shook his head slowly, "And what was this selfish purpose?"

Tyrone shrugged and sighed. "To discredit the firm Spencer worked for."

"Rubenstein Roberts?" said Clark.

Tyrone nodded. "It's a firm of some presence and reputation, as indeed has Spencer Livingstone, its chief analyst. Ronald saw them as a dangerous and powerful competitor, an obstacle to his building his own empire. He always spoke of his ambition to develop Hawkson Investments into one of the major players in the City. But his development plans were not materialising as he would have wanted. I suppose you could say the big firms got bigger and the smaller developing firms stagnated. Ronald took that as an insult, and as a challenge. He was determined to do all in his power to succeed, to drive his company further up the chain."

Clark shook his head again. "But why not just poach the successful analysts? Build his Company that way?"

Tyrone smiled. "I suspect he tried. And I suspect the main players turned him down. Again he would have been insulted. Maybe that was another reason why he did what he did with Spencer, to get back at him for turning him down, to discredit Spencer as well as discrediting his firm."

Clark nodded. It was making some sense. "Have you met Spencer Livingstone?" he asked.

Tyrone laughed. "Only the once, and how can I put this? I found him a... difficult character, antagonistic and aggressive. But everybody is different. Maybe that is why he has been so successful."

"Indeed," said Clark dryly, "Antagonistic and aggressive." Both men laughed briefly.

"And how did your brother Lance end up working with him?"

Tyrone paused for a moment. "Ronald again," he said, "Lance was with another company when Ronald came on board and Ronald introduced him to Spencer, persuaded him to take him on, no doubt with Lance instructed to dig for information to suit Ronald's agenda."

Clark nodded. "And when the guys arrived in Belfast to put pressure on me and my sister to leave it alone they were warning us off the investigation, in case we uncovered what they were doing?"

"Exactly," said Tyrone, "Ronald would have covered his bases. He would have checked you out, known of your reputation as a determined and dogmatic investigator, known even about your connections to the police, and maybe even concerned about what other unknown connections you might have had."

Clark nodded as he reflected how he had played into that uncertainty with Vince and Ryan, his neighbours. He reflected that Ronald had tried his befriending routine on him too, hence the club, but it had backfired. He thought about the coincidence that at each of the company offices he had visited he met with someone with a connection to the network. He then realised it was never a coincidence, but an orchestrated plan to intercept and control the information he was given. He thought of Sarah, Tyrone's daughter. He wondered for a moment if she had been briefed. But it was something he quickly dismissed. Sarah was innocent. All she had done was open a filing cabinet for him to take whatever he wanted. Maybe she was supposed to call someone. But he was sure she didn't.

He looked at Tyrone. His shoulders hung low and yet at the same time his eyes had brightened, his lips curled into a gentle smile. Clark nodded slowly, a narrow pursed smile of his own forming. He thought he understood. A great burden had been lifted. Tyrone had reluctantly and silently played along with Ronald to maintain the integrity of the network. And he'd had enough. Maybe he thought bringing his younger brother on board would be some form of legacy, some form of hand over. But that was not how it had turned out.

"There is one thing I still don't get," said Clark slowly, "I understand Brent and Wayne arriving in Belfast to follow us and to warn us off the investigation, but why encourage my sister to bail Spencer out financially? What would be in that for them?"

Tyrone shrugged and shook his head, the calm smile still evident. "Ronald wanted to cover his tracks. He wanted to protect himself from any internal Rubinstein Roberts or Financial Services investigation that would have exposed his manipulation. He heard that Rubinstein Roberts had offered Spencer a shot at redemption, a way to put the whole thing behind them."

"But why did Spencer not come clean? Why did he not make a case that he had been deliberately fed falsified information?"

The quiet smile left him as he looked towards the floor. "Alas Clark," he said softly, "I am sorry to say fear and intimidation might have played a part." His voice cracked. "Lance was close to him at all times. And I don't know what they did or how they managed to control Spencer but do not lose sight of the fact that they might have threatened to involve your sister."

It was the first time Tyrone had acknowledged coercion. And it was mentioned in relation to Amy. Clark winced. So that was why Spencer had been so secretive in handing over the disk. He was trying to protect Amy.

Clark looked at Tyrone. He was trembling, piercing sobs filling the air. Clark reached across and rested his hand on Tyrone's knee. The man looked at him. He slowly released a long breath. He nodded and ran hands across his face. And then he stood and left the room quietly, gently closing and locking the door behind him, leaving Clark in the darkness.

Clark lay on the bed kicking the polystyrene breakfast box onto the floor. He had much to think about. The network had turned out to be organised pretty much as he had considered. Ronald was the leader with Tyrone, Marybeth and Brent as 'lieutenants'. It seemed that Tyrone had been involved in initially creating the network but had stood down. He had once been the leader. That explained his power and influence, evident when Wayne, Lester and to a lesser extent Lance had followed his instruction.

Clark reflected too that not only was Spencer Livingstone innocent but that he had done what he could to protect Amy. But what about the club, what about the woman at the house in Greenwich? How much respect did he really have for Amy? There were loose ends.

He thought about Siobhan and Tracey. He thought about what Tracey had said to him after breakfast at the hotel, that they should follow their chosen paths. He thought about Siobhan and the path with her. But he could not shift Tracey from his mind. He wondered if she was thinking the same. He thought about Jackson, his best and oldest friend. He thought how it was Jackson Tracey looked to have chosen. He thought how happy Jackson was with her. He couldn't destroy Jackson. He couldn't destroy whatever it was Jackson and Tracey had. He would let them grow together. He thought again about Siobhan and wondered what she would be thinking at that moment. She had not seen him in twenty four hours. He thought about the jealousy when he had seen her with another. He wondered why he did not feel the same jealously when Tracey was with Jackson.

He knew then where his future lay, and more specifically who his future lay with. He closed his eyes while his mind filled with images of Siobhan. He smiled broadly and freely.

And then a thunderous crash emanated towards him. Loud shouts followed coming from somewhere close. He heard bangs and thuds and louder shouts. He sat up on the bed and tried to focus as best he could in the dark. He stared towards the door. But he couldn't see anything. He listened. He swung his legs to the floor. There was a deafening hammering from the outside of the door. He held his breath as it crashed open. He squinted, and shook his head laughing when Jackson ran towards him.

CHAPTER 26

Clark stood and Jackson fell into him, holding him tight. "I'm sorry Clark," he whispered into his shoulder, his voice breaking," I shouldn't have left you."

"Not your fault Jackson. How's everybody?" said Clark, his own voice faltering.

Jackson stepped back but continued to hold Clark shoulders. "We haven't slept all night. The girls are beside themselves. I've never seen Siobhan so drawn. She's really concerned. I'll tell you what, that's one girl who's going to be really pleased to see you."

Clark smiled and nodded, "And Tracey?"

Jackson smiled too. "Very worried and upset I must say, but sure she's got me." Jackson laughed and Clark managed to laugh along.

"Are you all right?" Jackson asked.

Clark nodded. "A bit sore and tired, and starving," he said staring at his friend. "How did you find me?"

Jackson smiled again. "The satchel," he said, "You had kicked it under the table, well out of sight. It was still there when I got back to the reception. Your phone was still in it." Jackson paused and laughed again. "We'll really have to get you a new model. Anyway you had a missed call earlier in the morning. You had the ringer turned off. It was from a Detective Inspector James. So I called him back from City House and told him I couldn't find you. He seemed to have some idea what we were up to and was very concerned for you Clark. He arrived at City House in no time and took your notebook. He said enough was enough, that it was time to stop shadowing these guys and time to make a move. He said there was enough in your notes to arrest Ronald Hawk on suspicion, which is what he did.

"And Clark, he broke him. Hawk revealed all. I have no idea what, why or how but he told it all, gave up all the names. And so, here we are."

Clark nodded again.

"Come with me," said Jackson and led Clark towards the light.

They arrived into an open plan kitchen, diner and lounge. The place was a mess, furniture upturned, lamp stands in pieces. And lined up against the wall with arms pulled tight and cuffed behind their backs were five men. Clark looked along the line of sorry figures, at the squat Wayne and Lester, at the bloodied Lance and at the crumpled and dishevelled Brent Hynes, the first time Clark had seen him since his parents' house. He held his eyes for the longest moment on Tyrone Oldfield. The man was distraught, convulsing, snivelling uncontrollably. The room was overrun with dark clothed men and women, all in tactical gear. At the door was a plain clothed couple who appeared to be in charge. Clark walked towards them with his hand extended.

"Clark," exclaimed DI Edward James stepping towards him and holding him in a tight embrace. "How are you son? You look good. Which is more than I can say about him," he said nodding towards Lance and his shattered nose. "I don't suppose you would know anything about that?"

Clark shook his head.

"Good man, enough said. Good notes Clark. Well done. There was enough there for us to lift the Hawk fellow. And he has given us enough to hold on to this lot, and a number of others I should add. We'll have forty eight hours to come up with a charge, but I am confident. Thank you again.

"And it appears that the Spencer fellow was not involved after all. Who'd have thought?"

Clark managed a tight smile and nodded.

"Right, we will need to debrief, but that can wait. Right now get back to the hotel and spend some time with that girl of yours." He winked at Clark. "Lucky man," he whispered. "Distressed she is, didn't stop talking about you all night. And the other girl wasn't much better, tired to consol your girl but ended up just as bad. You have good friends Clark, loyal friends. And in today's world that is something. You are indeed a lucky man." Edward turned and nodded at Jackson. Clark turned and nodded too. He grimaced as he thought of how he repaid the loyalty of these friends, the betrayal surfacing in his mind. He stepped towards Jackson and pulled him into a tight hold. He felt a tear drop on Jackson's shoulder.

"Sergeant Gunning will take you back to the hotel when you are ready," said Edward as he introduced Clark to the stocky woman beside him, fair hair pulled back in a ponytail and sporting a loose fitting black trouser suit. She had hard features that served as a warning. That all changed however when she smiled.

"Terri Gunning," she said extending her hand, "City of London Police. It's really good to meet you, and sterling work by the way."

Clark smiled and nodded.

"Let's go," she said.

Clark stepped towards the door and then stopped. He turned towards the five men lined against the wall. He moved towards the man at the end. "I'll do what I can for you," he whispered in Tyrone's ear.

The man nodded and managed a smile. "Sarah," he mouthed as a

235

huge tear meandered down his cheek.

Clark nodded.

It was nearly lunchtime, Monday lunchtime, when they arrived back at the Grange Hotel. Clark had arranged to meet with Edward and Terri later that afternoon to debrief but at that moment all he wanted was Siobhan. He knocked the hotel room door gently and stood back as it opened slowly at first and was then thrown vigorously against its frame. Siobhan jumped at him, her face a mix of concern, relief and joy. Clark held on to her, his face buried in her hair with tears freely flowing, Siobhan's face glued to his chest as she quivered in her own tears.

Clark lifted his head as Tracey came to the door. She too had tears in her eyes but she stood back. She wiped her face with the back of her hand and waved. Clark looked over his shoulder towards Jackson who was further down the corridor with his back to them. Clark looked back at Tracey and mouthed over Siobhan's shoulder, "Are you all right?"

She nodded and smiled, mouthing slowly in reply, "Yes." She paused for a moment before pointing at Siobhan's back. "Stay with her. She's the one for you. Everything will work out."

Clark inhaled and nodded. "Thank you," he said.

Tracey brushed passed him and gently placed her hand on his arm. Clark smiled and watched as she disappeared down the corridor hand in hand with Jackson. He blinked in an attempt to clear his eyes as Siobhan looked at him, managing to wink awkwardly and kiss her gently on top of her head before guiding her slowly into the room, kicking the door closed behind him. They sat together side by side on the edge of the bed holding hands and staring at each other, both with tear filled eyes.

"I missed you Clark," said Siobhan, "I have been so worried."

Clark smiled.

"I didn't sleep at all last night," she said, "In fact none of us slept. Are you all right? Are you hurt? Where were you? What happened?"

There were a lot of questions, all of which deserved answers. But Clark didn't want to answer them. Eventually he would, just not yet. He looked at Siobhan and pulled her towards him burying his head on her shoulder. "I'm sorry," he said softly.

"It's okay," she said as she too held on to him, "You don't need to apologise."

He thought for a moment about honesty, about openness, about coming clean and starting afresh. He drew back and looked at her, at her tangled hair and tear smeared eyes, at her relief and joy at having him safe beside her. He couldn't do it to her. He couldn't tell her. He closed the door in his mind, the corridor ahead with no diversions, a straight line with only person at the end. And that person was Siobhan. "I love you," he said quietly.

She smiled and sat back. "What was that?" she said.

"You heard," he said and they both laughed.

Eventually Siobhan pulled back, "There's something I have been meaning to tell you," she said.

He closed his eyes. He remembered her having said before that she had wanted to tell him something but he had put her off. He opened his eyes and looked at her. "What is it?" he said slowly.

She looked away. "My sister Vikki's moving out," she said, "Moving back with our folks." She paused and then turned to face Clark. "It's not just that... The landlord has given us one month's notice. He has sold the house and the new buyer wants to live there himself."

Clark watched her as her eyes fell away. He held her hand tightly. "What is it?" he whispered.

She looked at him again. "It's just... I thought...maybe..."

"What is it?" he asked again.

She tilted her head and shrugged. "I was thinking maybe with you in Ethel Street... on your own..."

Clark laughed. "You want to stay with me for while?"

She looked at him. "Well, yes I suppose... but I wasn't thinking about just for a while…"

Clark stopped laughing. Siobhan was suggesting moving in with him, moving into his house, the house he'd never shared with anyone other than overnight guests. But this was different. And this was not just sharing a house. This was living together. Is that what he wanted? He thought back to the night at the club and the anguish he had felt. He thought back to Siobhan arriving at the door of his hotel room, her timing perfect, how she made him feel, how he realised how in tune they were. He remembered having the thought that maybe it was time for him to think about sharing his life more fully with someone, with her specifically.

And now she was asking the question.

He looked again along the corridor in his mind and saw the same answer.

"Yes," he said nodding slowly.

She fell into him, crying.

They all ate lunch trying valiantly to talk about everything except Clark's experience, and for that he was grateful. It was however not over for him. He still has his debrief with the Metropolitan and City Police, and he wanted to see Spencer. He wanted to draw a line under whatever it was Spencer had got himself involved in with Ronald Hawk and Lance Oldfield now that he knew he was an innocent party, uncharacteristically and unprofessionally gullible maybe but not guilty. And he wanted to confront him about the woman on his doorstep.

Clark encouraged Siobhan to go back to Belfast that night on their scheduled flight with Jackson and Tracey. He didn't think he would make it in time and arranged at the hotel reception to hold onto their room for another night. He decided to forfeit his own flight and take a chance on availability the next day. Siobhan didn't want to leave him and Jackson too wanted to stay and help in any way he could. Tracey tried to hide concern and doubt behind a forced smile but Clark insisted, reminding them that they had work the next day. It was different for him, being freelance. In the end they reluctantly agreed and he exchanged embraces before leaving them to pack while he headed to meet Terri Gunning, his lift to the debriefing.

As he waited for the unmarked car he sent a text message to his sister on his repatriated phone telling her there was progress. He told her he was staying another night and had to finalise things with Spencer. He asked her not to contact Spencer until he had spoken with him. He told her he would explain all the next day when he was home. Amy texted a string of question marks but added that she was okay with that.

A car horn sounded and he looked up to see Sergeant Gunning waving enthusiastically with a broad grin across her face.

CHAPTER 27

They met in a small room at the City of London Police Headquarters. It was a comfortable room, not quite what Clark would have expected an interview room to look like. He suspected therefore it was something different, maybe a meeting room of some sort. There were four high backed plastic chairs with arms around a white rectangular table. In the corner was a white board with marker pens of all colours sitting on an attached narrow shelf. Light poured in from a small un-curtained window, no view but at least the light was natural.

A pot of coffee and a tower of paper cups were set on the table beside a recording device. DI Edward James sat beside Clark whilst Sergeant Gunning sat opposite.

And so the debrief commenced. Clark told the whole story right from the start, from Spencer giving him the disk, to meeting Ronald, to his inquisitive visits to each of the parent and subsidiary companies. He talked about the different people he met and how he established a connection between them all. He talked too about his outline structure and how he slotted everyone into it. But most of all he told the story of Tyrone Oldfield. He emphasised the remorse the man had shown, remorse that Clark had read and accepted as genuine.

DI James confirmed that Ronald Hawk had told a similar story. Despite the historic secrecy within and amongst such groups in the City he now had two high ranking members who were willing to talk. He was excited and thanked Clark for all he had done; even suggesting Clark might want to consider extending his freelance contract with the police in Belfast to include the Metropolitan and City of London Police forces. Clark was flattered and said he would consider it. DI James said he would set something up with DI McArdle in Belfast. He clearly wanted more of a commitment than flattered consideration.

DI James confirmed also that no one else from the group has spoken but that enough information was being gathered to press charges. He stated too that he had detected a difference in motivation from the two men who were talking, Ronald he deduced suspected there was a weight of evidence against him that would be impossible to deny. Damage limitation was therefore his motivation. DI James agreed with Clark that Tyrone appeared genuinely concerned about the direction the organisation had gone, a direction he did not agree with. DI James agreed also there was remorse and regret, a search for repentance, and concern about shame he had brought on his family. The family angle was something DI James had connected with. He told Clark he would do all he could to help Tyrone, and for that Clark was grateful.

There did not seem to be the same level of desire to help Ronald Hawk. And for that too Clark was grateful.

DI James agreed to let Clark speak with Spencer first but to let him know the police would want to speak with him at some point about the extent of his relationship with Ronald Hawk, Lance Oldfield and anyone else from the organisation.

It was Monday afternoon. Clark had no idea where Spencer would be. But he wanted his visit to be unexpected, unannounced. He thought he would try the house in Greenwich first. He stood and shook DI James' hand firmly, the policeman holding on for a long time. He said he would be in touch. Clark turned to shake the hand of Sergeant Gunning who raised herself on her toes and hugged him warmly. Clark left the room with a crimson neck and made his way outside to hail a taxi to Greenwich.

After paying the fare he asked the driver to wait while he climbed the steps to the front door. He rang the bell and waited. Footsteps quickly followed and the door opened to a surprised, shocked and ghost-like Spencer casually attired in corduroys, polo shirt and navy boating shoes. Clark smiled and nodded at him before turning and waving the taxi away.

"Hello Spencer," he said.

The small man looked at him curiously. He opened his mouth repeatedly in an attempt to speak, but nothing came out. He licked his lips, narrowing his eyes and trying to look over Clark's shoulder, quickly giving up and opting to look around him instead.

Clark watched him and continued to smile, enjoying the man's lost assertion, enjoying the fact he had been caught off guard.

"I owe you an apology," said Clark eventually.

Spencer looked at him. After a moment he sighed. "You'd better come in," he said and led Clark to small sitting room that looked to be used as a study. An enormous desk dominated the room, an antique effect desk with carved legs and routed drawers. A high backed burgundy leather swivel chair sat in front of the desk, a chair that Spencer sat on and pointed Clark towards a small matching burgundy leather sofa in front of the window.

Clark sat and repeated what he had said on the doorstep. "I owe you an apology. I doubted you. I thought you were up to something. I didn't know what but there was something fishy about you investing as you did and then seeking bail out from my sister. I investigated as you eventually agreed but to be honest I did think you were playing me. I now know different. It is sorted. The police are now in control."

Spencer's mouth fell open. Whatever colour he had in his face left him. He shrugged and held his hands out, still unable to speak. He began to tremble and breathe heavily.

"You wouldn't reveal your contact, your source," said Clark, "But it's okay I found him."

Spencer began to rock back and forth in his chair.

"Ronald Hawk is in police custody. And he is talking."

Spencer threw his hands to his face and shook his head. "What...why...?" he mumbled through fingers.

Clark was perversely enjoying it. "It was a power struggle Spencer," he said eventually. "Believe it or not but he was jealous of you, of your success. He was jealous of the reputation and success of Rubinstein Roberts. He wanted that prestige for his own firm. So he used you Spencer. In discrediting you he sought to discredit the firm. He thought he might capitalise on their failing reputation. So he massaged you for a long time Spencer, eventually sensing when the time was right to feed you falsified documents, encouraging and influencing you to invest. And he didn't do it alone. He was head of an organisation Spencer, a structured and clandestine organisation with insiders throughout the industry. Ronald was not the only one you allowed yourself to get close to. Lance for example?"

Clark watched Spencer. He kept his hands over his face, continuously shaking his head.

"But why you took the unethical decision to invest Rubenstein Roberts' money I have no idea. That is something perhaps you can tell me?"

Spencer gradually dropped his hands and began to tell Clark how Ronald had indeed befriended him over a long period of time. He found it hard to believe that it had all been part of a long term manipulation plan. He told Clark how Ronald had introduced him to Lance Oldfield and had arranged interviews and references to validate his pedigree. Spencer was equally distraught that this too was all part of the manipulation. He shook as he spoke, pausing frequently and rubbing his eyes. He rocked back and forth on his chair. He said he could not justify why he had invested the firm's money. He said it was something Ronald had suggested, and indeed something Lance had encouraged on one occasion during a general discussion about managing investment information. He said he had been sure no one knew Ronald had given him the disk, not even Lance. But that was something he was beginning to doubt. He was sure the information he got was sound and had invested on that information. He knew it was wrong but thought the he could spin the inevitable big win into a justification. It was a bridge he thought he would cross when he had to. But of course that chance never came. The opposite in fact happened. He had to justify a failed investment rather than spin a good one. It had nearly destroyed him. He said he couldn't have got through it and arrived at his current place of possible redemption and opportunity if it had not been for Amy. The man began to cry.

Clark almost felt sorry for him, almost but not quite. "Save me the adulation Spencer," he said, "In my book someone who sticks by someone though thick and thin, like Amy has to you, deserves respect. And while I accept you have been a victim here I do not accept the way you have treated Amy. Cavorting and groping innocent girls is not a way to show respect. And don't forget Spencer, Amy asked me to help you so she could satisfy herself that investing her portfolio in you is the right thing to do. I have yet to advise her one way or the other."

Spencer's face lost its colour, again. "Clark," he said in a soft voice, "I appreciate all you have done, I really do. Your sister was right. You are good. And I too apologise for any doubt I might have had in you. But you must understand this is the City of London. What you witnessed last week in the club is just part of the scene. Bankers, Investors and analysts visit these clubs as a matter of routine. A ritual if you like. Bonus time is a particular party time. And in the City party time means clubbing."

He shook his head. "And please Clark, do not think of the girls as innocent. They too are professionals. They know what to do and how to do it to maximise their own gain. And believe me they are well rewarded. They get what they want out of it."

It was Clark's turn to shake his head. "You can try to justify it all you like. But you shouldn't be exploiting any individual in that way. And I am not sure there are too many of those girls who grew up with that particular career path in mind."

Spencer held up his hands. "We may have to agree to differ on this one Clark. And I can assure you, Amy knows what goes in. She works in the sector herself. She knows how the boys like to let their hair down, so to speak."

Clark shook his head again. He looked at Spencer. "That doesn't excuse what I saw the other day outside this very house."

Spencer instantly tightened and held in a breath, lifting his hands quickly to hide his face. Clark thought he could see a redness shining through his fingers.

"That was not what it looked like," he said, "I was working at home and one of the associates dropped round with some paperwork. I just happened to be dosing on that sofa when she called, hence my unkempt appearance. She just dropped off the paperwork, stayed for five minutes to chat about some work stuff and away she went. It just so happened that you pulled up as she was leaving."

Clark continued to stare at him. "A fine looking woman," he said mischievously.

Spencer nodded. He paused for a moment and then asked, "Have you spoken to Amy?"

Clark shook his head.

Spencer nodded slowly.

Clark held the stare. "I would like to speak to the partners at

Rubenstein Roberts," he said slowly.

Spencer shook his head vigorously. "No, I don't think that will be necessary," he said.

"Perhaps not," said Clark, "But I would feel better. Square the circle. Complete the journey of you like. I would like to explain to them how things have turned out, how you were duped, that you are an outstanding member of their team and that you will never let anything like that happen again. What harm in doing that Spencer?" He raised his eyebrows and waited.

Spencer stood. "No Clark," he said, his voice rising, "I would prefer not."

Clark stood and nodded. "I'll see myself out," he said and walked out the door and down the steps, turning right on the pavement and walking briskly in search of a taxi rank.

CHAPTER 28

He had no idea where the offices of Rubenstein Roberts were, other than somewhere in the financial district of the City. He pinned his hopes on the taxi driver knowing, and he wasn't disappointed.

The taxi pulled up outside a corner building at Gresham Street and Old Jewry, between Lothbury and Saint Paul's. Clark was at least familiar with the general area. He was again in the heart of the City of London. It was late afternoon, hoards of suited and briefcase carrying workers scurrying in all directions in search of their transport home. Clark walked to the front reception and asked hopefully if he could speak with Mr Rubenstein or Mr Roberts. The young woman at reception laughed.

"I'm not sure about Mr Roberts," she said through her smile, "but Miss Rubenstein is certainly still here. I'll give her a call now. Who should I say is asking?"

He grimaced at his misogyny, a lesson learned. "My name is Clark Radcliffe," he said trying to ignore and avoid any embarrassment, "I'm an acquaintance of Spencer Livingstone."

"Oh yes," said the woman smiling, "And how is our Spencer?"

"Good," said Clark and turned away to leave the woman to make her phone call.

"Josephine Rubenstein will see you now. If you take the lift to the fifth floor she will meet you on the lobby," the woman said after a moment, still smiling.

He was met by a tall slim woman with hard features and shoulder length mousy hair in curls. She stood confidently in her Dolce and Gabbana knee length dress and extended her hand.

"Mr Radcliffe," she said, "Josephine Rubenstein. It is a pleasure to meet you."

Clark nodded. "Clark," he said and received her strong hand shake before following her into a small but beautifully furnished office. She sat at a small solid wood meeting table and invited Clark to sit beside her.

"I believe you know Spencer?" she said with a smile.

Clark nodded. "Yes, a friend of the family you could say. My sister has been living with him for the last few years."

Her smile widened. "So you are Amy's brother?"

Clark nodded.

"I've never met her," said Josephine, "but Spencer speaks often of her, and very highly too I should add."

Clark nodded again and smiled proudly. "I just wanted to say that I work from time to time with the police and as part of a current investigation I can confirm that Spencer was influenced unduly and coerced into doing what he did. It's not an excuse I know given his credentials but there were other forces at play."

The woman gave him a strange look. "I'm not following you," she said.

"Spencer's misguided investment of the firm's funds?" said Clark.

She shook her head. "What investment?"

"Investing the firm's funds, his loss of credibility and then your offering him opportunity to rebuild his career if he reimbursed the firm?"

She laughed loudly. "I really have no idea what you are talking about. Spencer is our Chief Adviser. His reputation is solid, and remains intact."

Clark sat in stunned silence.

"And Mr Roberts?" he said slowly.

She laughed again. "I can assure you there is nothing Bernhard Roberts and I do not share. We speak as one."

Clark shook his head and rubbed his face. "I don't understand," he said.

Josephine reached behind her and lifted a framed photograph from her desk. She set it on the table in front of Clark. It was group photo, a professionally taken photograph posed on the steps of some grand castle or stately home.

"This was our last company away day, something we do often to reward the team and to recognise their achievements. We are a tight unit. We work well together. And we know our ethics. We are respected and successful. Why would Spencer do what you suggested? We have even talked about expanding the partnership, to bring him in. Why would he compromise that?"

Clark continued to shake his head as he looked at the photo. He picked out Josephine in the middle of the shot standing beside a stooping older man. "Bernhard Roberts?" he asked as he pointed.

She nodded. "A founding member of the firm," she said, "Just as my father was before me."

Standing beside Bernhard was Spencer, small, squat and bald but oozing confidence. Beside him stood Lance Oldfield, his muscular torso barely contained within his short sleeved shirt. He stood tall and smug. Clark pointed at him.

"Lance Oldfield," Josephine said coldly, "Spencer brought him in. Not something we would normally condone but Spencer gave us the required assurance that due diligence had been carried out. He came with a good reputation and solid references."

Clark looked at her and nodded. If only she knew, he thought. He looked along the lines of other staff, stopping when he saw a tall woman at the edge of the group, a tall woman in a trouser suit and with her hair tied back in a ponytail, a woman he had seen before.

He pointed at her. "Who's that?" he said.

"Oh that's Stephanie," she said, "Stephanie Hawk."

Clark stopped and stared at her. "Excuse me?" he said.

"Stephanie Hawk, one of our associates. She's been here a long time too, works very closely with Spencer, very competent and very capable."

Clark stared at the picture. He said nothing. He sat back in his chair and stared at the ceiling.

"Are you okay?" asked Josephine.

He dropped his head and looked at her. "When was the last time you personally checked your company accounts?" he asked.

She shrugged. "I would formally review them twice yearly, so I suppose it's been a few months. Why?"

"And who does your regular financial monitoring?"

"That would be Simon Murdoch, our Chief Financial Officer." She pointed to a dark haired middle aged man with a tan standing in the picture behind Spencer.

"I need to speak with him," said Clark.

Josephine looked at him. "Just what is going on?"

"Maybe if I can speak with Simon I can tell you."

She shook her head and said slowly, "I'm afraid that won't be possible. Simon is away on business. He has been in Grand Cayman for the last three months."

Clark nodded and a smile spread across his face.

CHAPTER 29

He met Detective Inspector Edward James in the grand atrium of the Grange Hotel and outlined what he had just learned, together with how he then thought events had actually unfolded. Edward listened intently and made many notes in his pocket pad. He nodded enthusiastically but essentially let Clark do the talking. He liked it. There were a number of things he needed to check but there nothing that was beyond his capability or authority. He stood and shook Clark's hand and told him he would be in touch as soon as possible. He told him it could be a long night and to stay by his phone.

Clark waved him off and moved to the hotel's Novello Restaurant where he ordered a hefty steak. He phoned Amy and asked her if she had heard from Spencer.

"Just a quick call earlier," she said, "Asked me when I was coming home."

"Stay where you are and commit to nothing Amy," he said," I'll be home tomorrow and will explain all. It might be best also if you avoided talking to him." He hung up before he was asked to give any explanation.

He finished the steak and went to his room. It was after eight o'clock and he was tired, his head still pulsating with intermittent pain from the blow he had received. He felt for the lump and reminded himself to get it checked out when he got home. He lay on the bed and thought everything through. He allowed himself to smile. It was something that Ronald had said when he first met him that kept resonating.

He drifted off the sleep as he waited for DI James' call.

And at midnight the call came, the call that confirmed Clark's supposition. He drifted back to sleep with mixed emotions, contentment and satisfaction that it had all come together, and concern for how Amy was going to take it.

Tuesday morning came quickly and he showered, packed and checked out of the hotel, hailing a taxi at the door and fighting through the early morning traffic to Victoria Station and the train to Gatwick Airport. He was fortunate in finding availability on the nine o'clock flight back to Belfast, a flight where the time passed quickly as he stared out the window thinking about Amy, about how to tell her.

He took a taxi to Ethel Street to leave off his weekend bag and satchel and to collect his car for the journey to Ballydorn.

It was midday when he arrived, Amy running to the car to meet him. They embraced briefly and she led him along the corridor towards the kitchen, pausing momentarily at the door to the lounge so he could wave at his parents, his father waving and smiling in return, his mother sitting scowling with arms folded.

Amy sat at the kitchen table and Clark sat opposite.

"Well?" she said.

Clark grimaced and began to play with his hands. He looked out the window towards the fields. He looked around the room at the cupboards and the appliances. He looked everywhere except at her.

"Clark?"

He drew a deep breath. He couldn't avoid it forever. He turned to look at her and forced a smile. "Amy," he said, "Spencer has been playing us all."

He told her all about Ronald and the organisation. She sat silently and listened, shaking her head. "He did not invest the money Amy. He knew all along that his source was corrupt. He used you to involve me, even though at the start you were reluctant to open up to me he knew you would eventually. He even playacted himself to make it look like he was reluctantly seeking my help. He fed me what he wanted to tell me and used me to investigate Ronald and the organisation. He knew I would not give up until I found answers. And he knew I had connections with the police. He used me, Amy, to bring down the organisation."

"But why?" she managed to say, "If he didn't invest the money why does he need me to sell my portfolio?"

Clark reached across the table and took her hand. "Because Amy, he needs the money. He didn't invest the money, but he took it. He siphoned funds from the firm and channelled it into an overseas account. He needs your money to put back into the firm."

She shook her head and stared blankly at Clark.

He blinked and said softly, "Amy, he has been entertaining someone else, another woman. He has been planning a life abroad with her, but he could not leave his comfortable lifestyle. He needed a nest egg, a substantial nest egg. So he transferred funds from the firm, planning all along for Ronald to be a scapegoat. The irony was Ronald thought he was discrediting Spencer when it was actually Spencer who was stage managing. He planned for Ronald to take a fall."

"Why?" Amy whispered, Clark barely able to hear her.

"Because Spencer wanted him out of the way."

"Why?"

Clark said slowly, "Because Spencer has been having an affair with his sister." He squeezed her hand. "Spencer knew of Ronald's challenging relationship with his sister and that he would make life difficult for them both. And I can only imagine too that he wanted some compensation for Ronald's duplicity in befriending him. So he used me to get to Ronald, to collapse the organisation and to make sure Ronald was put out of the way."

Tears began to fill her eyes.

"He planned on using you too Amy. He intended to transfer the proceeds of your portfolio to the firm while the Chief Finance Officer was away. He thought the transfer to his overseas account might be overlooked or downplayed if the bottom line remained the same. Spencer had already transferred the money out while the finance guy was away and he knew the partners would not be doing any financial scrutiny in his absence. I imagine Spencer had some sort of a plan to explain the money out and the money in if it was raised."

Clark cupped his other hand over Amy's. "He planned then to resign, as did Ronald's sister, and move overseas to live their comfortable life."

Amy shook her head and sobbed loudly. "I can't believe it. He was using me. And for how long has this been going on? How could I not have suspected? How could I have been such a fool?"

"Amy," Clark said, "You are guilty only of trusting him, of loving him enough to have that trust. You saw only the good in him. You were not to know."

"But... why were the men here? Why did they ask us to leave it alone?"

Clark shook his head. "Ronald knew about me. He suspected you would ask me to investigate and he thought he would try to dissuade me. He didn't want me to find out about the organisation. And of course he thought Spencer was investing the firm's money and that he had him under control. Ronald wanted to maintain that control by keeping Spencer in Rubenstein Roberts. Ultimately Ronald intended to use Spencer to bring down the firm, to create a void for his own company to fill."

Clark laughed. "And all along Spencer knew exactly what he was up to. It was all a double bluff Amy."

She stared blankly at him, sitting upright and rubbing the tears from her eyes. "But Clark, what about Spencer investing his own money the second time to try and make amends, and what about Rubinstein Roberts offering him the opportunity to refund the company and allowing him to rebuild his reputation?"

Clark laughed again. He knew it was anything but funny, but could not help himself. "Who did you ever hear talking about that set of circumstances Amy? Wasn't it only Spencer himself? It was the situation Ronald and Lance wanted and it was the story Spencer perpetuated. Did you or anyone else ever see press reports, or did you just go by whatever you heard? Did you ever mention it to Leona, his secretary? Josephine Rubenstein confirmed she had never met you so you could not have got any corroboration from her. It was all part of the cover story, Amy. Spencer had presumably already siphoned his own money overseas."

Amy shook her head slowly, the tears drying. "Why did he not just con me out of my money directly? Why go through the pretence of moving money from Rubinstein Roberts and then having to replace it?"

Clark shrugged. "All part of the charade I imagine, should someone from the organisation know of, or corner, someone from Rubenstein's; the Finance Officer, for example."

"But Clark," she said, "Why was he not concerned that you as a competent investigator would find out?"

Clark shrugged again. "Arrogance presumably, hoping my focus would remain on Ronald Hawk and I would not be steered towards Josephine Rubenstein or Bernhard Roberts."

Amy stared into the distance. "Where is he now?"

Clark squeezed her hand again. "With the police," he said softly.

She paused for a long moment. "What will I do?" she eventually said, the tears returning.

Clark stood and walked around the table towards her. She stood too and he held her close and tight, feeling her fresh sobs against his chest.

"You will be strong," he said, "You have a life to live, a good life, a life that is beyond and better than this. Build your career, build your friendships. Enjoy yourself the way you want to."

He pulled away and looked at her. "And Amy," he said, "Don't forget you have a family." He blinked to fight against his own tears. "I will be here for you... We will all be here for you."

She smiled and reached forward, holding his face in her hands. She kissed him gently on his cheek. "Thank you," she whispered. Clark could not hold back the tears any longer. It hadn't been ideal but he had found his sister again.

Their mother came into the kitchen and stood with hands on hips staring at them both. He quickly ran the back of his hands across his face and smiled to himself. He knew he might have reconciled with his father and with his sister, but there was still some way to go with his mother. He knew it was something he would have to work on, and he knew also it was something he was determined to do.

He checked his watch. There was something else he had to do that afternoon. He made sure Amy was okay with his leaving for a while and asked his mother to stay with her. He checked on his father and told him he would back later.

Then he went out to his car and made for Belfast City Centre and the offices of Chesterton and Williamson.

CHAPTER 30

He found a pay and display parking space on Bedford Street and strode into Windsor House, climbing in the lift to the sixteenth floor. He kept his head down and walked straight to Charlotte's desk telling her he was going to see Fabian. He walked on giving her no chance to stop him.

Fabian looked up as Clark pushed open his door and sat himself on the visitor's chair. He apologised for not having been around for the last couple of days but that he had been involved in a police investigation that had taken him to London and had involved the Metropolitan and City of London police. Fabian sat back smiling as he listened, impressed no doubt not only by the story Clark told but also proud that one of his associates had been instrumental in it. His face however took on a graver shade when Clark outlined a connection to Chesterton and Williamson. He agreed however to let Clark deal with it. Clark thanked him and left for the meeting room. He sat in the far corner away from the door and the glass walls and made the phone call. He sat back and waited.

And in she came. Clark asked her to sit and unfolded a printed copy of the photograph of her standing alongside Marybeth Reid. He set it on the table and pointed.

She broke into tears. "I'm sorry Clark," said Deanna, "She called me and asked me to find the disk. She was a guest lecturer at my university and was a mentor for my dissertation. We built up a good relationship and became friends. We have stayed in touch. I'm really sorry."

Clark nodded. "I should have guessed," he said, "when you asked me how I got on in London. I didn't tell you I was going to London."

She dropped her head as tears continued to fall.

"I have agreed with Fabian," Clark said slowly, "that he allow you to resign voluntarily. He will take no further action."

She lifted her head and looked at him. "Thank you," she said quietly.

Clark nodded and left the room leaving her to her tears.

"It's done," he said to Fabian as he walked back into his office.

Fabian nodded. "Thank you, Clark. For all you have done for Annabel. I cannot believe the change in her in a matter of days. Her demeanour, her confidence... she is like a different person. She is talking a lot about a Jonathan Campbell?"

Clark nodded and smiled. "DC Campbell," he said, "DI McArdle's colleague. I introduced them last week."

"Oh yes, yes, of course. That explains it. DI McArdle called me to say the matter with the laptop has been sorted, that one of his colleagues had found what was needed along with the help of one of our trainees."

Clark laughed. Good old McArdle he thought.

Fabian pushed a few buttons on his mobile phone and some minutes later the door opened. In came Annabel eloquently but demurely dressed in a calf length skirt and with a blouse loosely fitted and buttoned high on her neck. Her hair was tied back and had minimal makeup. She came towards Clark and held out her hand. No embarrassment for what had happened before. He stood and took her hand.

"Thank you Clark," she said," Thank you for everything. Jonathan and I are for the cinema tonight." She smiled and nodded before turning and leaving the room.

"And Clark," said Fabian, "Forget about the Penny and Jimmy thing. Let's go back to where we were. You continue to work the way you work best and report directly to me. Penny and I'll sort something else out on the contingency and accounting front. And we'll deal with Jimmy."

Clark nodded and shook his hand. He left the office and walked across the floor to the lift lobby with his head down. He looked at no one but sensed many eyes glaring at him.

Out in the car he called Siobhan and told her he was home safe and would meet with her later to explain everything. He sent a text to Jackson saying more or less the same thing but that it might be the next day before they could catch up. And then he drove home to Ethel Street.

As he got out of the car Vince and Ryan were leaving their house next door. They raised their hands and waved. Clark waved back.

"Hi guys." he said, "Maybe you could do me another favour?"

"No problem, anything at all," they said together.

"Maybe if I hire a van you can help me move in some of Siobhan's furniture?"

"No problem," they said, "No problem at all."

ABOUT THE AUTHOR

Allan McCreedy lives in rural County Down, N Ireland with his family. A graduate of Ulster and York universities Allan has worked across a number of government departments. Systems Failing was his first full length novel and introduced Clark Radcliffe. Double Figures is a second novel featuring Clark Radcliffe. Social Insecurities, a third novel featuring Clark Radcliffe is coming soon.

25479252R00155

Printed in Poland
by Amazon Fulfillment
Poland Sp. z o.o., Wrocław